The Rogue's Pawn

A Novel

CARL SCHROERS

ISBN 978-1-953223-23-4 (paperback)
ISBN 978-1-953223-27-2 (hardcover)
ISBN 978-1-953223-89-0 (digital)

Rushmore Press LLC
1 800 460 9188
www.rushmorepress.com

Printed in the United States of America

SUMMER

2010

1

Experts in revenge weren't born that way.

Later he would blame himself for not paying closer attention to the guy who sold him the stuff. Later he would learn about the children who happened to be visiting the house at the time. Later he would discover that the big tank under the house was for propane not water. Finally he would recognize that he sucked at demolition and resolve never to do it again.

He'd planned to be gone long before any explosion. But the charge went off almost an hour early and carried a much bigger punch than intended. He never heard the blast before the shockwave caught him a hundred yards down the ridge as he stooped to grab his supplies. Feeling the earth tremble, he glanced toward the house only to see the world turn orange just as his feet left the ground. He was unconscious before his body slammed down.

He came to near the trunk of a dead pinion tree as dust and grit continued to fall, coating everything like filthy snow. Coughing, he tried to sit up, but pain from his right arm and rib cage blossomed. Choking, bleeding, and blinded by the dust, he pulled his face into his shirt then drifted, semi-conscious, until the predawn light roused him. Reaching for support from the dead tree, he finally stood, a dust-covered gray ghost, staring at the destruction up the ridge.

At least half of the house had been blown away, and a fire raged over the rest. Men dashed here and there, waving their arms and yelling. None of them looked down the ridge at the man standing by the dead pinion tree.

"Well, Carlos, ain't that a bunch of horse apples in your fruit basket," he whispered then huffed a quick chuckle before wincing in pain. "I hope ya'll is a'goin' up in that smoke."

SPRING

2015

2

A pawn is found!

Dorothy clapped her hands. "Shit, this is the one. He's going to want this one." She rose from the table and checked the data on the computer one more time then padded to the tiny kitchen. Opening the fridge, she pulled out the remaining four slices of pizza, a twenty-ounce bottle of Coca Cola, and for good measure, the rest of the chocolate pie. Back at the table, she elbowed the empty candy boxes to the floor to make room. "Wake up, Old Man. I know it's late, but you're gonna want to know about this guy." She squeezed her frame between the chair's armrests then began to type an email with her left hand, a slice of pizza in her right.

```
hey old man. got a long shot. start
with the news
```

She added a link to an article in the San Francisco Chronicle. Dated more than a year ago, the article revolved around a big drug bust. A dozen plots of marijuana had been found growing in the steep, rolling hills north of the Golden Gate Bridge. Apparently, it was the work of an unnamed Mexican cartel. While each plot was relatively small, the cumulative acreage was substantial. The find led to an operation that utilized the services of local, state, and federal agencies, ending in multiple arrests and seizures. Toward the end of the article, the agent in charge let slip that an anonymous tip had started the ball rolling.

take note of the anonymous tip

She sent the email then returned to her meal. Almost immediately, she received a response.

belly brain, this better be good. i'm not paying you anymore for crap

"Shit, he's awake." She laughed. "Well, let's string him along for a bit." Putting the pizza down, her chubby fingers flew over the keyboard.

nothing with the feds about the tipper except classified

no shit. it's late. quit fucking around.

Dorothy laughed again.

nothing with smokey or ma bell

belly, i know where you live. tell me what you've got

Her smile faded. She paused for a long time. The man scared her. She knew what he'd done in Mexico. Then she shrugged. There was no way he knew where she lived, she was far too careful.

ok ok ta da!! novato pd had 911 call in june of same year about mj in the hills but not in novato's jurisdiction so call forwarded to feebs, feebs to DEA, back to feebs,

```
etc etc etc. and then because of
fear of retribution 911 caller
maybe kinda likely classified as
anonymous tipper and was never
subpoenaed. but novato pd didn't
get the classification memo so 911
call was recorded on flimsy data
bank. do you want to know the name
of the caller?
```

yes, tell me please

```
double ta da!! the dude is a very
good citizen. yuck a thousand times!
I hate these anti-pot assholes. you
sure you want his name??
```

yes, pretty please

Dorothy chomped on her pizza and drained a third of her Coke before she sent:

```
harrison ross
```

After five minutes went by with no response, she added:

```
want to make me rich yet?
```

A minute later she received:

not yet. at least a box of Godiva. tell me more about your good citizen.

Dorothy clapped her hands. A box of Godiva meant big bucks.

not ready yet just started. uses
a po box in san rafael so haven't
found where he lives. don't know
his job or anything

get on it. this is definitely the best to
date. want to hear from you tomorrow.
will send compensation then

Dorothy raised her hands high. "Yes!"

AUTUMN

2015

THURSDAY

3

An old knight gets the boot.

Jorge sat, staring at the agent's face, but failed to get a read on the new guy. Periodically, the Bureau had pulled Jorge in to review the failure of his old task force. Like every other time, this agent focused on Harry.

"Mr. Morales," the agent said.

Jorge glanced at the thick file on the table. "Yes?"

"I need your answer."

"What was the question?"

Unruffled, the agent asked, "Has there been any contact between you and any members of the former task force?"

Jorge shook his head. "You people have asked me that every time. The task force I managed was disbanded years ago. People resigned or were reassigned, and it looks like I'm going to be put out to pasture."

"That doesn't answer the question."

"My point is, why would they bother to contact me?"

"So, your answer is no? Including with your former lead agent?"

"Harry? You're kidding. As far as I know, he's dead and gone. Your bosses aren't really still looking for him, are they?"

The agent ignored Jorge. "To your knowledge, how technologically savvy were the personnel on the task force?"

"That should be in the file," Jorge said. "Did you write these questions yourself?"

Oblivious to Jorge's taunts, the agent said, "Their training, the equipment they used while deployed, and the level of skill they displayed while on assignment are in the file. We're seeking to find out if any of the personnel had hacking skills."

"Hacking? God, no. Anyone like that would have been too valuable to send into the field. We'd have kept them here in D.C. Christ." Jorge laughed.

The agent jotted a note. "You refer to him by his alias. Why?"

Jorge shrugged. "I don't know his real name."

"Why not? You were his supervisor."

"Haven't you read the file?"

"I prefer to hear it from you."

Jorge shrugged again. "No one had access to another team member's real name. The program protocols didn't allow it. Each member selected one alias to use with the rest of the team, and that's how we knew each other. That's also in the file."

"Yes, it is. But I find it surprising that someone on your level and with your experience did not seek alternate paths to such basic information."

"That's not my problem," Jorge said. "I don't know his name, and I never really tried to find out. He was just Harry to us. Is his real name in the file? I bet it is. And I bet you have his background in there too, which is something else we had no access to. I wish I could have known his background. Might have saved everybody a lot of trouble if we knew we were dealing with a guy like Harry."

"And what kind of guy is that?"

"As I said, read the damn file. I'm sure there's more in it than I know."

"Mr. Morales, please stop pushing my queries aside. Answer them as completely as possible."

Jorge rolled his eyes. "Sure. What was the question?"

"I asked for your impressions of the missing agent."

"Competent but crazy, okay?"

The agent jotted another note. "Now then, when he went rogue, what did he do for money? He had to live somewhere, put food on the table."

"What you really want to know is how he financed his little vendetta."

"Of course that's the question. Please answer it."

Jorge smiled. "Well, the rumor is that Harry dug up some of the stashes Carlos had buried. That the financing of Harry's war against Carlos came from Carlos himself."

"Do you believe the rumors?"

"I don't necessarily believe rumors, but I do try to listen to them. Rumor has it that your bosses assume Harry set up his own drug cartel to finance his war. Of course, that's just one rumor. The main one is that he died in Mexico. That's all I've got now, rumors."

A full minute passed as the agent wrote a few notes. "Mr. Morales, I've actually read what he's done, what he's alleged to have done, and what he's rumored to have done. But I don't know him like you did. I need to *know* him."

Jorge paused. "Why?"

"That's not your concern."

Jorge rested his elbows on the table and slowly stroked the stubble on his cheeks.

"Mr. Morales?"

"Yes?"

"Can you tell me more about him?"

"Well…I don't think he's really from Appalachia. He's a hillbilly only when he wants to be."

"You're correct. He's not from Appalachia."

"Ah, well, what do you know." Jorge chuckled. "But he does have this hillbilly sense of loyalty."

"And what's that?"

Jorge leaned forward. "I found it important to understand that, when dealing with Harry in a situation where his friends were involved, well then, he was not someone you'd want to fuck around with."

FRIDAY, SATURDAY, and SUNDAY

***Just when the future seems clear, the
unexpected scrambles everything.***

Dressed in comfortable gray slacks and white blouse, Kay Morrell hoped she would present an air of confidence for her first meeting as the chair of the Redwood Academy English department. A stack of agendas sat on the table by the door, and her short presentation was ready on the Smart Board. Sixteen desks sat in a neat semi-circle, and a small cooler filled with ice, bottled water, and baggies of brownies sat by the windows.

She looked at the clock. Thirteen minutes until the first all-faculty meeting of the year. If Mrs. Cade kept on schedule, which was doubtful, then two hours and thirteen minutes remained before her meeting. *No more coffee*, she decided, as the butterflies fluttered in her belly. She sat in one of the student desks. *George will never understand this.*

The door opened and Rhonda entered. In jeans and a light sweater, she was dressed more casually than Kay. But then Rhonda was married with small kids and long past the days when she dressed to impress. She stopped by the cooler and picked up a brownie and an agenda. "Good God, Kay, you think everyone wants to go over all of this? My, oh my, you have been a busy girl."

Kay smiled and sighed. "Why don't you help yourself to a brownie?"

"Sure thing," Rhonda said with a chuckle. A history teacher, she was Kay's closest friend on the faculty. Sitting down, she looked straight into Kay's eyes. "Well?"

Kay smiled, turned her face away, and clasped her hands.

"C'mon, tell me, tell me, tell me," Rhonda said.

"Um…"

Rhonda glanced at the door to make sure it was closed. "He did, didn't he? I mean, come on." She pulled on Kay's left wrist and looked down at an unadorned ring finger. "Well, where is it? Did he ask? Or did he chicken out again?"

"No, he asked," Kay said.

"Hah! I thought so." Rhonda squeezed Kay's hand. "It's time you made an honest man out of Georgie. Good for you."

"Don't call him that."

"What? Georgie? Why not?"

They pulled apart and smiled at each other.

"So, where's the ring? Don't tell me he's too cheap to get a ring. I mean the guy must be making almost two hundred K by now."

"Oh, he had a ring, but—"

"Big smacking shiny rock, too, I bet. How big is it?"

"It's a really nice ring. But—"

"It didn't fit, did it? It's hard on guys, you know, figuring out a woman's ring size. I think it's a gender problem. I mean, when Stevie gave me mine, it didn't get past my first knuckle."

Kay sighed. "I didn't try it on."

Rhonda leaned back and pushed her glasses up her nose. "What?"

"I told him I needed some time. I just thought, you know, with Dad undergoing chemo and all."

"Huh. And how is your dad doing?"

"The doctor says he's doing well. But he's tired all the time and cranky. And he's lost a lot of weight." She paused. "Mom is struggling. Dad's always been so, I don't know, vibrant. It's hard on her."

"How about you? You okay?"

"Yes, actually. Dad *is* getting better, school's starting, and I'm probably getting married. So, yeah, I'm doing all right."

"Probably? You're really not sure, are you?"

"I think I am. I just need a little more time."

Rhonda nodded slowly. "You don't think hanging with a guy for, what, a year and a half is enough time? And just because your dad doesn't like him—"

"He likes him. Don't say that. They get along very well."

"Kay, I met your dad, remember? He's a knee-jerk liberal Viet Nam vet who can't stand Republicans."

"George is not a Republican."

"He's an investment banker, isn't he? There aren't too many Democratic investment bankers that I know of."

Kay laughed and shook her head. "And how many do you know?"

"Okay, good point. Maybe he's not a Republican. But hell, why are you taking so long? He's rich, he skis, he has a boat, and he flies all over the country. First class, I bet. And he's just gorgeous, which is rare for nice guys. And he *is* a nice guy. What's the matter with you?"

"I told him I want to marry him, but I just need a few days to let things settle. We made a deal."

"A deal?"

"We're going to let everything sit for a week, okay? So… nothing."

"Nothing? What does that mean? Like *nothing*?"

"Yeah, nothing. No phone calls, no texting, no, well, nothing. I just need time to think, okay? He's going to be out of town anyway, so…I don't know. It's not that big a deal."

"And he's cool with nothing?"

"You won't tell anyone, will you?"

Rhonda looked down. "Of course not. You know I won't." She paused. "How much are you worried about your dad?"

"The chemo is hard on him. And he has his heart thing." She looked away. "And you're right. He doesn't like George too much. I just need to find a way to tell him, and now is not a good time."

"You going out to see them this weekend?"

"Every weekend."

"All summer? You drove to Reno every weekend?"

Kay shrugged and nodded. "Almost. It's not that far."

"Not that far? Are you kidding? Not that far is from here across the Golden Gate Bridge to San Francisco. That's not far. Here to Reno is pretty far, Kay. My God."

"Yeah, I guess so."

"Yes, Kay, it is. Maybe you should take George with you."

Kay grimaced. "Well…George doesn't like going. It messes up his weekend work."

"Yeah, right." Rhonda sighed then raised both hands, palms up. "Whatever."

Kay looked at the clock. "We better get to the meeting."

"E-yup."

They rose together and walked to the door, but before they left, Rhonda said, "Okay, school mode. No more proposal shit, no more cancer shit. Let's get ready to slay the dragons."

"I think I'm ready."

"Nice pants, by the way. A little *too* nice for today's meetings, but nice. They make your ass look great."

Kay shook her head and punched Rhonda lightly on the shoulder.

They found a place in the back of the gym with their cadre of five other teachers, all of whom began teaching the same year. Mrs. Cade, the head of school, stood at the podium and ran through her welcome-back-to-school speech. It was the same speech every year, with dates and statistics altered to fit the accomplishments of the previous year.

The introductions of the new faculty followed. *Should be only two new teachers, history and math*, Kay thought. *Good for history. Rhonda could use some fresh blood in that department.* She hoped Mrs. Cade had not hired some fossilized retread of a college professor as she was prone to do.

The new math teacher fell into that category. An older gentleman stood briefly and accepted the mild applause from the faculty after Mrs. Cade read off his c.v.

"And joining the history department is a young man I think all of us will come to enjoy." Mrs. Cade paused and looked out at the teachers. "He is a former United States Marine and has both a BA and MA in US history from San Francisco State. While he has never taught high school, he has extensive teaching and training experience in the Marines and as a graduate assistant. Further, he has a background in wrestling, and he hopes to assist Coach Wilson with our team. Please welcome Mr. Harrison Ross."

Kay sat up with a jerk.

"Whoa," Rhonda whispered as the man rose and waved to the assembled faculty. "I don't care if he can teach or not. He's gorgeous. Holy cow. I mean, he's not very tall, but wow." She leaned forward and studied the man closer while Kay shrank in her chair. "But what's wrong with his ears?"

Harry. Oh my God, thought Kay. She failed to notice his ears.

* * *

As expected, Mrs. Cade went overtime. When she finally excused the faculty for a coffee break before the departmental meetings, Kay hunkered low in her chair, watching Harry walk toward the exit. "This is too much," she mumbled.

"What?" Rhonda asked.

"Nothing, nothing."

"You coming for coffee?"

"No, thanks. I…I need to prep for my meeting. You go ahead."

Rhonda gave Kay a look. "Okay, see you at lunch."

Kay nodded then hurried toward the exit. Cutting across the courtyard, she glanced over her shoulder and almost ran into one of the workers wheeling out a lawnmower. "Sorry, I…sorry."

The worker stopped, allowing Kay to step around the machine. "No problem."

"Thank you," Kay said. Glancing back again, she caught a glimpse of Harry with a group of history teachers. He stared at her, mouth agape, but Kay pretended not to see him and kept walking.

Back in her classroom, she gathered herself and the meeting went well. Several of her colleagues went out of their way to compliment her approach. As soon as the room emptied, she flipped through the faculty schedule and discovered that Harry taught US History and World Geography in a room not far from hers.

She stepped to her window and pressed her head against the glass. Thoughts of George, her father, and now, out of the blue, Harry tumbled through her head. Straightening up, she folded her arms across her chest then turned around and caught her breath.

Harry stood in the doorway. Dressed in black slacks, a light blue dress shirt, and a dark gray tie, he smiled nervously. Just as she remembered, his eyes blinked ever so slowly. "Hi. I see you still talk to yourself."

"What?"

"That's why I waited at the door." Harry looked away, then back at her. "I can't believe we're both going to be teaching here. I mean, whoa."

Kay could think of nothing to say.

"I saw you earlier on the courtyard."

"Oh…you did?"

"Yeah."

"Oh."

"Well, how are you?"

"I'm…I'm fine," Kay stammered. "Fine. How are you?"

Harry said nothing for a long moment. Just like the old Harry, he couldn't answer a simple question without prolonged consideration. "I guess I'm pretty excited."

"That's nice." Kay's stomach fluttered.

Another long silence followed, while Harry looked her over from head to toes. His sheepish smile returned. "You look spectacular."

The heat rose in her cheeks.

Averting his eyes, Harry said, "Oh, sorry. I shouldn't have said that."

"No. That's all right. I just don't know what to say."

Several more moments of tense silence passed.

"It's been a long time, Harry."

"Yeah, it has."

"You stopped writing."

With the barest of movement, Harry nodded.

Kay's stomach stopped fluttering and her eyes narrowed. "I don't…you quit answering my letters."

"Yeah, I know."

"Why? All of a sudden you just stopped."

Harry's blinking wrinkled his forehead.

"We were friends."

"Yeah, friends, I know. Best friends. I know."

"Was it…did I do something? Did something happen? You just stopped. I didn't know what was going on."

She watched impatiently as he mulled over her query.

He gave her an old look, the one that saw right through her. "I guess we both grew up and moved on. Stuff just happened, and well, I guess that's about it."

"What stuff happened?"

Again, Harry paused.

Kay used to count the seconds of Harry's conversational deliberations. "Well?" Yet again, she had to wait for Harry to answer.

His blinking stopped and his face relaxed. "I guess it's a stupid story. I really don't have any excuses."

"Well…you know…I'm sorry, but I have to go. You should've… never mind. I have to go."

"Oh, okay." He moved to the side of the door. "I really am excited, you know. Really excited. I've never taught in a place like this. Never really taught kids. But I don't know, I just get excited about, well, just about everything." He paused. "Can I see you again?"

Kay's stomach clenched. "I don't know. I have to go, okay? Maybe we can talk later." Without another word, she gathered her things and walked quickly out the door. A few steps later, she turned and walked back to the room.

At the door, she saw Harry's face brighten. "I have to lock up."

"Oh, yeah, of course." He walked out of the room and waited until she locked the door.

She looked one more time into his eyes. "Maybe later we'll see each other."

"Good. I'd like that."

Kay nodded and turned away.
Behind her, Harry said, "Bye, Kay."
Without looking back, she offered a brief wave of her hand.

5

A pawn can never really escape the game.

Ed Hoffman, exhausted after working a second site for his landscaping boss, walked into the kitchen of his tiny house, grabbed a beer from the refrigerator, and sat at the dining table. Rita had taken the kids to her mother's for the weekend, so he was stuck with frozen pizza for dinner.

"Eddie, it's good to see you again," a voice said.

Hoffman froze.

Two men approached. Both wore jeans and rumpled dress shirts. Both were armed. The older one said, "Carlos has a special task for you, compadre."

"Sergio, Juan," Hoffman said, his eyes darting from one man to the other. "I…I can't. I'm done. I've got kids. I'm—"

"Do you love your kids, Eddie?" Sergio said as he pulled out a chair.

Hoffman looked past Sergio and Juan and saw two other men in the front room. "What?"

"How about the kids' mama? What's her name? Rita? Do you love her too?"

Barely able to breathe, Hoffman whispered, "Please. No. Leave them alone."

Sergio slapped Hoffman then looked at Juan. "Make sure Estocio and Julio are keeping watch."

Juan sauntered into the living room.

"Okay," Sergio said, "it's like this. That landscaping company you work for has contracts with some of the schools in the area, right?" When Hoffman failed to answer, Sergio slapped him again. "Well?"

Hoffman nodded.

Sergio dropped a photo onto the table in front of Hoffman. "Ever seen this asshole?"

Hoffman shook his head.

"Look again. He works at the school where you mowed grass this morning."

Wiping his eyes, Hoffman looked. The shot showed a man standing by a bicycle. "No. I don't know this man."

"Doesn't matter. Memorize his face. Carlos wants him dead by Monday."

"What?"

"And if you love your little family, you're going to want him dead too."

In most decisions, emotion battles reason. Guess which wins.

Kay's weekend was miserable. Heavy traffic extended the drive time, and the temperature in Reno reached triple figures. Dad was thin, hairless, and morose, leaving Mom exhausted. Furthermore, Mom suspected something was amiss with George and pressed Kay hard for more information.

Somehow, Kay managed to avoid even mentioning Harry. But on Saturday night, she went out into the garage and rummaged through boxes of old yearbooks, report cards, and college papers until she found the old shoebox. She dumped the contents on top of the washing machine, scattering dozens of letters and cards. "Oh, Harry," she whispered.

She sorted the missives chronologically before carrying them to her room. Sitting on her bed, she opened the first of his letters.

> *Dear Kay,*
> *Thanks for seeing me off. It really helped me say goodbye. And thanks for letting me write to you. There are lots of people on the train who all seem to know what they're doing and where they're going. Me, I'm sitting here like an idiot with nothing but*

a duffle bag full of clothes and a brain full of second guesses. Sorry I missed your grad party.

Your friend,
Harry

His second letter was dated three weeks later.

Dear Kay,

I met some cool guys and the training is not nearly as hard as I thought it would be. I feel pretty focused and am doing better than most of the other guys. I get yelled at a lot, but so does everyone else. I think some of the instructors do it because it's all they know. I watched the sun set today. It was spectacular. It was almost as good as home. It is really hot here.

Your friend,
Harry

"God, Harry, why'd you have to be so banal?"

She stacked up all but the seven most recent letters and the one postcard. Each letter remained encased in an unopened envelope.

She looked at the postcard Harry had sent her for her 21st birthday, his final contact of any kind. It was a view of the Golden Gate Bridge from the Marin headlands. Fog hid all but the upper third of the two red towers, which glistened brilliantly in bright sunshine. Only the tallest spires of downtown San Francisco poked through the white blanket. Harry's message was brief as usual.

Happy Birthday, Best Friend. I don't know what I'm going to do without you.

Harry

She opened Harry's last letter, sent a month before the postcard.

> *Kay:*
>> *I think I understand now. I think you're right. And don't worry. I made them stop. Bye. Maybe we'll see each other again someday.*
>
>> *Harry*

Startled and confused, she read the other six letters.

"Oh, God," she whispered then gathered up the missives, returned them to the shoe box, and placed it in her car.

* * *

George, not quite willing to live up to their deal, called her twice over the weekend, leading to drawn-out conversations about their future. She managed to avoid a simple yes or no to the marriage question and begged him to stick to the deal. He promised to try.

At times, she wished Harry would call, but her cell number was unpublished. She tried to find his number and failed. An online directory showed many H. Rosses, but none of whom lived close to the school. She Googled his full name and found only old newspaper articles about his exploits as a wrestler in high school.

By the time she was on the road home, Kay had almost convinced herself that it was Harry who had quit communicating, not her. Almost.

MONDAY

Pawns have feelings too.

A little before six on Monday morning, Sergio picked up Hoffman at a bus stop on Lombard. "Good for you. I like it when people are on time."

"Why'd you leave Julio with my family?"

"Don't worry about it."

"You promised nothing will happen to my family."

Sergio dropped a drawstring bag on Hoffman's lap. "Carlos is a man of his word. Do your job and your family will be taken care of."

Inside the bag, Hoffman found a pistol, a suppressor, and three clips.

"You good with the piece?" Sergio asked.

Hoffman nodded. "Why does it have to be Julio in the house with my family? Why not Juan? I know Juan."

"Are you gonna give me shit all the way there, man?" Sergio said.

Hoffman shook his head and clasped his trembling hands together.

* * *

Sitting on a bench in a postage-stamp park, Hoffman glanced at his watch then wrung his hands around the bag with the gun. He'd been there for an hour. The bench and the adjacent exercise station stood in the opposite corner of the park from the main road and were partially hidden by a massive oak tree. According to Sergio, his target had been riding a bicycle to school every day the previous week and always stopped for a few minutes to use the equipment. Hoffman was to do the job there.

He looked down the hill toward the school that was just out of sight. A trickle of teenagers had already strolled past the park, adding to his anxiety. "Why here?" he mumbled. "What am I supposed to do if a bunch of kids wanna smoke dope here or something?"

He also wondered why he had been chosen to do the job. It made no sense. Sergio, Juan, Estocio, and even that kid Julio were stone-cold killers. Why couldn't they pull the trigger? When Hoffman had asked Sergio for the reason, the man had simply said Carlos wanted a local to do the job then shrugged.

But Hoffman had more important things to worry about than his confusion. His wife and his children were home with trigger-happy Julio standing guard, and Sergio had made it clear the job had to be done today.

He wiped his sweaty hands on his pants then checked the time again. Seven o'clock had come and gone and there was no sign of the target. More kids moved along the sidewalk. "Where are you, you fucker?"

Gainful employment offers no guarantee of safety.

Arriving early at school, Kay opened her room and, as always, buried her personal problems under the compelling aspects of her job. She laid out the day's lessons, fiddled with the layout of the desks, studied her rosters, stacked up her handouts, then arranged her grade book, all with a smile on her face.

Satisfied, she walked to the central courtyard and found her table facing the grass with one chair backed up to a classroom wall. The rest of the tables for the department heads lined the walkway to her right. To her left was a staircase that led to the second-floor classrooms. Past the stairs lay the administrative offices. She watched Mrs. Cade exit her office with her speech in hand.

Kay waved. "Good morning, Mrs. Cade."

"And it is a good morning, Kay." Mrs. Cade looked at the students gathering in the courtyard. "I love first days, don't you?"

"Yes, ma'am. They're wonderful."

"I see you're early. Are you ready to meet the whiners? None of the other heads seem too willing to confront that particular segment of our student body that is ever so hard to please."

Kay laughed. "I'm ready, Mrs. Cade. I'm ready."

Mrs. Cade smiled then moved out onto the grass where she greeted both students and faculty. Like the rest of the department heads, Kay spent the next twenty minutes meeting with students who wished to change their schedules.

Rhonda stopped by and placed both hands on Kay's table. "Hey, I hear you know the new guy. Is that true?"

Kay sighed. "Well, we were raised in the same neighborhood, and we went to school together."

Rhonda smiled. "I can see why you wanted some time to think about little Georgie Porgie."

Kay shook her head. "Please, don't call him that. Besides, I didn't even know Harry was going to teach here. Yesterday was the first time I've seen him in ten years. This has nothing to do with George."

Rhonda bounced her eyebrows. "Okeydokey, if you say so. Anyway, what kind of guy is he?"

"Don't give me that eyebrow stuff," Kay whispered as she looked around for eavesdroppers.

Rhonda laughed. "I didn't say anything. I just want to know what kind of guy he is. You know, professionally speaking and all that."

"I'll tell you about him at lunch. There's no big secret. We were just kids, okay?"

"If you say so." Rhonda wandered off toward the middle of the courtyard.

The excitement of the first day of school took hold of Kay. She laughed at the kids' antics, greeted other teachers, and relaxed in her chair. Across the courtyard, she saw Mrs. Cade walk toward the podium, concentrating on her opening address. In just a few minutes the new school year would begin.

* * *

Thirty more minutes had crept by but still the target failed to show. Panicking, Hoffman called home. No one answered. He called Sergio. No answer. Sobbing, he began pacing laps around the exercise equipment. Round and round he went before he stopped next to the big oak. He could see the school now. He could see people gathering in a courtyard. "The fucker's gotta be there. Gotta be." Taking a deep breath, he placed his hand on the gun under his black hoodie and headed towards the school.

* * *

Just before Mrs. Cade reached the podium, Kay saw a man jostle through the crowd. Students began to lean away and point, opening a gap for the stranger. The man kept his head on a swivel, his eyes darting everywhere.

Concerned, Kay stood and tried to catch the attention of Mr. Lee, but the Dean of Faculty was speaking to Mrs. Cade.

Suddenly, the stranger pulled a pistol out from under his sweatshirt. Raising the weapon high above his head, he shouted, "Where is he?" then fired repeatedly into the air.

Screaming, the students bolted.

Kay dropped into her chair, slamming it backwards against the wall as panic erupted. People pushed, shoved, and crashed into walls, doors, plants, and other bodies in their efforts to escape.

Frozen, Kay stared with wide eyes.

Breathing heavily and sobbing, the stranger spotted a few people cringing behind corners or under tables. Shouting, "Go away!" he fired several rounds into the ground. "I don't want you. Run!" One boy bolted. A moment later the rest followed.

Mr. Lee, a hand pressed tightly to his forehead, rose from behind the podium then took a wobbly step toward the man. "Sir, please..."

The man whirled and emptied his clip.

Mr. Lee crumpled. Without thinking, Kay rose and shouted, "Stop it! Just stop it! You can't do this!"

Spinning around again, the man pointed his weapon at Kay and pulled the trigger, the hammer clicking uselessly.

Kay pushed back against the wall, slipped, and fell heavily into the chair. "Stop! Don't do this. You have to stop!"

Wiping his eyes, the man somehow managed to insert a new magazine then took a step toward Kay.

"Put the gun down!"

Distant screams roiled the air.

Sobbing and talking to himself, the gunman shook his head, took another step toward Kay, and aimed.

"No! You can't do this!"

The gunman lowered his pistol, turned completely around, and stared into the distance.

Kay dropped to her belly, knocking the table over, its far edge coming to rest on the opposing chair. In the silence that followed, she raised her head.

The gunman gestured into the distance with an uplifted palm then began to turn back just as Harry sprinted by her table.

The gunman opened fire. Instantly, the wall behind Kay exploded, showering her with dust, grit, and chunks of concrete, but she could not pull her eyes away from Harry.

Lowering his body, her old friend plowed into the gunman's thighs. Both men flew for a few feet before crashing onto the grass. Harry wrestled the gunman onto his belly, slipped his arms under the man's shoulders, and locked his hands over the man's head.

Kay wiped the dust from her eyes and watched as Harry repeatedly slammed the gunman's face into the turf. The man kicked and bucked and somehow continued to fire. A window above Kay burst, showering her with tiny cubes of tempered glass. Again, she dropped to the floor, covering her head with her arms.

A few moments later the shooting stopped and was replaced by the desperate grunts and muffled thumps from the battle in the courtyard. Slowly, Kay raised her head. The two men rolled over several times, writhing and twisting on the grass. Keeping his hold on the stranger's head, Harry locked his legs around his adversary's thighs, then, attached like a snake, rode out the man's flailing effort. Again and again, the gunman tried to gain purchase on the ground only to have Harry roll him back to his belly then smash his face into the sod. As they wrestled, tiny explosions of grass erupted around them. More glass dropped from above, forcing Kay to cover her head again.

Sirens blared in the distance.

Holding her breath, Kay saw a cop crouching by the stairwell, pistol in hand and frantically signaling her to come his way. She shook her head and pointed to the courtyard where, head down, Harry sat on the grass with the gunman draped across his lap.

The next thing Kay knew, the cop grabbed her armpit and the belt of her skirt. With her feet leaving trails in the concrete dust and shattered glass, she was dragged to safety. Once out of view of the courtyard, the cop hefted her to her feet, grabbed her hand, and pulled her deeper into the hallway.

"Here! Over here!" a voice hissed. The cop changed direction and burst into Mrs. Cade's office. Once inside, he released Kay and hustled back to duty.

"Harry's out there!" Kay whispered.

"Kay," Mrs. Cade said, "we're in lockdown. We are to stay here and remain quiet. Can you remain quiet?"

"Okay, okay." Shaking from head to toe, she sat on the couch.

Mrs. Cade wrapped an afghan around her shoulders. "Here. Your blouse is torn.

Sometime later, Kay borrowed Mrs. Cade's cell phone and called her parents' home. When no one answered, she whispered a message into the answering machine.

* * *

Shortly after nine, someone pounded heavily on the office door. "Mrs. Cade? This is Officer Cornish. We're still in lockdown, but we're moving everyone to the gym. Please unlock the door, and I will escort you."

Mrs. Cade walked apprehensively to the door. "Charlie? Is that really you?"

"Yes, ma'am, it's me. Will you unlock the door?"

"It's Charlie Cornish, Kay. Remember him? He always helps us with security at the games."

Kay nodded.

"He's the one who pulled you in here."

"Mrs. Cade?" Charlie said.

Mrs. Cade unlocked and opened the door. "Is it all over?"

Charlie stepped into the room. "Yes, ma'am, we think so. But we're still running a room-to-room search."

"What about Harry?" Kay asked from the couch.

"Harry?" Charlie asked.

"He went out there," Kay said. "He went after the man with the gun. He went out there and—"

"Oh, that was him? His name is Harry?"

"Harrison actually," Mrs. Cade said. "Harrison Ross."

Charlie stammered for a moment. "Huh." Turning away, he huffed a quick sigh. "Right. Well, he's quite a guy, but we need to get you to the gym."

"Where is he? Is he okay?" Kay asked.

Charlie shuffled his feet. "He's on his way to the hospital. That's all I know. But c'mon, we need to move quickly now."

Kay bolted upright. "Hospital? But I saw him. He was sitting up, and the man with the gun was just lying there over his legs. Why is he going to the hospital?"

Charlie looked toward the ceiling then toward Kay. "He was shot, ma'am. We think the gunman broke free, shot your teacher friend, and then committed suicide."

"Shot?" Kay's hands trembled. "Shot Harry?"

Charlie said nothing.

Mrs. Cade dropped her head. "Oh, Lord. Anybody else?"

"No," Charlie said. "No one else."

"What about Mr. Lee?" Kay blurted. "I saw him fall."

"No, ma'am," Charlie said. "He wasn't shot. He had a heart attack or a stroke or something. He's at the hospital too." Charlie shook his head. "Look, I don't know a lot, but the paramedics seem to think that Mr. Lee…he's a dean or something, right?"

"Yes," Mrs. Cade said. "He's our dean of faculty."

"Yeah, well," Charlie said, "the paramedics seemed a lot more worried about him than Mr. Ross. I hear he was conscious the whole time. So, you know, maybe it's not too bad."

"I'll call the hospital."

"Mrs. Cade," Charlie said. "We gotta get to the gym so we can do our job. You can call from there."

"Yes, of course. You're right. We've taken too much time already. Come on, Kay. Let's let Charlie get on with his duties."

Kay rose off the couch, gingerly walked to Charlie, and hugged him. "You pulled me out. Thank you."

"Yeah." Charlie patted her back and noted her torn collar. "Sorry if I hurt you, but we gotta move now."

"Give me one more minute," Mrs. Cade said. She hurried to the attendance office through a side door and picked up a stack of binders. She nodded to Charlie. "Sorry. These hold student contact information. We're going to need them."

9

Some people are players; others are just played.

The ringing phone jerked Jorge out of his nap. He looked at the clock, huffed, and debated answering. He walked over to the desk, shoving stacks of papers around until he found his phone. "Hello?"

"You see the news?"

Jorge pushed his thinning hair back, looked for his glasses, and yawned. "Who is this?"

"It's Cobb. Have you seen the news?"

"Cobb? It's been a while."

"Hey, I think Harry's up to more shit."

"Cobb, you've been retired for almost five years. If Harry's up to something, let someone else worry about it."

"I got pushed into early retirement. So what? At least you kept your job."

"Not anymore. I'm done."

"Really?"

"Yup, done and done. Anyway…good luck and everything, but I'm going to finish my nap. Something I will be doing more often now."

"Just turn on the news," Cobb insisted.

Jorge rolled his head around to loosen up the kinks. "Perhaps you should just tell me what's on your mind."

"Shit, okay. I'm out here in the Bay Area, up in Marin County—"

"I know where you are…unless you moved away from San Rafael. Did you?"

"No. But, anyway, I think we need to get on this."

"This *what*? Forget about Harry. We can't be working off the books. You know that."

After a pause, Cobb said, "There's been another school shooting."

Jorge found his glasses on the carpet by the couch and put them on.

"You still there?" Cobb asked.

"Yeah, but I don't think I will be much longer."

"You going to listen to me or what?"

Jorge tapped his forehead with two fingers. "Okay, fine…tell me what's what."

"This shooting was different. The shooter was stopped by a teacher. According to witnesses, the teacher ran out and tackled him and—"

"Great. So we have a hero. Wonderful. The world loves heroes."

"Hey, shut up and listen! I'm working here, and I haven't got much time."

"I'm waiting for you to say something important."

"Christ, okay. Somewhere in the fight, the gunman broke free, shot the teacher, and then committed suicide."

Jorge massaged his temples.

"And you know what else? There were no other casualties. He didn't hit anyone but the teacher."

"So, no one else got shot. Huh. The shooter probably used a pistol. Notoriously inaccurate in crazed situations, pistols are. But I'm sure you know that."

"Yeah, he used a pistol. So what? The scene was crammed with potential targets, and he was in the middle of the damn crowd. He couldn't have missed, but there's only one gunshot victim, which doesn't make any sense."

Jorge pursed his lips as he shook his head.

"The teacher will probably need surgery, but it looks like he'll live."

"Well, score one for the good guys."

"And get this…the teacher's name is Harrison Ross."

"Shit," Jorge whispered.

"You still there?"

"Yes. I'm thinking maybe you should've said that first."

"I don't have anything more yet, but it looks like some of the other shit you told me about."

"That was months ago, Cobb, and I never should've said anything anyway. Back then I still had a job even though no one would listen to me anymore."

"You told me to keep my eyes open."

"Like I said, that was months ago."

"The teacher's name is fucking Harry Ross, Jorge. How many times has that name come up?"

"Christ…I don't know how to tell you this, but in reality, you have nothing. There must be tens of thousands of middle-aged men named Ross, and thousands with a first name of Henry or Harry or whatever. And there's not a situation on Earth in which *our* Harry, even if he were alive, would use that name. None, none whatsoever. It's not him."

"Of course, I know that, I know it's not him. The teacher's a young guy in his late twenties. I'm just saying I'm here, and you know Astor is near."

"Astor won't call me anymore."

"What? Who cares? I'll contact—"

"Do *not* contact Astor."

"Why not? Astor probably already knows. Maybe we should check it out. Maybe Harry's out there working solo again."

Jorge controlled a surge of anger. "That is a particularly bad idea. Do not, I repeat, do not do that."

"This thing reeks, and you know it."

Jorge took a deep breath and let it out slowly. "I know nothing of the sort. We are a discredited group. We no longer have anybody to cover our backs. The only time anyone lets me in the building is to be interviewed about Harry's fuck-up." He paused. "So…leave Astor alone. Do *nothing*. Am I clear?"

"Yeah, you're clear. I'm just saying, this has a bad smell to it."

Jorge nodded. "Listen. You're lucky to be out of it. Now, go out and have a life."

"Yeah, whatever." Cobb hung up.

"A smell," Jorge mumbled. "All that's left are damaged people and their noses." He closed his eyes. "We're done and done, thanks to fucking Harry."

* * *

The lockdown ended shortly after Mrs. Cade and Kay entered the gym. Only a few teachers and students remained. Most had fled the campus during the shooting. While the cops began escorting people out of the building, Mrs. Cade asked Kay and two other teachers to stay back. They spent the next several hours on the phone verifying the whereabouts of students and faculty.

The majority of Kay's conversations with parents were perfunctory although some vented angrily about the school's lack of security. More often than not, Kay found a way to lower the angst of these parents, and almost every parent, angry or not, ended the call by thanking her.

She was interviewed twice by the police and submitted a handwritten account of the incident. An FBI team entered the gym but never asked to speak to her.

Occasionally, Mrs. Cade relayed news reports she monitored on her smartphone. Initially, only the basics came out: a shooting at a private school in Marin County where only the gunman was confirmed dead. As time passed, more information, some confirmed, some not, flowed over the internet. Harry was identified as the wounded hero of the day and Kay as a teacher who narrowly escaped a hailstorm of bullets. Mr. Lee had suffered a heart attack but survived.

The as-yet-unnamed gunman was described as a white male with light brown hair and brown eyes. A composite picture of the dead man circulated online. By early afternoon, the gunman had been identified. Edward Hoffman carried a criminal record for the distribution of drugs. His common-law wife and their two small children had been found murdered in their house in Richmond.

Kay wondered if the world could get any sadder.

At one point, she moved to the far corner of the gym and, blinking back tears, answered a call from her mother. "Hi, Mom… Yes, everything is fine. I'm okay. I mean, I got some cuts on my legs, but they're okay. Nothing too deep… Yes, they're all bandaged up… No, I don't think I need stitches… No, Mom. I'm okay. *Really*… Oh yes. God, I was so scared. Very, very scared… No, I'm fine now. How's Dad doing? Can I talk to him?… No. Let him sleep. I'll talk to him later… Yes, it's really him, our Harry… Actually, he was hired to teach history… Yeah, I know. Out of the blue… Absolutely… Oh, my God, he was heroic. Unbelievably heroic… Yes, he was shot, but they say he's going to be all right… No, I haven't seen him yet but hope to soon… Yeah, I'll give him your love… No, I don't think I'll be able to visit you this weekend… Yes, Mom, I know it's hard to believe, but it *is* Harry… No, I haven't had time to talk to George yet. I'll call him next… Okay, love you, Mom. Tell Dad I love him… Bye."

She closed the connection. Drained, she decided not to call George.

By late afternoon all students and school employees had been accounted for. Kay helped Mrs. Cade collect the binders and carry them back to the office. Charlie escorted them.

"Are you hungry, Kay?" Mrs. Cade asked when she finished locking up the office. "Charlie, how about you? Would you like something to eat? I'm sure I've got something at home." Mrs. Cade lived in a house on campus that the school provided.

Charlie shook his head. "No, thanks. I'll escort you home then I have to get back to the station."

As they walked by the courtyard, Kay stopped and gazed at her table. Cordoned off, it remained exactly as she had left it, standing on two legs with the opposite edge resting on the facing chair. Concrete, dust, and glass debris covered the floor below the pockmarked wall. Most of the holes were two or three feet away from where she had sat. However, two were directly behind her chair. She looked at the remains of the window, shuddered, then walked on.

Once they arrived at Mrs. Cade's home, Kay hugged Charlie again. "You deserve a medal."

"Well, I'll take a hug like this anytime. You folks okay, then? I mean, we're gonna have people on campus all night."

"Thank you, Charlie," Mrs. Cade said. She also hugged the skinny cop. "You get home and get some rest."

"Thank you, ma'am. I'll do that." He hesitated. "Did the detectives tell you what to expect from the reporters? I mean, there's a bunch of them out there in front of the school."

"Yes, they did. Our board chair, Mr. Abramson, has been handling the press."

"Okay, good. It's quite a show out there. Well then, I guess I'll be on my way."

"Bye, Charlie," Mrs. Cade and Kay said.

Charlie waved as he walked away.

Mrs. Cade glanced at Kay. "Well, are you hungry?"

"Actually, I'm famished. But shouldn't you be seeing to your husband?"

"Will's in Philadelphia. I've spoken to him a couple times. Right now, he's at the airport, trying to get a flight. Come on in, and we'll find something to eat."

Kay nodded. "He saved me, didn't he?"

"Mr. Ross?" Mrs. Cade asked as they entered the house.

"Yeah. I can't believe he attacked the man." She heaved a long sigh. "I guess you should know that Harry and I went to school together."

Mrs. Cade stopped abruptly. "Really?"

"Yeah. I haven't seen him in ten years, and the first thing he does is this. God, he just went out there. The guy had a gun."

Mrs. Cade also heaved a deep sigh. "I believe he saved a lot of people today."

* * *

The phone rang again just as Jorge had begun his dinner. "Christ." He slammed down his fork, pushed his chair back, and stomped into his study to answer the phone. "Who's this?"

"It's me again."

"Cobb? What are you doing?"

"You seen the news yet?"

"I'm not doing news anymore."

Cobb huffed. "I told you there was something strange about this situation. But there you are, probably drinking wine and not giving a shit about anything."

"We don't even exist anymore. We don't have a budget, and everyone's gone. You're retired. Astor and the rest of the support staff have been reassigned. And Harry's…whatever." Jorge stopped and took a deep breath.

"They ID'd the shooter. White male, late twenties, a long record of pushing and distribution. The guy's name is Edward Hoffman and—."

"So?"

"So, nothing. Listen, will you? First of all, witness statements say Hoffman was seeking a particular target and not trying to wipe out a bunch of kids. Other statements have him firing into the air or into the ground and yelling, '*Where is he?*' several times. That's why there were no other casualties from the gunfire."

Jorge said nothing.

"And another thing, the hero teacher got air-lifted to San Francisco General for surgery."

"So what?"

Cobb huffed. "Jorge, the transfer was ordered by the FBI, not the doctors…and *you* and I know why that happened. Local P.D. is pissed because the transfer occurred without notice."

"Oh fuck."

"Yeah."

Jorge began pacing. "Let me think for a minute."

"I'll bet the goddamn moon Harry's got something cooking."

Jorge massaged his forehead and squeezed the phone until it shook.

"You know Astor—"

"I told you, Astor won't call me anymore."

"This is gonna get ugly," Cobb said.

"Okay… Let's say you're right. Astor is obviously already working on it. Give it a day. I'm sure you'll get a call."

"So, you want me to just wait?"

Jorge took a deep breath then slowly exhaled. "Yeah. Wait for the call and while you're waiting, check into everything you can and keep me informed."

"Okay."

"Christ," Jorge whispered, "if it *is* Harry, Astor's going to need help."

"No shit," Cobb said. "Maybe it's nothing. Maybe the teacher's name is just a coincidence."

"I doubt Astor thinks it's a coincidence."

"Yeah, right. You know I owe Harry. Even if he's gone crazy, I owe him."

"So does Astor." Jorge closed his eyes. "I just got the final heave ho."

"Christ. Sorry, man."

Jorge rubbed his eyes. "Ahhh, fuck…what else am I gonna do? Tell you what, I'm coming. I'll catch a flight." He looked at the clock. "Probably be there by tomorrow. I'll text you the details."

"Okay, good. I'm worried, man."

Jorge put down the phone then flipped open his laptop to book a flight. "Shit, Harry. Are you ever going to stop?"

10

The complexity of chaos demands planning,
both before and after the mayhem.

Mr. Abramson, without bothering to knock, burst through Mrs. Cade's front door and into the living room. "Mildred! I checked the gymnasium, but it was empty. Are you here? An officer said you went home, and he even escorted me all the way. Is everything all right? Well, are you here?"

Kay rose from the sofa, but the focus of the chairman of the school board lay elsewhere.

"I'm in the kitchen, Levi," Mrs. Cade answered. "Please make yourself at—"

"It's utterly mind-boggling, you know...the press, that is. Talking to them is like teaching kindergarteners. They all ask questions at the same time and won't wait for an answer before they ask another. And, of course, I don't really have any answers, at least not for the questions they're asking. Mildred? Where are you?"

"I said I'm in the kitchen, Levi."

"Kitchen? Good. Do you have anything to eat? I'm terribly hungry. You should hear my stomach. If the microphones had been any lower, my stomach would have been quoted." Levi finally noticed Kay. "Who are you?"

Mrs. Cade strode into the room. "Now, Levi, I need you to get a grip on your horses. This is Kay Morrell. She's—"

"Morrell!" Mr. Abramson barked. "You're the one who almost got shot! The press keeps asking about you. They say you were shouting at the bastard. Shouting at him to stop shooting. Is that true? Have you spoken to the press? They're champing at the trough to hear your story. I heard the bullets missed you by inches, just inches." He paused briefly. "Your legs are bandaged. What happened? *Were* you shot? Are you all right?"

"Levi!" Mrs. Cade said. "You're babbling. Let Ms. Morrell say hello."

"Yes, of course." Mr. Abramson reached forward with his hand. "How do you do? Levi Abramson at your service."

"How do you do, Mr. Abramson," Kay said, shaking his hand. "We've already met several times. Christmas parties, workshops, and I taught your granddaughter."

Mr. Abramson studied Kay's face. "Ha! English teacher! Am I correct? English teacher?"

Kay offered a simple smile. "Yes, sir."

"Ha! Never forget a face." Mr. Abramson turned to Mrs. Cade. "Mildred, is that coffee I smell? I could use some. We've got a lot of planning to do, and we best get at it. I've called the rest of the board, and we're going to meet tomorrow." He turned to Kay. "Ms. Morrell, would you be so kind as to serve the coffee? We'll take it in the dining room. Oh Mildred, the entire board has gone off on their normal cowardly way and wishes for us to present an action plan before they open their mouths. Where's Will?"

Mrs. Cade shrugged. "Would you mind, Kay?"

As Kay walked toward the kitchen, Mr. Abramson shouted, "Will! Are you home?"

"Will's out of town, Levi," Mrs. Cade said. "He's at—"

"Oh? Well, that's too bad. We could use his amazingly level head, and we certainly need all the leveling possible in the present situation. Wouldn't you say so, Mildred?"

* * *

They met for three hours. Within the first five minutes, Kay had become the official note-taker. Ten minutes later, she offered her first opinion, a simple one, but one that seemed obvious to her. "Don't you think we should get the word out about the school being closed tomorrow? Teachers and parents are wondering right now what to do."

"Hah! Of course, you're right." Mr. Abramson jerked his cell out of his pocket then punched in a number. "Bertha!" he bellowed. "Levi here. I need a favor. Call the media and tell them we're closed tomorrow... No, no, Bertha. Tell them the *school* is closed. The school... Yes, the radio stations would be best. But hit the TV stations too... Yes, the papers too, but do them last. We need to get the word out... Good girl."

Mrs. Cade raised her hand.

"Wait, Bertha, wait."

"Have the parents check the school website for further information," Mrs. Cade said.

"Website! Of course! The website, Bertha. Tell the media about the website... What? Look it up, girl, Google-ize it!"

Mr. Abramson hung up and took a deep breath. "Great girl, Bertha. Not the sharpest knife in the barn, but give her a task and it gets done." He shook his head. "Damned exciting! Don't you think? Pardon my language, ladies."

Soon it was no longer Mrs. Cade, Mr. Abramson, or Ms. Morrell. Instead it was Mildred, Levi, and Kay. When finished, they had a long list of tasks prioritized and placed on a timeline. The meeting of the board was set for the next morning at Levi's house. Then each went off to a corner of the room to make the necessary calls.

A little after eight, the three sat quietly around the dining table, staring at the oaken top. Eventually Mildred rose. "I can't thank you both enough. But duty calls. I'm going to go to the hospital now to see how our people are doing."

Little new information had been released. Earlier, Levi had called the head of the hospital and discovered Mr. Lee was out of danger, having suffered a stroke, not a heart attack. There was no significant information about Harry other than his injuries were not considered life threatening.

"May I come along?" Kay asked.

"Certainly, dear," Mildred said. "Levi, I can't tell you how much your support has meant to me."

"Mildred," Levi said, "normally I don't stop folks from telling me how wonderful I am, but this was a situation that needed all hands on the grindstone."

"Well, yes. Thank you," Mildred said. "And I'm sorry I didn't get word to you earlier when I left the gym."

"Water under the dam, water under the dam."

Mildred moved toward the front hall. "Let me get my things, Kay, and we'll be on our way."

Levi raised his hands. "You ladies will need an escort. So, in that I refuse to ride in that rattletrap you call a motor vehicle, Mildred, we'll go in my car."

Because the fog had rolled in, Kay exited the house wearing a comfortable, dark-green school sweatshirt, courtesy of Mildred. Kay looked out from the porch through the windows of the nearest classroom wing and could see the courtyard lit up by portable flood lamps. A cop met them at the end of the walk and escorted them to Levi's car. As they approached the front of the school, media vans and flood lamps burned orange halos through the fog.

"I ought to go over there and give them a piece of my mind," Levi said. "Heart attack? No wonder people don't trust the media. They can't even tell the difference between the head and the heart."

"Oh, Levi, don't pretend. You enjoyed dealing with them," Mildred said.

"Ha! Can't fool you, can I? How about you, Kay? Want to have a go at the fourth estate?"

"Not tonight," Kay said, shaking her head. "Not tonight."

"Good thinking. They're going to hound you, but don't worry, we'll sneak out and leave no scent."

When they reached the Marin County Hospital, they were informed that Mr. Lee was not receiving visitors, so the trio met with

Mrs. Lee and their three adult children. All expressed relief about the cautiously optimistic prognosis and gratitude for the visit.

Harry, they learned, had been airlifted to San Francisco General. Levi spoke briefly with the head of the hospital, upset about not being informed. Then they were back in the car, heading for the Golden Gate Bridge.

* * *

Traffic was light but slowed to forty-five miles per hour with the increasingly dense fog. The soft murmurs of Levi and Mildred's sporadic conversation and the dull rush of tires pushed Kay deeper into the back seat. Levi kept the heat running, and soon Kay doffed the bulky sweatshirt to use as a pillow against the window. "Harry Ross," she whispered under her breath as she thought about her childhood with such an undersized, uncoordinated, and socially inept friend.

How many times did she tie his shoes, redo misaligned buttons, fix an inside-out shirt, or whisper in his ear to pull up his fly? How many times did she sit by him because no one else would?

She remembered how she often escorted him to and from school to protect him from a small gang of bullies. She remembered how those bullies loved to surround him and play Toss-the-Baby, shoving his little body back and forth until he finally hit the ground. She remembered their laughter when they finally sauntered away. Then she remembered Harry on his knees, tears rolling down his face as he jerked out tufts of grass and angrily flung them away.

Kay bolted upright as the image of flying tufts of grass brought her out of her reverie. "I need to call the police."

"What's that, dear?" Mildred asked.

"I remember something about the shooting. It just came to me. I need to call the police. Mildred, do you have Charlie's number? Should I just call 911?"

Mildred rummaged in her purse. "Kay, the FBI is in charge of the investigation now. I have the card of the special agent in charge. Give me a moment. Levi, turn on the dome light, will you?"

"The FBI?" Kay asked, closing her eyes against the light.

"Homeland Security, Kay," Levi said. "They think it might be a terrorist act."

"Terrorist? The man was white. Oh, that was stupid. Terrorists can be white, can't they?"

"Lots of them are," Mildred said. "Didn't the FBI interview you in the gym?"

"No. I don't know why. I spoke to two policemen but not to the FBI."

"Well, they must have a copy of your statement," Mildred said. "Here it is. Special Agent Cabrera. Do you have your cell? Never mind, I'll use mine." She dialed. "Agent Cabrera? Mildred Cade here… Yes, we're okay… Well, I have Kay Morrell with me and… Yes, that's her. Well, Ms. Morrell has remembered something that she feels you need to know… Yes, please hold." Mildred passed the phone to Kay.

"Ms. Morrell, this is Special Agent Maizie Cabrera," a female voice said. "Mrs. Cade said you remembered something that might be important."

Kay took a deep breath. "Yes, at least I think so. When Harry and the man, the man with the gun, were fighting, I remember tufts of grass flying up. Not by their feet or anything but close to them, little explosions of grass."

"Can you tell me more?"

"I don't know how else to say it. Little chunks of grass that just kind of…erupted."

"Okay. How many little explosions did you see?"

"How many? A few. It wasn't continuous. There'd be a little puff maybe a few inches from the fight, then a little while later there'd be another."

Agent Cabrera said nothing.

"A cop told me that the man broke away then shot Harry before he committed suicide."

"Yes, that's the prevailing theory."

"I had a hard time with that when I heard it, but there was so much going on and I was so scared, I pushed it out of my head. But it doesn't make sense."

"And why is that?"

"Harry was a wrestler, a really good wrestler. He had the man in a double vine and a full nelson. That man could not have gotten away from Harry."

"Double vine?"

"It's a wrestling thing. It's when a wrestler wraps his legs around his opponent's legs. It's very tough to escape from. And Harry was known for his vine."

"How do you know all this?"

"I watched Harry wrestle a lot in high school."

"I have a report indicating you know him," Agent Cabrera said. "How well do you know him?"

Kay ignored the question. "I saw Harry sitting up with the man draped across his lap. He was trying to push the man off but couldn't. The man would roll a little bit then flop back onto Harry's lap."

"Yes, I read that in your statement."

"Agent Cabrera, the man was already dead by then, wasn't he? The little explosions of grass were bullets that missed, weren't they? Bullets from another gun, right?"

A long silence followed. Kay heard, but could not understand, muffled conversations through the phone. "And something else," Kay added.

"Yes?"

"Before Harry came out into the courtyard, the man, the gunman, stopped shooting for a little bit."

"Stopped shooting," Agent Cabrera said.

"Yes. And he was crying."

"Yes, that's in your statement."

"I know. Anyway, he stopped, and then he turned around. I mean, he completely turned away from me. While he was facing away, he made this gesture. He just kind of…raised his hands."

"Like he was surrendering? Were the cops there yet?"

"No, not like that. He wasn't surrendering. The cops hadn't arrived. Harry hadn't even shown up yet. It was more like, well, he had his palms up, like everything was all messed up and he was saying, 'What do you want now?' Or something like that. I don't know."

"Signaling someone."

"Yes. I think so."

"This wasn't in your statement."

"I just remembered. It all just kind of came back."

"Did you see any other person during this signaling?"

"No. I mean everyone had run away already."

"Okay. Can you tell me what else was in your line of vision?"

"What?"

"Imagine the man signaling, look past him, just straight out, what else was there?"

"Oh, you mean if there was a hiding place or something?"

"Anything. Think back. What was in front of you?"

"Well, the parking lot. The courtyard opens onto the parking lot. There's a fence there, but it's short. You can see the cars. I guess someone could have hid behind one of the cars."

"What else? What's beyond the parking lot?"

"Well, the street and across the street, there's an apartment building. But that's pretty far away. I didn't see anyone else. I'm sure of that."

Agent Cabrera paused. "Mrs. Ross, are you in a car?"

"Uh, yes, I am, but I'm not—"

"Where are you headed?"

"We're going to look in on Harry, Mr. Ross. He's at—"

"San Francisco General, yes. I just spoke to him."

"How is he?" Kay asked.

Agent Cabrera sighed. "He's out of danger, barring infection. He lost a lot of blood and a part of his ear, but the doctors say he should recover."

"A part of his *ear*?"

"One of the bullets just grazed his left ear lobe."

Kay gasped.

"Are you okay, Mrs. Ross?"

"What?"

"You sound distressed."

Kay exhaled. "I'm fine."

Another silence grew stale before Agent Cabrera said, "Mr. Ross confirms your statement, except for the bullets kicking up the grass. He has no memory of when or how he got shot. He was stunned to find out he was wounded."

"That sounds like Harry."

"Mrs. Ross, have you spoken to the press yet?"

"Agent Cabrera, my name is *Morrell*. Please stop calling me Mrs. Ross."

"I'm sorry. I don't know why I called you that. Have you spoken to the press?"

"No, I haven't. Mr. Abramson, the chairman of our board, is handling all the press inquiries."

"Mr. Abramson, yes, I saw him on TV. He did an excellent job. Please be advised that the media have set up camp around the hospital, and I think it would be best if you could avoid them for the moment."

"I don't want to talk to the press."

"Excellent."

* * *

After giving Kay instructions, Maizie ended the call and turned to Tom Henderson, her partner. "She knows."

Leaning against the wall of the small conference room, Tom said, "About the second shooter on the roof of the apartment building?"

"Yeah. Maybe not where the shooter was positioned but definitely about a second shooter. She hasn't talked to the press yet."

Tom shrugged. "Probably doesn't matter. Where is she?"

"We're in luck. They're on their way here. She and the school principal plus one of their board members. You know, visiting the wounded troops sort of thing. I told them I'd meet them at the loading dock and help them avoid the press."

"Okay. How long before they get here?"

"They just cleared the Golden Gate. Maybe fifteen, twenty minutes." Maizie made no move toward the door. Instead, she put her hands on the conference table and studied the shiny, faux-wood top.

Tom's cell chimed. "Henderson here… Hey, Pauli, thanks for getting back to me… Ahh, yeah… No problem… Yeah, it's a funky case with a shitload of loose ends… Thanks again… Yeah, I owe you one."

"What'd you get from Pauli?"

"Guess what? Ross was the confidential source in that big Bay Area drug bust a couple years ago, the one that took a bite out of the Carlos Cartel."

Maizie's head snapped up. "You're kidding."

"Nope."

"Christ…I never knew that, and I worked on that task force."

"Ross is the guy who found where the marijuana was growing. Maybe that's why someone is gunning for him…someone from the Carlos organization."

Maizie stared at nothing.

Tom shrugged. "Naw…that sounds weak. I can't see Carlos going after a citizen this side of the border just for reporting the locations of his crops. More likely, he'd go after the people he trusted to keep the crops secure."

Still silent, Maizie nodded.

"Besides, Ross never had to testify, and all of his statements had his name redacted." Tom shook his head. "And for him to become a target of Carlos, someone would have had to leak his name."

Maizie's head dropped. "That would've been the shits." She sighed. "But I don't see anyone from that task force being that kind of an asshole."

"Well, we can ask Ross for more information about that situation next time."

Maizie nodded. "Yeah…maybe."

"Anyway, his landlords didn't offer much about Ross's background."

Earlier, they had interviewed the family who rented a small cottage to Mr. Ross. The cottage sat on a small farm that specialized in providing fresh produce for pricey restaurants.

"Well," Maizie said, "they know about his service in the Marines and his years in Chicago. But they don't *know* him." She closed her eyes and slowly shook her head. "Maybe Ms. Morrell can offer more."

"Maizie, you okay?" Tom asked.

"What? Yeah, fine. Why?"

"I don't know. You look kinda beat up about this case."

"Nah. Just tired, I guess."

Tom huffed a short breath. "Maizie, I know you. You don't get tired. What's the matter?"

Maizie laughed. "Why, Tom, I didn't know you cared."

Tom also laughed. "Okay, whatever. You better get down there. I'll meet you later. I need to finish my report." He sighed. "Pretty funky case, you know?"

Maizie turned to the door then stopped and faced Tom. "Ms. Morrell knows the guy."

"I know. So?"

"My sense is that she's pretty attached to him. And the way Ross talked about her, well, you heard him. He seems really close to her. Hopefully, she can fill in some details about our hero."

"That's why you called her Mrs. Ross."

"What? No. That was stupid. I don't know why I did that."

Tom chuckled. "Bullshit. You call people by the wrong names all the time. And I think you do it to get inside their heads."

Smiling, Maizie punched Tom on the arm. "Lordy, Tom, whatever makes you say such things about little old me?"

Tom laughed again.

Maizie shrugged. "They're connected though. Really connected."

"I'm sorry I missed her at the school. We all thought it was a single shooter, and I had her statement. It looked pretty complete. She didn't even try to run for it. The whole school was in a panic, and yet, there she was, yelling at the guy like he was a misbehaving student."

"I know," Maizie said. "The problem is that we worked on an assumption…the lone gunman thing. Doesn't matter. We need to move forward. Hopefully, we can keep some of the shit out of the news until we've made some progress. Maybe that's why they gave me the case. You know, another spreading of their gender wings. They assumed it was just another single crazy guy shooting up a schoolyard and we'd solve it in a day or two." She shrugged "Then they could show the world my pretty face on TV. It'd look good for them."

"Well, okay. But I don't think you're very pretty. If they want a pretty face, maybe *I* should brief the press."

Maizie laughed then again punched Tom on the arm.

11

Best friends remain best friends for a reason.

Agent Cabrera's short stature surprised Kay. A little over five feet tall with a trim torso and muscular legs, the agent had dark hair that reached just below her collar and wore a knee-length gray skirt with a gray jacket.

After quick introductions, Cabrera led the trio down several hallways to the elevator. "Ms. Morrell, I'd like to go over your statement."

"Again?" Levi barked. "Do you realize what the poor girl has been through already?"

"Yes, sir, I do. But the next few hours may prove critical, and we need all the information we can get."

Before Levi could reply, Kay waved him off. "Of course. I just think we should see Harry first."

Cabrera nodded. "Mr. Abramson, I thought you managed the press quite well. You were honest, you didn't elaborate, and, most importantly, you didn't speculate."

Levi subtly rocked back on his heels. "Thank you, I appreciate that. I'm sure those people work hard, but their barrage of questions was insane."

"And Mrs. Cade," Cabrera said, "all of the officers I spoke to were impressed with the way you handled the school's reaction to this horrible event."

Mildred shook her head. "Thank you, but all I did was hide and follow administrative procedures."

"Oh, don't be so damned modest, Mildred," Levi said. "Agent Cabrera's quite right, you were outstanding."

"Levi, please, enough."

"And we appreciate that you managed to avoid the press, Ms. Morrell," Cabrera said. "With all that you've been through, I find it amazing you're still functioning."

"The press never approached me. We were in the gym and they weren't allowed in. It's just the way it was." Tired as Kay was, she recognized Cabrera's efforts to enter everyone's good graces.

When the elevator opened, Cabrera pointed toward a hallway. "Mr. Ross is in 505 at the end. You need to check in with the officer on duty. He'll ask to see your ID."

"There's a policeman guarding Mr. Ross?" Levi asked.

"It's procedure in this type of incident," Cabrera said.

At the waiting area, Mildred brought everyone to a stop. "Kay, dear, you go ahead. We'll wait here."

"Oh, we can all go together. Harry and I were friends once, but that was a long time ago."

Mildred gently pushed Kay forward. "Go on, Kay. We'll wait."

As Kay walked away, she heard Levi expound further on the media. The officer rose from a chair in front of 505 as she approached. "May I help you?"

"I'm here to see Harry Ross. I'm Kay Morrell."

The officer looked at his clipboard. "Morrell, hmm. Yeah, here you are. May I see some ID?"

A painful moan drifted out of the room when Kay proffered her license. Her heart bumped solidly against her breastbone.

"Okay, Miss Morrell, you can go in."

On top of the moaning, Kay heard a female voice. "I'm sorry, Harry, but doctor's orders are doctor's orders."

Then she heard Harry's weak whisper. "No, wait. It's not time yet. Wait."

"Sorry, Harry. Say goodnight."

Kay, eyes wide, looked up at the cop, who smiled gently. "He's been struggling ever since they brought him up from recovery. He's hurting."

Kay nodded and entered.

Harry's room contained a single bed with a curtain shielding all but Harry's legs, which twitched as he moaned.

"More time, please…wait," Harry mumbled.

Kay walked around the curtain. The nurse looked up and smiled. "Well, hello. Look who's here, Harry. You have another visitor."

Harry slowly rolled his head toward Kay. As his bandaged ear met the pillow, he winced in pain. His bloodshot eyes met Kay's, and he smiled.

A lump grew in Kay's throat.

"Hi," Harry slurred.

The nurse backed away. Nodding at Kay, she whispered, "He won't be awake much longer."

Kay wrapped her hand around two of his fingers, carefully avoiding the IVs stuck into the veins on the back of his hand. "Hey, best friend."

Harry was fading fast. "Bess frenn," he murmured. He forced his eyes open then whispered, "You 'kay?"

"Yeah. I'm okay."

But Harry was already gone.

The nurse moved forward and read the data off the monitors. "He's been in a lot of pain and kept squirming until he popped a couple of his staples. The doctor ordered him sedated because he's allergic to most of the normal painkillers." She shook her head. "He should feel better when he wakes up. He'll hurt, but he's young and extremely fit. He should recover pretty quickly. Six weeks, and he'll be as good as new."

"Thank you. I'm Kay."

"Yeah, I know. We all know. He's quite the blabbermouth about you."

Kay opened her mouth to speak then shook her head and said nothing.

The nurse finished and began to move toward the door.

"May I stay a few minutes?"

"Sure, no problem." She held out her hand. "I'm Lei. I'll be here all night."

Kay took the outstretched hand. "Thank you, Lei."

"Rough day for you."

Kay nodded.

"Rougher for him. He's lucky to be alive. Could've bled to death before the paramedics got to him."

Kay nodded again. The lump in her throat grew larger. "Thank you."

Lei nodded. "You need anything?"

"No, I'll just be a moment."

"Okay. I'll be right down the hall."

Turning back to Harry, Kay took his hand again. As he softly snored, his mouth hung loosely open, giving him that naïve look she remembered so well. She noticed his lips were chapped. On the rolling table next to his bed, she found a small vial of Vaseline.

She closed her eyes and remembered the last time she saw Harry in a medical facility…how she had turned to him instead of her parents or other friends to drive her to the abortion clinic.

She remembered how he blushed when her hospital gown slipped from her shoulder, and how she cried when her clueless friend mentioned her halitosis, and how gently he applied Chapstick to her dry lips.

She picked up the Vaseline, unscrewed the top, and used her finger to apply it to Harry's lips. Replacing the vial, she took a final look at her long-lost friend and noted his unbandaged ear was permanently lumpy and swollen. "You kept wrestling, didn't you? You promised to always wear headgear so you wouldn't get cauliflower ears. And now look. I suppose the one under the bandage is worse. You promised."

With one hand pushing the baggy sweatshirt to her chest and the other resting on the bed frame, she leaned over and imagined she smelled the Harry who had spent so much time on her grandparents' farm—a mix of leather, hay, and sweat. Leaning over a bit further, she softly kissed his forehead then walked out the door.

* * *

In the waiting area, Levi and Mildred were locked in conversation with an elderly Asian couple. A boy about four years old slept, cradled against the woman's chest. Dressed alike in red plaid shirts, jeans, and work boots, the couple looked away from Levi and Mildred as soon as they saw Kay. The man pushed steel-framed glasses up his nose then doffed a battered baseball cap, exposing a glistening silver crew-cut. He stood and smiled. The woman remained on the couch, cuddling the boy. She wore her gray hair pulled back in a tight bun, and a pair of black-framed glasses hung from a chain around her neck.

Kay's eyes were transfixed on the slender, dark-skinned boy. She thought him beautiful.

Levi and Mildred sat on an adjacent couch while Cabrera leaned against a wall, talking quietly into her cell phone.

Mildred rose. "Oh, Kay, This is Alma and Kenji Toma. Harry rents a cottage on their farm. And this is Vincent, Harry's son."

"Son?" Kay whispered, still staring at the boy. "Oh my goodness."

"Hello," Kenji said, his eyes merrily greeting Kay's as he offered his hand. "It's something to actually meet you."

Kay shook his hand. "Um, hello."

Alma shifted Vincent until his head rested on her shoulder then stood. "Harry talked all weekend about you."

"Really?" Kay said.

Alma gently adjusted Vincent's position until she could lock her arms under the boy's rump then approached to within inches of Kay. The child began to stir. "Shh," Alma hushed. Squinting, she leaned closer to study Kay's face.

"Alma," Kenji said. "Your glasses."

"What?" Alma said. "Oh yeah. Stupid glasses." She took a half step backward then adjusted Vincent onto a single arm. A moment later, glasses on her nose, she again closed in on Kay's face. The crows' feet by her eyes crinkled deeply.

Levi and Mildred glanced at each other.

"Well, are you his best friend or what?" Alma asked.

Kenji laughed. "Alma, let the lady be."

"Hush, Kenji."

Kay pursed her lips. "I…I haven't seen Harry in ten years, so—"

"Alma," Kenji said, "come on now, we need to get Vincent home. Let's go say goodnight to Harry."

"But he's sleeping," Kay said. "The nurse gave him a shot."

"That's okay," Alma said, eyeing Kay and resting her cheek on Vincent's head. "We'll still say goodnight." She stroked the sleeping boy's head again then reached up and pulled Vincent's arms from her neck. Vincent stirred and opened his eyes as Alma turned him toward Kay. "Here, hold Vincent." She thrust the boy out until he touched Kay's chest. "He's almost done with a cold. The doc doesn't want a sick boy to visit his pops. So here, hold him while we say goodnight to Harry."

Too close to back away and with the child already pressed against her chest, Kay's arms encircled his small body. "Wait, I'm—"

Alma released her burden, grabbed Kenji's hand, and together they marched toward 505. "We'll be right back," Kenji said.

Transfixed on Vincent's face, Kay smiled softly. The boy placed his hands on her shoulders and sleepily returned her gaze. Satisfied, he wrapped his arms around her neck, nestled his head against her shoulder, and closed his eyes. Cabrera returned from her call and began a conversation with Mildred and Levi. Their voices dwindled to white noise as Kay hugged the boy and fell into the warmth of Vincent's body and the silkiness of his dark curls against her cheek.

The Tomas returned all too soon. Kenji took the boy, winked, and gave her a kind smile.

Kay returned the smile.

Alma nodded towards Agent Cabrera, Mildred, and Levi then took both of Kay's hands. "Best friends are best friends. Time means nothing."

12

Finding a way forward is helped by looking to the past.

For her interview, Kay sat across from Agent Cabrera at a table in a small hospital conference room. Fifteen minutes into the interview, Agent Cabrera turned off the recorder and asked Agent Henderson to inform Mildred and Levi that a ride would be provided for Ms. Morrell and that they could go home. "Don't let them protest, Tom. They're probably running on empty. I don't want them to have to wait."

"How much longer are we going to be here?" Kay asked.

"Not much longer. Thank you for your patience," Cabrera said then resumed the dull, repetitive questions that forced Kay to stifle yawn after yawn. How far from her position was the gunman? How many shots did she hear? Why did she think the gunman was white? Was she sure about the words the gunman shouted? Was there anything else she heard from the gunman? When did the window explode? When did the officer pull her to safety? On and on it went.

Sporadically, Agent Cabrera threw in questions about Harry. What was the gossip about him? Who were his friends on the faculty? Did she know any of his non-faculty friends? Kay had very little to offer.

Thirty minutes later, Agent Cabrera turned off the recorder.

"Are we done?" Kay asked.

"For now. I'll get my things and drive you home."

Kay nodded but said nothing.

In the hallway, Maizie told Tom, "I think she's tired enough."

"Okay, but you better hope she doesn't nod off while you drive."

"She'll talk. I don't think she's going to add anything, but maybe I'll find out a little more about our hero in 505."

"Case is definitely funky."

"I already said that."

"Whatever. You know? For the life of me, I can't see Ross as a target, even with his status as a confidential source."

Maizie opened her mouth to speak but said nothing and stared off into space.

"Do you think Ms. Morrell knows about his status?"

"No, not a chance. Ah, well, what a funky case." She turned away.

* * *

By eleven, with Kay slouching in the front seat, Agent Cabrera drove while silently glancing at her passenger. Soon Kay closed her tired eyes and slid into a troubled doze. Only when Agent Cabrera opened her door and gently shook her shoulder did she awaken. "We're there already?"

"No. Sorry," Agent Cabrera said, proffering a paper cup. "But I thought you might like some tea."

Kay straightened up and took the tea. She took a sip and felt the tingling warmth all the way down to her stomach. "Thank you. Sorry about dozing off."

"It's okay. You've had a day, haven't you?"

Kay nodded as she took another sip.

"Kay," Agent Cabrera said once they were moving again. "May I call you Kay?"

Kay took another sip. "Yes, that's fine. What may I call you?"

"Well, I prefer Agent Cabrera."

"I thought so."

"How's the tea?"

"It's perfect, but look, you don't need to play me, okay? I know you're just doing your job, but I think you already know everything we went over tonight. Except for…" She trailed off.

"Except for what?"

"I think you're trying to find out more about Harry, and I don't know what to tell you. I haven't seen him for years."

"We're just beginning the investigation, so we're looking into everything."

"I understand that. But the way you asked all those peripheral questions about Harry makes me wonder. Why don't you just ask me directly?"

Instead of answering the question, Maizie said, "We need more information because so far, nothing makes sense."

"So, what happened to that prevailing theory?"

"There are a number of theories, none of which answer all the questions."

"Earlier you said the prevailing theory was that the man got away from Harry, then shot him, and then committed suicide."

"Did I say that?"

"Yes, you did."

"Well, it's not prevailing anymore."

Kay nodded and had another sip.

They drove in silence for two blocks before Agent Cabrera said, "My name is Maizie. Indirect questioning is a technique I've found to be useful. I won't use it anymore with you."

"Thanks."

"You're not a panic-stricken, little schoolmarm, are you?"

"Oh…I was scared out of my wits. I'm just happy to be alive."

"The reports indicate you shouted at the shooter. That doesn't sound scared to me."

"Maizie, I'm a teacher. I recognize your little manipulative tricks. I have to use a lot of the same tricks working with teenagers. But today…" A lump formed in Kay's throat. She wiped painful tears from her face. "Damn." She sniffled.

"Kay—"

"I'm just saying it was hard today, really hard. I don't like things to be like that." She inserted her tea into a cup holder. "Do you have any Kleenex?"

"Glove box. Don't worry, it's okay."

Kay blew her nose, wiped her face, then grabbed her cup and drank more tea. "There, all better. Well, what else do you want to know?"

"How well do you know Mr. Ross?"

Kay laughed without humor. "I can't say that I know him at all anymore."

"Did you ever think he could do the kind of thing he did today?"

"You mean run straight at a man who was shooting at him? Yeah, that's Harry all right, no surprise there."

"So, you do know him a little bit."

Kay sighed. "We grew up together, but I haven't seen him in such a long time."

"Has he ever done things like that before?"

Kay's thoughts turned back to high school, to the times Harry had gotten into fights.

"Kay?"

Kay rubbed her eyes. "I'm sorry, what did you ask?"

"Has he ever been involved in something like this before?"

"No. I mean, he got into fights as a kid, but nothing like this. I know he joined the Marines, but I don't know if he ever went to war."

"How long have you known him?"

"I went over that already."

"I know. I saw it in your statement. But I'd like to hear it from you."

Kay sighed. "Well, I was born around 11:30 pm on December first, almost twenty-nine years ago. Harry was born a little over three hours later in the same delivery room. His mom and my mom shared a room. They were both Japanese-Americans and found out they lived only a couple blocks apart. And, well, they became friends. And then my dad and Harry's dad became friends. Whenever my parents went out, I stayed with the Rosses. Whenever Harry's folks went out, he stayed with us. We grew up together. Our families became more than friends, I guess. My grandparents owned a farm up in the foothills outside of town, and Harry and I would spend parts of our summer vacations there." She paused. "We were really good friends, that's all."

"What happened?"

"What do you mean?"

"Everything you said was past tense. Why aren't you still friends? What happened?"

"Oh, I thought you meant if it became sexual or anything. Did it get ruined because of sex." Kay paused. "Well, it didn't. It never got close to that. I mean, we hugged each other a few times and we helped each other a lot. We even argued. But nothing sexual, never."

"So, why aren't you still friends?"

Kay closed her eyes. "I just blabbed, didn't I? I just went off about something you never even asked about. Damn it."

"Kay, I really don't care about any sex you may or may not have had with Mr. Ross. I really don't. I'm just trying to get a picture of the man to see if there's anything, anything at all, that would make him a target."

"God…growing up, he was always a target. He was different and children can be cruel."

"His childhood doesn't concern me. When did you last hear from him?"

Kay sighed. "He quit writing. I got a card for my twenty-first birthday and then, poof, nothing. Well, he wrote my dad, but it was just the business about his house. After a while my Dad didn't even let me see the letters. So we quit communicating. Not another word. Then on Friday he showed up at school, and on Monday he charged that madman with a gun."

"He used to write?"

"Yes. Letters. It's funny, you know he hand wrote every one of his letters or cards…never even used email. He was so backwards sometimes."

"Interesting. Did you keep any of the letters?"

Kay hesitated.

"Kay?"

"No. Well, I suppose after a few years of moving from one small apartment to the next, one tends to dump things."

"How about your dad? Did he keep any letters from Mr. Ross?"

"Oh, I don't know. Please don't bother him with all this. He's undergoing chemo, and it's very hard for him right now."

"But it may be important. And I'll tell you what's bothering me. You knew him in his youth, until he was twenty-one or so."

"I never saw him after high school," Kay said.

"Yes, but he wrote. You had contact, right?"

"Yes."

"During the time he was in the Marines, right?"

"Yes, but he rarely wrote about his service. Well, I mean, he did, but I guess he didn't have a normal experience in the Marines."

"How's that?"

"He made some Marine wrestling team. I didn't even know the Marines *had* a wrestling team, but anyway, he made it and spent a lot of his time training or going to tournaments. He wrote a bunch of short, little notes about his wrestling and the countries he went to compete in."

"He served in Iraq."

Kay squirmed uncomfortably. "I didn't know that."

"We have access to his records. He did a tour there in his last year of service. He remained mainly in the Green Zone as some sort of analyst."

"That sounds like Harry. I guess that's around when he quit writing to me."

"My point is, we have that time in his life fairly well identified. Plus, we've spoken to his wife."

"He's married?"

Maizie nodded. "She's listed as his emergency contact. She's a lawyer in Chicago, but I believe they're separated. She's on her way here and should arrive tonight sometime."

After a long silence, Kay said, "Oh."

Maizie glanced at Kay then shrugged. "So, we have his time when he was married and his time with the Tomas. He's been living with them for almost three years, but—"

"Three *years?*"

"Yes, three years. He's been working on the farm, going to school, and raising his kid. Apparently, he's making ends meet with a decent nest egg saved from his service time and the sale of his parents' house in Visalia a couple years back." Maizie sighed. "While we didn't get much from Mr. Ross during our first interview, he said a great deal about you. So, we're turning to you. Anything you can tell us may prove useful. The thing is, there are more than two years of Mr. Ross's life where we know nothing. From the time he got out of the Marines to the time he married. We're trying to find out about those years to see if there's anything that would make him a target."

They drove in silence for a while before Kay said, "Like I said, Harry was a target his whole life. An easy target."

TUESDAY

13

When little makes sense, focus on simple tasks.

Before Maizie dropped Kay off at her apartment complex, the two women exchanged cell numbers. While in the car, they had solved nothing, adding more frustration and confusion to Kay's exhaustion. After all that had happened, dredging up long lost memories of Harry had burned the remains of her energy. Worst of all, Kay felt strongly that Maizie was hiding something about Harry.

She thumped up the stairs, entered, and walked to the kitchen. Huffing, she returned to the door and set the deadbolt. She stripped to her underwear in the tiny laundry area and decided a shower could wait for morning. As she headed for bed, she looked at her phone. Numerous people had called, including her mom, George, and others whose numbers she did not recognize.

Clicking on the light, Kay froze when she saw a man sleeping in her bed then sighed heavily. "George! What are you doing here?"

George bolted upright. "What? Kay? What time is it?"

"What are you doing here?"

Pivoting his feet to the floor, George cleared his throat. "I called and called. You never answered." Dressed in boxers and a t-shirt, he rubbed his eyes and shook his head.

Arms crossed, Kay leaned against the doorframe.

"I was worried. So…I came over. I was so worried."

Kay remained mute.

"Why didn't you answer? It's all over the news. *You're* all over the news. I—"

"My phone was on vibrate." Kay shrugged.

"What?"

She held up her phone. "It was on vibrate. I didn't answer because I never heard it. I had a lot of calls."

He walked toward Kay and pulled her into an embrace. "Hey, it's okay."

She folded her arms across her chest and let George hold her for a moment before gently pushing him away. "George," she whispered, "we had a deal."

He staggered half a step back. "Did you think I would stay away after all this? There's no way. You know that."

Kay dropped her head then patted his arms. "Yeah, okay. I'm sorry."

He took her hand and led her to the bed, where they sat side by side.

Kay blinked back a few tears. "George, I'm sorry, but I have to go to sleep now. I'm so tired, and I have a meeting tomorrow. You can stay here if you want, but not here, not in the bed, okay? I need to sleep alone tonight. I don't mean to sound like this, but I just need some time."

George shook his head. "No, I don't think leaving you alone tonight is what you need. I'll sleep on the floor or on the couch or something. That's okay. But I also think, I mean, I have something to tell you. I think it'll be good for you."

Kay shrugged. "What?"

"You know I'm going to New York."

Kay had forgotten but nodded anyway. The fact that he was going to be out of town had made their deal more palatable.

"I want you to come with me. I think it's important for you to get away right now. I mean, you're all over the news."

Kay sat up straight and leaned away from George.

"I bought your ticket. The flight's not until tomorrow afternoon. It'll be..." George trailed off.

Kay sadly shook her head.

"You're not going to go with me, are you?"

"The school's in trouble now, George. I…how could I possibly leave?"

"I don't know. Stupid of me to think you would, I guess."

Kay sighed. Reaching up, she placed the palm of her hand on his cheek. "No, not stupid. And thanks for trying. But this is who I am. I think that's why you love me, isn't it?"

George covered her hand and gave a small smile. "Absolutely."

They remained locked together, cheek and hand, until Kay's cell chimed.

She pulled her hand away from George and looked at the screen. "It's the FBI agent."

"The FBI? Now?"

She answered just as she heard a siren in the distance. "Maizie?"

"Kay, you still at home?" Maizie asked.

Kay heard urgency in her voice. "Where else would I be?"

"Good, stay there. An officer will be there shortly. His name is Officer Cornish, Charles Cornish."

"I know Charlie." The siren grew louder. She stood up. "What's going on?"

"Stay clear of your windows. Is your door locked?"

Kay glanced at her window. It overlooked the wooded ridge across the street. "The door's locked. What *is* going on?"

"What's going on?" George echoed frantically.

Kay held up a finger. "Maizie, talk to me."

"Don't answer the door unless Officer Cornish identifies himself. Do you understand?"

Pacing now, Kay almost shouted, "Maizie!"

George stood, mouth agape.

"Someone tried to kill Mr. Ross again," Maizie said.

Kay's stomach clenched. "What?"

"He's fine," Maizie said. "Look, Officer Cornish will be there shortly."

Kay nodded.

"Kay?"

"Yes, I'm here."

"Wait for Officer Cornish, and stay away from the windows, okay?"

"Okay."

Maizie cut off the connection.

Kay let her arm fall, dropping the phone. It bounced quietly on the carpet. "Someone tried to kill Harry at the hospital."

"Kill? Kill who?"

The siren screamed to a stop outside.

"I have to get dressed," Kay said, picking up her phone.

"What? Kay, what's happening?"

Kay looked at George. "You better get dressed too."

By the time Charlie pressed her door buzzer at the building's entrance, Kay had donned clean jeans and a long-sleeved t-shirt. She let him in at the street entrance then waited at her door for his knock.

Once inside, Charlie darted around the apartment without a word, pulling down window blinds and turning off lights. When finished, he turned on a small lamp next to the couch where Kay sat. George, now fully dressed, sat nervously at the table in the adjoining dining area.

Sirens continued to blare.

"More people are on their way," Charlie announced, looking at George. "Who are you?"

"Halliday, George Halliday. I'm…I'm here to see Kay. I was worried about her."

Charlie nodded and spoke into his shoulder mike, identifying George.

"He's my friend, Charlie," Kay said quietly from the couch. "What happened?"

"Don't know, Ms. Morrell, don't know," Charlie responded. "We've all pulled double shifts from the thing this morning, and then I got called to come over because the FBI said you might be a target." He paused. "That's all I know."

"Target?" George said. "Kay? A target? Why? How could that be?"

Kay looked at Charlie. "An FBI agent called me and said someone tried to kill Harry at the hospital."

"The Ross fella?" Charlie asked.

Kay nodded.

"Okay," Charlie said. "We're all gonna sit for a while until the cavalry arrives. Everyone got that?"

Kay slouched and let her head drop onto the backrest. George sat still, staring at the lowered window blinds.

Minutes later, Charlie opened the door for Maizie.

"Kay," Maizie said, "we're going to move you. You need to pack a bag with enough for three days. I don't know where we're going yet, but we'll find out in the car."

Kay remained sitting.

"Kay, we need to hurry."

"Is Harry all right?" Kay asked sharply.

"He's unhurt. We have more people on him now."

Kay closed her eyes and nodded.

George remained seated, his head swiveling from person to person.

"Kay, we need to hurry, please."

"Fine." Kay shook her head and walked toward the bedroom.

"Mr. Halliday," Maizie said, "an officer will escort you home. Are you ready to leave?"

"I want to stay with Kay," George said.

"I'm sorry, sir, but either you can drive yourself home with an escort, or I'll have an officer drive you home in a squad car. This is for your own protection."

"I live in San Francisco. Is this really necessary?"

"Officer Cornish," Maizie said.

"Yes, ma'am."

"Please set up transportation for Mr. Halliday. I really don't have the time for this."

"Yes, ma'am, no problem. I'll get right on it," Charlie said. "Mr. Halliday, this way, sir."

"Kay! Talk to them," George shouted.

"George," Kay said then paused. "I'll call you. Go home. It's best for now."

Charlie spoke at length on his shoulder mic then escorted a reluctant George out of the apartment. Kay stuffed clothes into a small roller bag. She stared at the wadded mess as Maizie entered.

Maizie adjusted her Bluetooth earpiece. "Ready?"

"I don't know. Almost, I guess."

"We need to hurry." Maizie went back into the living room.

Kay spent a few minutes packing an array of toiletries then remembered Harry's letters. Impulsively, she stuffed the large manila envelope into her bag before wheeling it into the living room. She glared at Maizie. "This has been a really long day, you know? A really long, really bad day."

Maizie nodded. "Yeah, it has. And all we can do now is try to keep the damage minimal until we get the chance to make the day better. Ready?"

They left the apartment and took the stairs to the main entrance.

"We're approaching the lobby," Maizie said into her Bluetooth. "Are you ready outside? Yes, that's good… Pull in front, you'll see the main entrance… Yeah, get as close as you can. Use the opposing lane."

"This is crazy," Kay whispered. "It makes no sense."

Maizie nodded. "Just stay calm. We'll get you out of here."

"Why is this happening? It makes no sense for anyone to be gunning for me or Harry."

They met another agent at the front door. His gun was drawn and pointing at the floor. He stepped out onto the walkway in front of the entrance and scanned the area.

Some sort of signal must have passed between them because suddenly Maizie said, "Okay, straight ahead, the big van in the street. Climb in and move to the far side, got it?"

Kay looked between the parked cars and saw the van sitting in the near lane, heading in the wrong direction. The engine was running and the sliding door on the driver's side was open. She shrugged and nodded.

"When we go, move quickly, but don't run."

Kay nodded.

"Here we go." Maizie stepped behind Kay and grabbed a wad of her sweatshirt between her shoulder blades. She gave a little push with her fist, and they moved out onto the sidewalk. They stepped off the curb between a Toyota and a Volkswagen and took one more step before a bullet shattered the side glass of the Toyota's backdoor. The window exploded, sending tiny cubes of glass flying in every direction.

"Move, move, move!" Maizie shouted.

The other agent shouted, "Gun! Gun!"

Propelled forward by Maizie's fist, Kay scrambled into the van.

Just as Maizie had a foot in the door, she lurched sideways and slammed her hip into the wall of the vehicle. "Shit!" she screamed as she hunched over and dove inside. Kay caught her by the shoulders.

"Go! Go! Go!" Maizie shouted with her head on Kay's lap. The van surged forward with the sliding door still open.

"Get your feet in the door!" the driver shouted.

They slid into a hard right turn. Kay screamed as she felt Maizie sliding toward the opening. She grabbed the agent's collar with both hands.

The van straightened out before Kay could pull Maizie inside.

Maizie, screaming through clenched teeth, rolled onto her side and pulled in her legs. The sliding door closed. "I'm hit, goddamn it, I'm hit," she said between bursts of rapid, heavy breathing.

The driver picked up his radio mike. "This is Doman. Cabrera's been hit. I repeat, Cabrera has been shot. We're southbound on Pine. I need a twenty on the hospital."

The radio crackled. "Agent Doman, this is Officer Cornish. I'm on your six. Slow down and let me pass. I'll escort you to the hospital."

Kay craned around and saw the flashing lights of Charlie's squad car. The van decelerated. She could just make out Charlie as he sped past in a blaze of blue lights. Maizie continued to wince and huff.

"Here," the driver shouted as he tossed a small box into the back seat. "See if you can help her!"

"What?"

"First Aid kit."

Kay opened the kit then took a deep breath and leaned close to Maizie's ear. "Where are you shot?"

"My ass," Maizie whispered through clenched teeth. "Bastard shot me in the fucking ass."

Kay nodded. "I have to… I'm going to move down into the foot well, okay?" As she slid to the floor, Maizie continued to hiss through her teeth. With her knees settled uncomfortably on the floorboard, Kay reached up and turned on the dome light. Blood covered the seat and trickled down to the floor, soaking the knees of Kay's jeans. The van took another hard turn, throwing Kay painfully over the drivetrain hump.

Hands shaking, Kay took another deep breath then twisted her body to face Maizie, who lay prone on the seat with her face buried in her hands.

Carefully, Kay tugged at Maizie's skirt until her buttocks were exposed. Even in the dim light of the dome lamp, she saw the small, round hole in the woman's left cheek. Blood seeped steadily out of the puckered opening. With badly shaking hands, she rummaged around in the first aid kit until she found gauze pads wrapped in waxed paper envelopes. Clumsily, she tore open several, placed them on the wound, and pressed.

Maizie hissed and mumbled something into her hands.

"What?"

Maizie lifted her head and muttered, "Exit wound. There's gotta be an exit wound."

"Hold on," the driver shouted. "Five more minutes."

"Exit wound, of course," Kay whispered. Carefully, with one hand still pressing down on the entry wound, she used the other to push on Maizie's hip and roll her onto her side. Not much larger than the entry wound, the exit wound poured out blood.

"Oh, God," Kay whispered. She took another handful of gauze pads, released the pressure from the entry wound, and used both hands to tear off the waxed paper coverings. Wadding some of the pads into a tight ball, she stuffed them into the exit wound and pressed. She used her free hand to replace the pads over the entry wound and rode the rest of the way to the hospital, covering each of the two wound sites. In the background she heard excited chatter over the radio but understood none of it over the screaming siren.

The van bumped hard onto the hospital driveway, roared to the emergency entrance, and skidded to a stop. Even before the vehicle had settled, the door slid open. A man in surgical scrubs climbed in beside Kay. "What do we have?"

Kay looked at her hands. "She's been shot. I've been using direct pressure and, like that. Direct pressure."

"Okay, good. Excellent, in fact. Keep the pressure on." He turned and shouted, "Bring the gurney to the door!" He turned to Maizie. "Ma'am, can you hear me? I'm Doctor Truong. Can you hear me?"

"Yes," Maizie said hoarsely.

"Good, we have to move you, and I'm afraid it's going to hurt a bit. You understand?"

Maizie nodded. "Do I have a fucking choice?"

The doctor offered a one-syllable laugh. "Okay, miss, you can let go now."

Kay nodded, jerked her hands away, then pressed herself against the opposite door.

"Her legs," the doctor said to the people outside. "Take her legs and we'll slide her out onto the gurney. I'll take her upper body. Go on my count." Two people from outside the van grasped Maizie's legs, while the doctor slid his hands under Maizie's torso. "Okay, one, two, three!" Maizie slid along the seat and onto the gurney.

Kay watched until the gurney entered the building. The agent who drove the van came into view. "Ms. Morrell, will you come with me, please?"

Kay looked up. "May I sit for a while, just a minute or two?"

The agent turned and signaled to someone. "I'm going to leave this officer with you while I make arrangements. When you're ready, please come inside."

Kay nodded and the agent walked away.

Charlie poked his head into the van. "You all right, Ms. Morrell?"

Kay, blinded by the lights behind him, nodded. "Yeah, I think so. I just need to sit a bit. Is that all right?"

Charlie straightened up and looked around. "Sure. I'll be right here."

Kay gave a wan smile.

Charlie leaned against the vehicle, avoiding the blood puddles on the pavement.

A few minutes later, a lean man dressed in scrubs, a scrub cap, and a surgical mask approached.

"Oh shit," Charlie whispered. He faced the man. "Um…Doc, can I help you?"

Moving out of Kay's view, Charlie and the doctor talked for a few moments before returning to the van.

The doctor toyed with the mask covering his nose. "Excuse me, Ms. Morrell, we need to get you inside. Will you come with me, please?"

"Do you know what's happening?" Kay asked.

The doctor shrugged. Backlit by the bright lights, he was a dark mass. "I don't know much, just that Agent Cabrera asked me to fetch you. I believe they're setting something up for you here."

"How is she?" Kay asked as she started to rise.

"The wound doesn't appear to be life-threatening."

She nodded, got out of the van, and followed him inside. Charlie accompanied them to the door then said, "I gotta stay near the unit, Ms. Morrell."

Kay stopped, turned around, and hugged Charlie tightly. "Charlie, please call me Kay."

"Sure, Kay, sure." Charlie walked away.

Once inside, the doctor led Kay to a group of three men, all wearing black FBI sweatshirts, including the van driver. "Excuse me."

All three stared at Kay in her blood-soaked clothes.

"Ms. Morrell, I thought you wished to stay in the car," the driver said. "I left a cop with you. Where is he?"

"He went back to his car," Kay said.

The doctor added, "Agent Cabrera asked the hospital to accommodate Ms. Morrell. Would you please escort her to the third floor. The nurse on station will help you."

The driver asked, "Agent Cabrera said that? She's supposed to stay here? In the hospital?"

The doctor nodded and offered a slip of paper. "I have a note from her."

The driver read the note while the doctor walked away. "Okay. Cabrera wants you here tonight. Probably better anyhow. Shall we go, Ms. Morrell?"

The third floor stood empty, except for one heavyset woman who manned the nurses' station.

"Excuse me," the agent said. "I was told we could house Ms. Morrell on this floor. Do you have a room somewhere?"

The woman, busy typing on her computer, barely glanced at the agent. "You one of them G-Men with all that commotion downstairs?" She looked up and saw Kay's haggard face.

"Yes, ma'am. I'm Special Agent Donigan. If you could—"

"Lordy, sister, are you hurt?" the nurse asked.

"This is Ms. Morrell," Agent Donigan said. "Presently, she is in protective custody, and we need a room where she can stay until we—"

"Custody?" Kay asked.

"Sister," the nurse said, "are you doin' okay?"

Kay looked at her bloody hands, bloody sweatshirt, and bloody knees. "It's not my blood. I'm fine."

"Can you find us a room?" the agent asked, looking at the nurse's name tag. "Nurse Bette."

Nurse Bette held up her ring of keys while she stared at Kay. "You're the one, aren't you, honey? The one they were shooting at this morning at the school."

Kay closed her eyes and nodded. "Yeah, that's me."

"Would you like a shower, honey? I mean, you look like you could use one."

"I…yes…but I don't have a change of clothes. I—"

Nurse Bette raised her finger to silence Kay. "C'mon, honey. Follow me. We got showers, and I'll find you something to wear."

"Ma'am, where are these showers?" Agent Donigan asked. "I've been assigned to watch over her."

Nurse Bette glared at him with her upraised finger. "You can put your tiny little ass by the door, Mr. Special Agent Donigan. Come on, honey, it's right down here." She moved out of the station and walked down the hall.

Kay looked at her bloody hands and turned to Agent Donigan. "A shower will help. You don't mind, do you?"

"No, ma'am. It's all right. I'll stand outside the door." He paused and looked at Kay. "Ma'am?"

"Yes?"

"You did real well today."

Kay shook her head, sighed, then nodded.

"Hey!" Nurse Bette called, already halfway down the hall. "Special Agent Donigan, the lady needs to shower."

"I'll be right outside the door," Agent Donigan said.

Kay smiled softly and moved away.

She caught up with Nurse Bette at a door with an etched plastic sign that decreed, "NURSES ONLY."

"You go on in, honey. The showers are in the back." She pulled a plastic bag off a roll from a nearby cart. "Put your clothes in here and set them outside the shower door. I'll see if we can get some of that blood off before it sets."

"Thank you. I don't know what to say."

Agent Donigan, cell phone to his ear, said. "Excuse me, Nurse Bette, is there another entrance?"

Nurse Bette put her hands on her hips. "No, sir." She took Kay's elbow and led her into the nurses' domain. Five steel-framed beds with cheap mattresses lined one wall, a row of lockers stood on the opposite wall, and a wooden bench ran down the center. A frosted glass door led to the lavatories and showers. Nurse Bette gave Kay the plastic bag, opened the glass door, and gently pushed her in.

"I'll wait here for the bag. You go on now. There ain't nothing like a hot shower to start feeling like yourself again. You've had a tough day, and you don't want to end up giving another part of yourself to the day or to them morons with the guns or the federales. They're all trying to take a piece of you. Don't you let them do it.

Now, go on and git. Towels are inside the shower room on a shelf. I'll wait here for your clothes."

"Thank you. I just—"

"Go on. I've gotta lot of other crap that needs attention."

* * *

Kay washed and rewashed. Grit and light gray mud foamed out of her hair, leaving a dirty path to the drain. Staring at nothing, she found it difficult to believe that the shooting—the first shooting—had occurred less than twenty-four hours earlier.

Her mind kept drifting back to Harry. "I saw you," she whispered. "I talked to you. You seem like the same guy. But you're not, are you? Oh God, Harry. What's going on?"

She leaned against the wall and let the hot water pound her head, neck, and shoulders. When tired of standing, she sat under the cascade. Soon, the hard tile floor pained her backside, so she stood, shut down the water, and dried off. Outside the shower room, she found a pile of neatly folded surgical scrubs atop a bed. Under the floppy green garments were undergarments and ankle socks. Everything was too large but comfortable.

She finished dressing, stared wistfully at the beds, then padded to the door. In the hallway, she spied Agent Donigan and Nurse Bette chatting about baseball. Both stopped talking when Kay appeared.

Nurse Bette held blankets and a pillow. "C'mon, sister. Let's get you to bed."

Kay smiled sadly.

A clock on the locker room wall read 2:14 by the time Kay finally lay on her side and pulled the blanket to her chin. Though exhausted, she found sleep difficult. Nurse Bette's little words of wisdom sounded too much like Harry's *Don't let anything take you from you*, the little maxim he repeated *ad nauseum* through childhood.

Kay remembered a time when she had a boyfriend for whom Harry had little respect. Harry wanted her to break away from the guy and had prodded her with the *you-from-you* thing until she blew up and iced him out of her life for a few days. Then she learned her boyfriend had been two-timing her. "Okay," she whispered, "I guess I went out with a few turds in disguise. Yeah, you saved me back then too. I guess we needed each other."

She forced her eyes closed only to have more memories of Harry march through her head.

In the seventh grade, her dad encouraged Harry to go out for wrestling, thinking it might toughen the boy up. During his disastrous first season, Harry's only success came at the conclusion of his final match when he somehow managed to avoid being pinned. He shook hands and jogged off the mat, muttering, "You from you. You from you."

Under her dad's advice, he spent that entire summer on her grandparents' farm. He took to the hard, repetitive, physical labor like a fish to water. Milking their one and only cow, building fences, baling hay, and digging trenches should've kept him busy all day.

Her father, however, had other ideas. He gave Harry a regimen of daily exercises. Harry never missed a day. If Grandpa wanted to start the day before dawn, Harry rose an hour earlier to work out. When Kay and her parents visited on weekends and farm work was curtailed, Harry doubled or tripled his regimen. Come nightfall, while everyone else chatted happily in the living room, Harry would fall dead asleep on the rug.

By the end of summer Harry could pump off sixty-pushups, fifteen pull-ups, and hundreds of sit-ups. She remembered because she had to serve as the scorekeeper when her dad tested Harry. He'd also grown three inches to five feet four and had gone from something under eighty pounds to a little over a hundred pounds.

The next wrestling season, the two dads and grandpa went to all of Harry's matches. Even Kay attended some. Harry won more than he lost and was never pinned. His coach said he had potential and offered him a more intense regimen of exercise, one that included weight lifting and running. The coach emphasized the never-miss-a-day philosophy.

The everyday thing bothered Kay. Harry had turned into a maniac. When she confronted him on his narrow focus on life, he thought for a long time then simply offered, "Don't let anything take you from you."

The physical and verbal abuse of Harry died as he developed his wrestling prowess in the ninth grade. Instead, Harry was essentially ignored. His exaggerated blinking, his long conversational pauses, and the way he could stare at a person's face made most people uncomfortable. Kay remembered this subtle shunning hurt her friend the most.

Wrestling, no doubt, helped. The number of people he associated with slowly grew. He could almost be social. People respected him. The sport not only changed his outlook; it also changed his physique. At the same time, Kay was beginning to notice boys, and boys were beginning to notice her. And Harry, for the first time in his life, had a body that Kay found interesting.

14

One sly move and a rook can no longer hide.

Fuming, Sergio walked quickly through the cold, predawn light. Already four blocks from the hospital, he still had to stifle his urge to run. "Why did they use that weak-ass Hoffman? And why did I have to be the guy who fucking backed him up? What was Roman thinking? Fuck!"

Roman, the middleman with the money, had said, "It's all in the message. Carlos wants the guy to deliver a message to the target before taking him out. So, it's got to be done, you know, up close and personal."

"A message."

"Yeah. A fuck-you message."

"Hoffman's never done this kind of thing before," Sergio had said.

"He will. We're leveraging his family."

"That's not what I mean. He won't be able to pull the trigger."

"Well then, that's where you come in."

"Okay. But if I've gotta do it, it won't be personal. I'll be on the roof."

Roman shrugged. "Carlos knows you might have to improvise. Oh, and understand that either way, when it's over, Hoffman has to go. He's expendable."

The plan should have worked. Sergio's position on top of the apartment building gave him sightlines to the school's courtyard and the park where Hoffman had been ordered to hit the target. If Hoffman balked, then Sergio would have a clear shot as the target rode by on his bicycle. The position also provided easy escape routes.

When the day arrived, he watched from his perch as Hoffman waited in the park. But the target never rode by. Soon Hoffman began pacing and punching the air. He even pointed toward Sergio's position on the roof. The situation worsened when, inexplicably, Hoffman walked to the school's parking lot and drew the attention of both students and teachers. Only when Hoffman began to walk away did Sergio take an easy breath. But then Hoffman turned, crossed the parking lot, and barged into the crowd of kids in the school's courtyard.

Sergio called Roman. While he waited for the call to connect, Hoffman pulled out his piece and began shooting. Roman answered, listened, then immediately ordered Sergio to take Hoffman out. But by that time some fucking hero was locked onto Hoffman, and the two were rolling around on the grass. Sergio missed several times before Hoffman lay dead across the hero's lap. Hoping no children had been shot, Sergio scrambled down the fire escape.

Once he was clear of the area and he could think, he figured there would be no follow up for at least a month. But later that day, Roman called and said that the fucking hero was Hoffman's intended target. It had become a cosmic situation according to Roman. Calmly, he ordered Sergio to finish the bastard off in his hospital bed. Sergio briefly thought the man had to be kidding. But Roman never joked about anything regarding Carlos.

Roman had also said it would be simple. Walk in, do it, and walk out. But he never said one word about a fucking cop standing guard at the door. As soon as Sergio approached, the cop figured out the play, and pulled his weapon. Sergio ran. Fortunately, the cop never left his post, and Sergio managed to hide in the laundry room until the lockdown ended. Trashing his doctor togs, he slipped into his handyman clothes and walked out with the rest of the crowd.

While relieved that he had escaped, he wondered how he was going to explain everything. As deep as he was in Carlos's organization, he knew Carlos did not abide failure. He knew what had been done to Hoffman's kids and old lady, but Sergio had no family. More important, he had come to believe the guy in the hospital was not the legendary Harry who had bombed Carlos's home. The guy was just too young. Explaining that to Carlos after all that had happened was going to be tough. For now, he was going to rest, get a bite to eat, then think about his next message to his boss.

He turned into an alley past the small mom and pop store on Hastings and shivered. Something wasn't right. He backed up against the dirty white clapboard wall and peaked around the corner. "Nothing, nobody. Get a fucking grip." He crossed the street and hurried into his apartment on the second floor of the old row house.

* * *

Across the street, hidden in the shadow of a recessed doorway, a wiry old man watched. "Gotcha, ya bastard," he whispered then walked away.

15

"You from you" takes on new life.

Nurse Bette jostled Kay's shoulder. "Come on, sister. I hate to wake you, but that FBI lady wants to see you."

Kay opened her eyes and cleared her throat. "What?"

"The FBI lady, that lil' thing that orders everybody about, well, she's leaving in a bit and says she needs to see you."

Kay sat up and rubbed her eyes. "Cabrera? She wants to see me? She's okay?"

"No, sister, she ain't okay. She's a mean-ass bitch in my book. A tough old bitch, but a bitch just the same. She's moving about on her crutches and snapping at every damn living soul."

Kay pushed the hair out of her face. "When?"

"Now, sister. She's pretty adamant."

Kay slid off the bed and looked at the wall clock. "God, it's after nine."

Two agents escorted Kay to a first floor, glass-enclosed office. Maizie leaned on a pair of crutches next to a counter as she shuffled through a stack of papers while talking on her cell phone.

Kay stepped in just as Maizie finished her phone call.

"Well, I heard you got some sleep," Maizie said.

"Yes, I did. I'm surprised to see you on your feet. What's going on? Has something happened to Harry?"

"No, he's fine."

"Well, what happened?"

Maizie shrugged. "A man in surgical scrubs tried to gain access to Mr. Ross's room. The cop on duty smelled a rat and challenged the individual. The guy took off and disappeared down the stairs. The cop remained on station and called for help." Maizie paused, took a breath, and wiped a film of perspiration from her forehead. "Anyway, the hospital locked down, but it's a big place and the man escaped. We have a good description of him and, well, we just might get lucky and find him."

Kay stared at the woman.

Maizie shifted her weight. "Mr. Ross slept through the whole thing."

"He was sedated," Kay said.

"Yeah, I know. You all right?"

"I'm okay. What about you?"

"Fit as a fiddle. Now, the reason I asked to see you is to apologize for leaving you unattended in the car last night. So, and I do mean this, I apologize."

"I wasn't left alone. Officer Cornish was with me."

"The agent should not have left you. He should have waited until he was relieved."

Kay stared at Maizie but said nothing.

"Kay, this is what we train for, and we screwed up. I screwed up. You know, the only thing saving my ass from being fired is my ass. After what you did for me, I'm really sorry."

Kay nodded.

"Okay," Maizie said. "The shooter last night, the one at your place…well, he's dead. The local cops figured out that he must have stashed his getaway vehicle on a road on the other side of the ridge from where he fired his weapon. There's an unfinished development there."

"I know. I've walked over the ridge and seen it. There's a trail. They look like they would've been nice homes."

"Yeah, it's the times, I guess. Anyway, they found the suspect's vehicle and waited. The guy came out shooting, and they had to put him down."

"Oh God."

"Yeah, I'm sorry too." Maizie sighed. "We're in the dark with this case, and not having the chance to interview him is a lost opportunity. Anyway, we're working on his ID and hope it will lead us somewhere."

Kay shifted her weight. "And just where does all this leave Harry and me?"

Maizie pursed her lips. "All I can say at this point is that you and Harry will be under our protection. As of now, we don't understand enough to know what's what."

Kay shook her head. "It's...it's so hard to believe. Why? Why would anyone want to do this?"

Maizie shifted painfully on her crutches and wiped her face yet again. "I can't answer that yet." She took a few deep breaths. "Enough of that. My agents tell me a doctor escorted you into the hospital."

"Yes, he did. He had a note from you."

Maizie sighed. "I remember writing the note. But I don't remember who I gave it to. It should've been an agent, not this doctor. Anyway, I didn't want to wait for some safe-house to be ready." She sighed. "We needed to protect you, and I thought it would be better here. At least for the night. God knows we had enough personnel on site, and the hospital had a place for you to sleep. I need to thank that doctor. Do you remember his name?"

Kay sighed and closed her eyes. "I wasn't really paying attention. He came to the van and said you wanted me to come inside."

"Could you tell me what he looked like?"

Kay thought for a moment then shook her head. "The lights behind him were really bright, so I didn't see any nametag. I couldn't even see his face. He was thin, though. Not just trim, but thin, skinny. Charlie saw him. Maybe he remembers."

"Officer Cornish? Hmm. I'll check with him later." Maizie looked away from Kay. "I wasn't myself last night."

"You should be in bed."

Maizie wiped more sweat from her head. "This is what I do, Kay. In this outfit, with a case like this, you don't let anyone or anything take it away from you. You do that, you may never get another. It's what I do."

Kay said nothing but thought, *you from you.*

Maizie pointed toward the wall. "Your bag is over there. You need to get changed. We have a safe place for you, and we need to get a move on."

"Wait, I'm expected to be at a meeting at ten."

"You can't go to some meeting. You know that, don't you? You were shot at. We have to find out why. And Harry's shooter is still on the loose. You know you can't go."

Kay stared at Maizie. "No, I don't. The school's in trouble, and I was asked to help. This is who *I* am."

Hesitating, Maizie wiped her face. "Where's this damn meeting? The school?"

"At Mr. Abramson's house. He's the—"

"I remember." Maizie crutched over to the window and banged on it with her knuckles.

* * *

Dressed in jeans and a long-sleeved collared shirt, Kay again sat in a black van. Maizie reclined on a stack of pillows in the front seat, while Agent Henderson drove. Their vehicle was second in a caravan of three.

"Mr. Abramson is going to be surprised," Kay said.

"I called him. He knows we're coming."

"He knows three cars full of people are coming?"

"Maybe not that part. But most of us are heading to the city and won't be there long. I told him you're with us and we might be a little late. Then I asked him if his board would like a briefing on the progress of the case. He seemed very excited about the idea." She paused. "Kay, I can't emphasize this enough…you're still a target. So, please listen and follow all instructions from your security detail."

"I…" Something flashed in the back of Kay's mind. She tried to focus on it, but it slipped away.

"Kay? You understand?"

"Yeah…of course," Kay mumbled as she wrestled with the fleeting thought.

"Good. Now then, during the briefing, I'm not going to mention your part in the shooting outside your apartment."

Kay hesitated. "But why? It must be in the news already."

"Right now, the press is unaware of your involvement. Their focus is on the other side of the ridge where the shooter was killed. The man had drug paraphernalia in his car, so we're going to insinuate that it was a drug-related situation. If asked, we'll say it might be related to the school shooting, but it's most likely just a coincidence."

"But why?"

"Basically, it's just a small effort to confuse the bad guys."

"Won't they see through that?"

"Maybe. Probably. But you'd be surprised how stupid people can be. So, we'll take a chance on confusion. The local cops are on board. They know it's to protect you, so they'll keep quiet. Can you live with that?"

"Do I have to lie?"

"No, I don't think so. If I do it right, they won't even consider the possibility." Maizie thought for a few moments. "How many of the people at this meeting know where you live?"

"I just moved into my apartment at the beginning of the summer. Of course, the school has my address, but only my boyfriend has ever been there."

"So, no one's going to ask us about the proximity of your apartment to the shooting."

"No…I guess not."

"Good."

They turned up the long drive way to Levi's house. "I'm putting them in danger, aren't I?" Kay asked.

Maizie took a pain pill and washed it down with coffee. "Not likely. The bad guys have two shooters dead and have to be scratching their heads about what happened. They're going to need some time to figure out their next step. Hell, they might even call the whole thing off. Who knows?"

As they parked, Kay blurted, "I need to visit Harry—today. I'm sorry if that causes trouble, but it's something I have to do."

Maizie huffed angrily then said, "Fine…I'll speak to your security people. They will be a combination of FBI and local law enforcement personnel."

16

*The knights see the moves but don't
understand the old rogue's strategy.*

As Jorge stepped outside the gate at SFO, his phone chirped. He studied the other passengers then stuffed a Bluetooth into his ear. "Yeah?"

"You okay to talk? A lot of shit's been happening," Cobb said.

Jorge's breathing quickened as he felt a sharp pain in his abdomen. "Just arrived, heading for the rest room. It's crowded, but yeah, go ahead."

"You were right. Astor called me."

"And?"

"Some guy tried to hit the hero teacher. But there was a cop at the door so the guy ran. God, every cop in the Bay Area is antsy about the shooting, and the morons send another hitman in broad daylight to the fifth floor of the fucking hospital. I don't get it."

Jorge massaged his stomach as he continued to walk. "Well, thank God for small favors. Do we know anything about the guy?"

"No. Nothing."

Jorge croaked then looked around for a restroom. He exhaled with a tiny squeal.

"You all right?"

"Forgot to take my pills. I just need…nothing. What else?"

"You don't sound so good," Cobb said. "Maybe you better get some rest and I'll fill you in later."

Jorge spotted a restroom. "No, fill me in now. I'll rest at the hotel. But make it quick."

"Well, there was a big shootout in San Rafael early this morning. Astor said it looks like an attempt to take out the teacher witness, the woman…the one from the school shooting."

"Christ! She better not be dead."

"She's alive. The shooter missed but Astor said…hey, I gotta go."

Jorge could hear voices in the background. "You're no longer alone, are you?"

"Correct." Cobb's voice trickled into a whisper. "I…" Cobb hung up.

After relieving himself, Jorge bought a newspaper, found an empty table at a food court, then perused the article about the San Rafael shootout. Besides the implication that drugs had been involved, a yet-to-be-named law officer had been wounded. Apparently, the wound was not serious as the officer had been released from the local hospital. No mention was made of the teacher.

Jorge slapped the paper down, whispering, "What a useless article. Why in God's name would Carlos target the woman teacher? That makes no sense at all. Harry, you fucking, fucking bastard." He pulled out his cell and dialed, even though he knew Astor would never answer his call.

17

If you need to get something done, ask a busy person.

Maizie led off the meeting of the school board by explaining away her crutches as a slip in the shower and a severely bruised tailbone. After a bit of polite laughter, she proceeded with her briefing. Other than the shower story, she told no more outright lies, but by the final question, Kay was aghast at the false story that Maizie had woven.

The applause Kay received when Maizie introduced her as a hero of the school shooting and as a significant contributor to the investigation sent her into a tailspin of disgust. Blushing bright red and clenching her teeth, she backed away and headed for the washroom. Angry and frustrated, she spent several minutes splashing cold water on her face. Maizie and many of the FBI personnel left before she exited.

Once composed, she headed back to the meeting only to be intercepted by Mildred at the entrance of the dining room.

"Kay, I need a huge favor."

"Mrs. Cade—Mildred—I'm here. You need me to do anything, just ask. You need me to serve coffee? Help with the typing? Anything? You don't have to worry about my ego." She stopped and peered into the dining room. "There are probably enough egos in the room already."

Mildred smiled. "Oh, Kay, I'm afraid it's a little bigger favor than that."

"Anything, Mildred."

"Good. I need you to assume Mr. Lee's position as Dean of Faculty."

"What?"

"Just until he returns to duty."

Dean of Faculty was the number-two position in the administration. If the Head of School was gone or incapacitated, the Dean of Faculty assumed the post as the interim.

"We'll be bringing Evie Dirkson out of retirement to cover your classes while you're busy saving the school from catastrophe."

"She…she was my mentor." Kay couldn't think of anything else to say.

"I've already spoken to Robert and Bill, and they think you're a great choice." Robert Jones served as the Dean of Students and Bill Chen kept the school in the black as a tight-fisted business manager. "Levi, of course, thinks you're terrific. In fact, he thinks it was his idea in the first place. So please, make sure you thank him."

Kay nodded and stared at Mildred for a long time. "Okay. What about Mrs. Shim?"

Mildred smiled softly. "Millie will be your greatest asset. Now, I need to reintroduce you to the Board. Please don't be embarrassed and leave the room again. We have much to do and very little time to do it."

"You really think it's a good idea?"

Mildred shrugged. "I'm way past that worry. Levi and I made the decision this morning. We don't have time to worry about things already decided upon. Right now, we have to get the next things done." She paused. "Are you ready?"

Levi tapped Kay on the shoulder. "Exciting, isn't it, Kay?" he said. "It's just so damned exciting, just like the storm before the calm."

* * *

That evening, Agent Donigan drove Kay to the hospital. During the ride, Kay propped open a yearbook and studied the names and faces of the faculty. In the eight previous hours she had made dozens of phone calls, sent numerous emails, planned a speech for the following morning's assembly, calmed the fears of several faculty members, found substitutes for those teachers whose fears could not be assuaged, ordered updates to the school's website, and listened to the complaints of a few teachers who thought she was too young and inexperienced for the job.

Early on, she had brought Mr. Lee's legendary secretary, Millie Shim, to Levi's house. The two spent an efficient half-hour going over the basics of Kay's new position then worked side-by-side, phoning, emailing, and discussing their next moves.

All in all, she felt good about the day. Even George, once again reneging on their deal with a text message, brought a smile to her face.

doing great. think I will get an offer. in wining & dining phase. love me. marry me.

Most of all, she felt an urge to see Harry. In the past she had dominated almost every aspect of their relationship, especially their conversations, using Harry as both a sounding board and as a pressure valve whenever she needed to vent.

She hoped he would still listen to her like he used to. She never realized how important it was to have a friend who listened as intently as Harry. The urge was downright stupid and silly, she told herself. Regardless, it hummed along in her head.

Agent Donigan broke into her reverie. "I understand Mr. Ross was a wrestler."

"Excuse me? Oh, yes, he was. In high school. He was really very good. His junior year he placed second in the state."

"Really? What state?"

"California. He's from Visalia in the central valley.

"Wow. He must've been something. How'd he do as a senior."

"Um…not as well. He, uh, he had a difficult year."

"Oh, well, too bad. I used to wrestle, so I know how tough it can be."

"Yeah."

They drove for several more minutes before the agent asked, "How close were you two?"

Kay suddenly realized Maizie was behind the agent's questions. "Well, when we were young, we used to walk to school together."

"So, you must have been pretty close."

Kay leaned back and closed her eyes. "Uh huh. Look, what does Maizie want from me? More about Harry? She knows I haven't seen him for a long, long time."

"Not too subtle, was I?"

"Did she choose you because of your wrestling background?"

The agent shrugged. "Probably." He sighed. "She wants me to find out anything I can about Mr. Ross. Can you help me, please?"

Kay remained quiet for a long moment. "Agent Donigan, thank you for the direct approach. I'll do what I can."

"Thanks. May I record you?"

"Fine, whatever."

"I was briefed about her interview with you," Agent Donigan said. "As you know, we're trying to find out why he's a target of a criminal enterprise." When Kay said nothing, he added, "There are only a few reasons for this to occur. One is that the target is involved with criminals. Another is—"

"No way."

"Pardon?"

"He'll never become a criminal. With every choice he makes, he always thinks it through then evaluates possible outcomes. He'd choose to avoid a life of crime because of the damage it causes."

"How do you know this?"

"Because he told me so. We were friends, Agent Donigan. We talked all the time. What I just said was a paraphrase of his actual words. I can remember those words because he said the same thing about working for a tobacco company or a strip-mining operation or any number of other professions."

"Okay. But that's the talk of a teenager from ten years ago. People change over a decade."

"Of course they do. As did Harry. As he grew older, his social skills improved. But most of the improvement came from Harry's own discipline. He had to train himself to interact reasonably with other people. He worked so hard at this that I can't see him changing his basic foundation."

"Train himself?"

"Yes, exactly. Take conversation as an example. By high school he had trained himself to think before speaking. Which was not really great because his pauses during conversations could be lengthy. But it was a huge step forward. He even started to accumulate a small cadre of friends."

"That's not really describing an unarmed guy who made a snap decision to charge a man with a loaded gun."

"Oh, it does, believe me. You can tell Maizie that Harry has never lacked courage."

* * *

Agent Donigan escorted Kay all the way to Harry's room. A duty cop still sat in a chair outside the door.

Harry reclined in bed, his half-opened eyes staring blankly at an iPad resting on his table.

"Hey," Kay said.

Harry turned, smiling broadly even as his eyes drooped. "Hey, whoa. Give me a sec, okay?" Chortling, he held up a hand and triumphantly pressed the nurse's call button numerous times.

Nurse Lei entered. "Harry, this is not a hotel."

"Ha! I told you Kay would come. You owe me."

"Hi," Lei said.

"Hi," Kay said but could not take her eyes off Harry, who grimaced while raising his knee. "What's going on?"

Lei shrugged and smiled. "Harry doesn't like our ice cream. To shut him up for a while we made a deal."

"Ben and Jerry's Cherry Garcia coming my way," Harry croaked. "I knew you would come."

Kay smiled. "I hope you've been behaving."

Lei retrieved a pint container of Ben and Jerry's Cherry Garcia ice cream from her pocket and placed it with a spoon on Harry's table. "We're always going to be a step ahead of you."

Though Harry continued to smile, his head bobbed gently as if he didn't have the strength to hold it up. "Hey, thanks."

"You must be feeling better," Kay said.

Harry rubbed his eyes with his knuckles. "I was dozing when you came, but I'm okay now. I just get so sleepy. You and Ben and Jerry woke me up."

"Harry, you were reading your iPad."

"Huh? Really?"

Kay nodded.

Harry folded the iPad closed then picked up the ice cream. "Okay, I guess I'm more awake now." His hands trembled as he struggled with the lid. "You see how these nurses get even? They probably glued it shut." After one last futile effort, he put the container on his table. "Darn."

Kay took the container, pulled the lid off, and set it back.

"Thanks." Still trembling, he managed to scrape a tiny wafer of ice cream off the top. Turning the spoon upside down, he placed the wafer on his tongue.

"You okay?"

"Not yet. But I will be. I was frustrated with the lid and the ice cream is frozen like a rock but it doesn't pay to argue with Ben and Jerry." His eyes cleared and his voice strengthened.

"I don't remember you being like this before."

"Like what?"

"Oh, I don't know. Funny, I guess. You used to be so serious."

"I think being shot helps. I always wanted to be a stand-up comic, but once I got shot I had to settle for being a lie-down comic."

Kay smiled weakly.

Harry noted her face. "Yeah...I know. That's always been my downfall. One good line followed by a lame one. Anyway, I, um, I gotta say this, so listen okay?"

Kay nodded.

Harry took a deep breath and his eyes blinked. "I really missed you, okay? And I'm sorry I quit writing."

Kay blushed. "I…Don't be, please" she whispered. "I…" she trailed off.

Smiling, he slid another wafer into his mouth. "I'm so glad you came."

Kay's blush deepened.

Harry looked away. "Okay, sorry. I'm calling a timeout. Let's talk about something else. So, how about school? How did the first day go? Were the kids okay? Whoa, that was stupid. I bet everyone was nervous."

"Um, we canceled school for today. We had to so we could map out what's next. We're starting up again tomorrow."

Harry nodded then closed his eyes. "Yeah, that makes sense. Well, what does the map look like?"

That was all the prompting Kay needed. For twenty-five minutes she spoke about her day sorting out the trauma at school, stopping often to answer Harry's questions or to backtrack because she knew she had skipped something. She never mentioned the assault at her apartment, her time with the wounded Agent Cabrera, or her night spent at the hospital. Instead, she kept the focus on the school. Her elevation to the administrative ranks, even if only temporary, thrilled Harry.

Somewhere in the middle of her discourse, she laced her hand with his, using his fingers to count off points. She did not let go until she noticed his eyes drooping.

"Oh God, you're tired. I've been rattling off like an old woman and—"

"No, uh-uh. I'm good. Don't stop. Except I've gotta use the toilet. They pulled the catheter out this morning, and, well, now I gotta go."

Kay smiled. Talking about bodily functions had never been taboo with Harry.

Sweat beaded on his forehead as he raised the back of the bed as far as it would go. "Darn, this is so embarrassing."

"Do you want me to call the nurse?"

"Darn, darn, darn," he whispered, his voice cracking. "Call button's by your hand."

When Nurse Lei entered, Harry said, "I gotta take a leak, but I'm having trouble getting out of bed."

"You don't need to get out of bed," Nurse Lei said.

"Bathroom. I'll do it in the bathroom." He eyed Kay. "Sorry. Please don't go. This takes more time than it should. Can you wait?"

"Of course, Harry, sure." Kay stepped to the foot of the bed.

Nurse Lei gently swung Harry's legs off the bed then, slipping an arm under his shoulder, helped him stand.

Harry's gown, open at the back, slid off his shoulders as he hobbled to the restroom. Yellow tape secured a white pad on his low back just above his buttocks. Higher up, a dozen pink scars crisscrossed his shoulder blades.

"Oh, God," Kay whispered when the door closed.

"Yeah," a voice said. "I've been wondering about those scars too." Maizie stood at the door, leaning on her crutches.

Kay looked up. "What?"

"Those scars on his back. Pretty raggedy, don't you think?" Maize shifted her weight and winced. "You know, he never saw combat when he was in the Marines. Oh, he served in Iraq, but as an analyst in the green zone. So, I don't think those scars came from any war time experience."

Kay stared at her.

Maizie crutched over to a spot by the bed. "According to his record, he did well in the Marines." She shrugged. "Basically, a solid record, nothing spectacular. And, it turns out, you were right. Much of his time in the service was spent on the Corp's wrestling team. He trained and competed all over Europe and Japan. Mostly military tournaments. So, when did he get those scars?"

Kay used a tissue from Harry's nightstand to wipe her eyes. "I don't know."

The toilet flushed. Maizie shrugged as Nurse Lei escorted Harry out of the bathroom. He pursed his lips when he saw Maizie. "Well, Inspector, what happened to you?"

Kay wadded the tissue in her hand and stuffed it in her pocket.

"Slipped on the stairs and bruised my tailbone," Maizie said.

Harry walked his eyes over Maizie's face as Nurse Lei helped him return to bed.

"Okay now?" Nurse Lei asked, wiping the sweat from Harry's face.

Breathing with difficulty, Harry nodded. "Way better than yesterday."

"Do you want something for the pain?"

"No, thank you."

"I'll check on you later," Nurse Lei said then left the room.

Maizie crutched closer to Harry. "Mr. Ross, we're still trying to understand why people are shooting at you. So, I need to ask you a few more questions. Are you up to it?"

Harry took several slow breaths.

"Perhaps I should come back later."

Kay, recognizing Harry was in one of his conversational pauses, almost smiled.

"Well," Maizie said, "I'll check again tomorrow."

Just before Maizie turned away, Harry said, "No, I'm okay."

Agent Henderson entered and leaned against the wall. Harry glanced toward him then focused on Maizie.

"Excellent," Maizie said. "Let's start with this. Tell me how your back became so scarred."

Never taking his eyes off Maizie, Harry wrinkled his forehead in concentration.

Unfazed, Maizie returned the stare.

"Well," Harry said then paused as his head tipped forward and his eyelids drooped.

"Mr. Ross?"

As if there had been no pause, Harry said, "It's kind of a stupid story." He raised his head and opened his eyes. "I'll tell you how I screwed up my back if you tell me how you really hurt your butt."

Agent Henderson coughed.

Not missing a beat, Maizie said, "Fine. You first."

Harry paused again. "Well, after I got out of the Marines, I decided to be a history teacher." He took a few short, shallow breaths.

"I have always been fascinated by our country." He glanced toward the ceiling then shrugged. "Really fascinated. It's such a crazy place. Good and bad, great and horrible, but always incredibly interesting." Sweat beaded on his forehead. "My idea for research was to walk across the country." He drifted away for a moment. "It was much harder than I thought it would be. Imagine all the pioneers and Native Americans that did it." Again, his head drooped.

Maizie leaned forward. "Mr. Ross, I'm trying—"

"Oh, did I tell you I started in Visalia? Well, I did. Hometown and all. Anyway, I started there then hiked across the central valley. Took me a while to hit the Sierra foothills."

"Mr. Ross, excuse me," Maizie said. "I just want to know how you got the scars on your back. Do you have a short version?"

"Oh. Sorry. Well, the short version is I got shot."

Kay's body jerked. "You were shot?"

Harry shrugged. "Told you it was a stupid story."

Maizie held up her hand to silence Kay. "Maybe not that short of a version, Mr. Ross. Who shot you?"

"Big Sluice."

"Who?"

"I don't know his real name, but everyone called him Big Sluice." He closed his eyes closed and softly rolled his head. "Now, what happened to you?"

Maizie shifted on her crutches and glared at Harry. "The short version is I was shot. Maybe you read about it. The drug thing across the bridge."

"I read about it." He took his eyes off Maizie, looked at his IV lines, then glanced at Kay. "So, you're the officer who got shot."

Kay's face heated up.

"Yes," Maizie said. "Bad timing on my part."

Harry nodded. "You have a position of some authority. You shouldn't be lying."

Tensely, Maizie said, "I apologize. I didn't do it to exert authority. I did it because I'm trying to protect some people."

"Agent Cabrera," Agent Henderson said quickly, his eyes darting toward Kay.

Maizie glanced at Agent Henderson. "Yes. Yes, of course. Sorry."

Tom shrugged.

Kay took a step back and crossed her arms.

"Mr. Ross," Maizie said, "what really happened to your back?"

Harry took a ragged breath. "Thirsty. Can I have some water?"

Kay found his cup on the side table, filled it with water, and held the straw to his lips. "Drink slowly, Harry, slowly."

"Perhaps we *should* come back later," Cabrera said.

With his hand on Kay's, Harry shook his head. "No. No, I'm okay."

Kay nodded. "Harry, you need your rest. They can come back."

"No, I'm okay." Harry blinked slowly. "Anyway, Big Sluice was drunk and beating up on his daughter, a little twelve-year-old girl. So, I made him stop. And then I carried her away."

"Made him stop? How did you make him stop?"

Harry paused again.

"Mr. Ross?"

"I shucked him down to the floor then, when he stood up, I shoved him into his bedroom. He shot me when I was carrying Alice away…shot me twice." He held up two fingers. "I didn't know he had a shotgun. I was pretty far away, but a bunch of pellets hit me. Not too deep, but it hurt really bad." He paused yet again and shook his head. "Alice was lucky. Only a few pellets hit her boots."

Everyone remained silent.

"Anyway, Big Sluice felt bad about everything so he took me and Alice to one of his uncles who was supposed to be a doctor." Harry shrugged. "I'm not sure about that, but the old man got the birdshot out of me and stitched me up." His forehead wrinkled with a long blink. "Oh, and then the doctor found a relative who agreed to take care of Alice."

"Where did all this happen?" Maizie asked.

Harry glanced toward Kay. "Outside of Shelby, Montana."

Maizie winced as she shifted her weight. "This happened on your cross-country tour?"

"Yeah."

Maizie nodded. "And how long did you tour the country?"

"Two years."

"Two years?" Tom said. "You walked across the country for two years?"

Shaking his head, Harry blinked twice, eyed Kay again, then chortled. "Naw…I gave up walking. I bought a bike and rode. Well, in bad weather I hunkered down wherever." He looked toward the ceiling. "And sometimes I hitchhiked. Had to be a pickup, though. Needed a ride that could carry my bike." Again, he dropped his chin and seemed to lose focus.

Maizie slowly nodded. "Mr. Ross, Agent Henderson is going to continue the interview. Kay, would you come with me? I have a few more things I'd like to go over."

* * *

Once again, Kay sat with Maizie in a small room answering questions, most of which she had already answered numerous times. After ten minutes, Kay finally blurted, "You know, if you wanted me out of the room so Agent Henderson could be alone with Harry, you should have said so." She lowered her chin but kept her eyes on Maizie.

Sitting on a pillow, Maizie huffed a brief chuckle. "Is that how you look at your students when you catch them without their homework?"

Kay continued the look.

Mazie shrugged. "Okay, yeah. I needed Tom to have a go at Mr. Ross without anybody else in the room."

"I told you, I don't like being played."

Maizie shrugged again. "Does this cross-country thing sound like the guy you used to know?"

"Do you think Harry is lying about it?"

"I have no idea, but then, I don't know him at all."

"To answer your question, yes, it does sound like the Harry I knew." She raised her chin. "And you know what? I think you believe he's telling the truth."

"I do, but I've learned to be skeptical of what I believe. Anyway, Mr. Ross has become a target and needs protection. Furthermore, whether it's because of your past with him or what you did at the school, you also need to be protected. That's my job regardless of what I'd like to believe. So, I'm going to probe into anything and everything."

"That's fine. I just prefer a direct approach."

Maizie smiled. "No problem. It's like this: We're still researching Mr. Ross's past so I'm going to probe your memories. I want you to look back and see if there's anything that strikes even the smallest chord in regards to this situation."

Kay huffed then looked away. "Fine. Fire away."

The probing went on for twenty minutes.

18

An ex meets cosmic propinquity.

By the time Kay returned to Harry's room, his face had collapsed with exhaustion.

"You okay?"

"I'm tired. It must be the drugs."

Kay nodded.

"Did you see her hands?" Harry asked as he massaged his forehead.

"Whose hands? Maizie's? No, I didn't notice them."

"The knuckles are all swollen, and her left forefinger is bent. I was going to ask about it but didn't want to be rude. But it makes you wonder what happened, doesn't it?"

"Why? Could've been anything."

"Yeah, I suppose. Actually, I kinda like her. But I hope she won't lie to me again."

"I don't think Maizie's dishonest."

"Maizie? You call her Maizie?"

Kay hesitated. "Um, yes. We get along pretty well for the most part. Anyway, she's just trying to do her job. But I do know what you mean. She plays little games with her questioning."

"I bet that went over well with you."

"She got better at being direct. But like I said, I think she's just trying to do her job. She's got inquiries going on all over the place.

She even has access to your service record. She also asked a lot of questions about our past."

"Whoa," Harry whispered. "*Our* past?"

"Yes, Harry. Our past. Anyway, did you hold something back from her or Agent Henderson?"

Harry took a long time to speak. "I need to think about that."

"What? Think about what?" After another lengthy pause, Kay sighed. "Well, you better think about it."

Harry nodded. "I need some time on this, okay?"

"Fine. Well then, I guess I should go."

"Anyway, I'm really happy talking with you again."

Kay smiled. "Other than all this terrible, terrible stuff…yeah. Me too." She leaned over and kissed his forehead. "Night, Harry."

Harry blushed and his eyes slowly blinked over and over again.

* * *

Kay found the Tomas and Vincent in the waiting room. Vincent sat on Alma's lap, staring at a book. Alma nodded a greeting while Kenji rose and waved.

"Hello," Kay said. "Were you waiting for me? You could have come in. Harry and I were just talking."

"Hello, Miss Kay," Kenji said, smiling and looking over his wire-rim glasses. "It's all right. We don't mind waiting."

Alma moved Vincent to the floor. "Hey, friends need their time together. Old folks like me and Kenji, we've got all the time in the world." She gave Vincent a tiny shove in the back. "Go say hello to Auntie Kay, Vinnie."

Vincent, dressed like his elderly friends in blue jeans, flannel shirt, and running shoes, did not need prompting. He walked quickly to Kay and raised his arms. As soon as Kay picked the boy up, he wrapped his arms around her neck, squeezed, and kissed her cheek. "Hello, Auntie Kay."

"My goodness." Kay ruffled his soft black curls. "This is the nicest thing to happen to me today."

"Read to me, Auntie Kay, read to me."

"Vinnie," Alma snapped.

"*Please* read to me."

"Oh my, he's going to break a lot of hearts, isn't he?" Kay said.

"Well," Kenji said, "he's well on his way. He had a little wrestling match with a girl in preschool this morning."

"She pushed me first," Vincent said.

Kay laughed. "Vincent, I can read to you for a little while, but then I have to go. Okay?"

"Alma, let's go see Harry," Kenji said. "Vincent, after Auntie Kay finishes reading, you can go see Pops."

After Kay set Vincent down, he ran the two steps to the small couch and picked up the book. "This book, Auntie Kay. This book."

Kay sat and took the book. "Absolutely."

Vincent climbed up and settled next to Kay, his feet not reaching the edge of the cushion. She opened the large picture book across both of their laps.

"Lazy lions lounging in the local library," Vincent said. "L. Look for L."

Kay smiled when she realized how the clever author-artist had embedded numerous items in the work that all began with the letter L. "This is amazing."

"Focus, Auntie Kay, focus." Vincent pointed to an elfin creature on the page. "Leprechaun, L is for leprechaun."

Kay glanced abruptly at Vincent. In her mind, she heard Harry say, *Focus, Kay, focus.*

They had reached Six Slithering Snakes Sliding Silently Southward when a female voice said, "Hello, Vincent."

"Mama!" Vincent slid off the couch and ran to a tall black woman. She scooped him up and received a hug and a kiss just like he had given Kay. "Mama," he said, kissing her again.

"Hey, big guy," the woman said. "I've missed you so much."

Kay rose and offered her hand. "Hello, I'm Kay Morrell."

Clinging to Vincent with one arm, the woman shook Kay's hand. "Elizabeth White," she said. "I'm Vincent's mother."

Kay smiled. "I can tell."

"Auntie Kay's reading to me, Mama. We're finding S's."

"How nice." Elizabeth looked at Kay. "Are you helping the Tomas with Vincent while Harry's laid up?"

Kay smiled again. "Um…no. I'm just here visiting Harry. Alma and Kenji wanted some time alone with him, so I'm watching Vincent."

"And how is Harry?" She paused and grimaced as her throat caught. "I came last night, but he had been sedated already. Is he okay?"

Kay sighed. "He's tired, but he's much better than yesterday. He and I talked for a while, and he had an interview with the FBI."

Elizabeth brushed her eyes with the back of a hand. "I was told he was going to be all right, but when I came, he looked so terrible and…Thank you. That's excellent news."

"He seems to be recovering rapidly. He's very lucky."

Elizabeth nodded with closed eyes as she gently rubbed Vincent's back.

"He's a really bright child," Kay said.

"Thank you." She nuzzled Vincent's neck, and the boy squealed in delight. "He certainly is. Aren't you, my little man?" She shifted the boy to her hip. "How do you know Harry?"

"We, um, we teach at the same school."

Elizabeth stopped staring at her child and focused on Kay. "Wait. You said your name is Morrell."

Kay sighed and nodded.

Elizabeth's mouth opened. "You were there. The news calls you the prime witness. Oh my God, you could've been shot. That must have been terrifying."

"Well, I screamed a lot. I know how lucky I am."

"Harry saved you."

"Yeah…he did," Kay said then repeated a line that had become a common response. "He saved a lot of people."

"Yes, of course. Oh my God. Harry."

"Vinnie!" Alma called from the hallway. "It's time to see Pops. Come to Nana."

Elizabeth turned and released the squirming Vincent who ran toward Alma.

"Alma," Elizabeth said.

"Lizbet," Alma said then retreated with Vincent into Harry's room.

Elizabeth watched her son disappear. "Harry's surrogate mother is the queen of the realm." She took a few steps to the couch and sat heavily. Slender, close to six feet tall, and dressed in designer black pants and white blouse, the beautiful woman wore her long hair in multiple cornrows bunched into a braided ponytail that fell down her back. "You know, I've tried very hard with Alma. And I'm still trying. I don't think she'll ever understand what happened between Harry and me. Kenji seems to understand." She sighed. "That man is a saint."

"I don't know exactly what to say, Ms. White. I really don't know them very well."

Elizabeth nodded. "Yes. I'm sorry. I shouldn't have burdened you with that little bit of drama. That was inappropriate."

"You must be tired. It's a long flight from Chicago."

"Not that long. Besides, I arrived last night. And then I didn't find out he had been transferred until after I went all the way to the San Rafael Hospital." Elizabeth paused. "How did you know I was from Chicago?"

"Oh, last night when I was visiting Harry, the FBI agent said you were coming in from Chicago."

Elizabeth pursed her lips. "Yes, I spoke to one of them on the phone before I left. Some woman—a very assertive woman. Kind of like Alma, I think. It's funny, she kept calling me Mrs. Ross, and I kept telling her we were never married. It just went right over her head."

Kay's eyes momentarily widened.

Elizabeth shrugged. "And yes, I am tired. When the firm gave me time off to see Harry, they also found a way for me to meet with some west coast clients. I've been in meetings all day." She paused. "I can't believe I'm unloading on you. You're the one who had her world turned upside down, and here I am whining about a couple of meetings. God, you must think I'm an ass."

Kay smiled. "Not yet."

Elizabeth returned the smile and, for a long moment, neither spoke.

"I know Harry's new to the school, so it's really good of you to visit him." Elizabeth said to break the silence. "Did you know Harry always wanted to be a teacher?"

"Oh, I never really understood what Harry wanted," Kay said then quickly winced.

"Really? Huh, that's interesting. How well do you know him?"

Kay could think of nothing to say.

"Excuse me, I'm really sorry, but is it possible you're the Kay from Harry's childhood?"

"Well…yeah, that's me." She started to say more but instead tightly closed her mouth.

"Uh huh. This has been the strangest day."

"It's been very strange for a number of days now." Kay picked up her sweater. "It's been very nice to meet you. I'm glad you've come to see Harry and your son, but I really must get back to school. My poor driver has been waiting for a while now."

Elizabeth rose and offered her hand. "You were Harry's best friend."

Kay looked up and saw the woman's eyes well up again. "That was a long time ago."

"Holy Mary Mother of God. This has indeed been the strangest day."

19

A trap is set by capturing a rook.

After a brief nap and shower, Sergio went to a diner and ate a burger and fries. As always, he returned with his head on a swivel. As he reached his building, he checked the street one more time. Seeing no one, he entered and climbed the narrow staircase to his apartment. At the door, he checked the tiny wedges he had left in the jam. Finding them untouched, he unlocked the deadbolt and entered.

The job had become increasingly difficult, not only because of the failures of his crew, but also because the man in the hospital was not the ghost Carlos wished to destroy. He understood and believed strongly in the value of revenge, but this ridiculous effort made no sense. He booted up his laptop and logged into his encrypted email site. He needed to brief Roman with the identity of the man in the hospital. Before he could start typing, he heard a muffled sound behind his chair.

"Evening, Sergio," a voice said. Sergio reached for his gun as he spun on his chair. Just as he caught a glimpse of a scarecrow of an old man, nodes of a Taser struck him in the ribs and blackness overwhelmed him.

While he whistled a little ditty, the wiry old man stripped Sergio to his underwear then injected him between his toes with a sedative. Sitting at the desk, the old man searched Sergio's pockets and found a slip of paper with an address he recognized. "Well, you dirty, rotten sons of bitches," he whispered. "But this has gotta wait." He retrieved a laptop from his rucksack, rubbed his hands together, then typed out an email. "Belly, darlin', time to go to work."

20

***Somebody has to save the Boy Scouts, Girl
Scouts, and Tess Truehearts of the world.***

Tom eased the Ford out of the hospital parking lot. "Been a long day."

"Yeah," Maizie grunted from the passenger seat.

"At least we know Ross isn't lying. He really did take a cross country tour. And he never knew Hoffman."

Maizie hissed in pain. "Yeah. Did you press him on that marijuana-plots-in-the hills thing?"

Tom shook his head. "Didn't have to press him at all. I asked him and he went off on a story about finding the plots while running. It took a while to get him to shut up."

Maizie shrugged. "Ms. Morrell said that's how she remembers him…either as super quiet or unstoppably verbose."

"Verbose?"

"Her word, not mine."

"It still doesn't make sense. Carlos is a vengeful sonofabitch, but putting a contract on a nobody who did nothing but report some pot fields is crazy…even for Carlos. I mean, two attempts? That's nuts."

Maizie shrugged. "We can only confirm him as a target at the hospital. We can't confirm that he was the target at the school shooting."

"Don't nitpick. If Ross wasn't the target at the school, then why the attempt at the hospital?

"Beats the shit out of me."

They drove in silence for a few moments before Tom asked, "What was all that guff that Ross laid on you when we first got there?"

"No idea. Christ, my ass hurts."

"Well, you should've kept your puny butt in the hospital."

"No fucking way. This case is…" She squealed through compressed lips as the Ford made a turn. After a few gasps, she said, "This case is gonna get huge, Tom, huge."

"Maybe…maybe not. I'll say this, Ross's got some skills, and regardless of what Ms. Morrell says about his slow thought process, he didn't think twice before going after Hoffman."

Still breathing through her mouth, Maizie said, "Yeah, whatever. He was a Marine, you know."

"Yeah…true."

"He's also a fucking Boy Scout…just like you."

They arrived at Maizie's building. "You need help to get to your apartment?"

"Oh…God. Would you mind? I mean, I know you should be home, but—"

"Relax. I'll get you up and settled."

"Please, please, please don't tell anyone."

"Goddamn it, don't be an ass."

"Sorry, sorry. I know I'm a pain in the ass sometimes."

"In more ways than one." Tom found street parking, then held onto Maizie's arm as they negotiated the few stairs to her building.

Breathing hard, Maizie leaned heavily on Tom as they walked through the narrow foyer of the apartment and into the living room. Carefully, Tom eased her onto the sofa, belly down.

"Tom," Maizie said.

"Yeah."

"I need another favor. Don't laugh."

Tom said nothing for a few seconds. "Well, I'm not laughing, but you're not asking any favors either."

"Can you, um, can you bust up some ice from the freezer, and, um…"

"What? You want me to put ice on your ass?"

"I can't do it myself. The doctors said it would help."

Tom marched off to the kitchen. "Sheezus."

Maizie could hear the freezer door opening and the ice jangling.

"You got something to smash the ice with?"

"Rolling pin in the top, left hand drawer."

After enough pounding to turn rocks into sand, Tom marched in with a large plastic bag filled with crushed ice. Maizie had her skirt up around her waist, her buttocks split by a thong. Numerous tiny, dark, round scars pockmarked her cheeks. Two white dressings, secured by yellowish adhesive tape, failed to cover the massive bruising surrounding her bullet wounds.

Maizie said something, but with her face pressed into a pillow, her words were completely muffled.

"What?" Tom asked, his eyes on Maizie's buttocks.

Maizie pulled her head out from the pillow. "I don't know if the bandage should come off…before the ice, I mean. I don't think I can get it off anyway. It really hurts. I can't believe they used tape."

Tom stared for a few more seconds. "I think we'll just leave it on for now, okay?"

Maizie nodded and plunged her face back into the pillow.

"You take your pain pills?"

Maizie raised her head. "Yes, goddamn it. Four of them. And they aren't working for shit."

"Four?" Tom gently laid the ice over both wounds.

Maizie gasped, then, moaning through gritted teeth, drove her head deeper into the pillow.

The ice failed to stay aloft and slipped to the floor. Tom retrieved it. "Can you roll a bit to your side?"

Maizie tried but winced and sucked in her breath before she turned an inch.

"Okay, okay, wait," Tom said. He went to the bathroom and returned with a towel. Carefully, he stuffed one end of the towel under Maizie's hip then placed the ice back over her wounds. Finally, he wrapped the towel over the ice and stuffed the free end between her buttocks and the cushioned backrest of the sofa. "There. Just don't move for maybe twenty minutes, okay?"

Maizie nodded in the pillow. "It's fucking cold."

"Yeah, should be bearable in a couple minutes. I'm going to—"

Maizie jerked her head up. "Tom, please, please wait. Just until the ice is done. Okay? Can you wait that long?"

Tom pulled up an ottoman and sat next to Maizie's head. "I was about to say that I'm going to wait until you get in bed. Okay?"

Maizie nodded. "God. Thanks."

"Yeah, whatever." Tom pulled out his phone.

Maizie's eyes widened. "Who're you calling?"

Tom held up a finger and pointed to her mouth. "Shh, I'm on the phone. Hi, babe, it's me... Yeah, I'm late... Yeah, I know, sorry. You been watching the news? Yeah... Yeah, they might be connected... Yeah, I know the agent who was shot. Maizie, it was Maizie... No, no, she should be okay. Anyhow, I'm gonna be later yet because... Yes, I should be able to take the kids to school tomorrow... Babe, listen for a minute. You listening now? Good. I'm going to be late because, well, Maizie was shot, right? Anyhow, she was shot in the butt... The butt, babe, you know, in the ass... Yeah, it is kinda funny... Yeah, okay. Anyhow, I'm at her apartment, applying ice to her wound... Babe... Babe, you there?... Because she couldn't do it herself, and she doesn't want the office to know she's really, really hurting, okay?... No, I'm not going to tell anyone... Yeah, it is... No, no way, not nearly as good as yours... Yeah, I'll be home as soon as I get her settled... Yeah... Love you too... Bye.

Tom closed his cell and looked at Maizie who had risen to her elbows, staring at him. "You are such a fucking Boy Scout."

"I don't hold things back from her anymore."

"Such a fucking Boy Scout."

"You must be feeling better."

"I'm not sure if it's the pills, the ice, or that phone call, but, yeah, a little better. Does she know I could hear you?"

Tom shrugged. "Maizie, I need to ask you something."

"What?"

Tom sighed. "I know what makes those little round scars like you have on your butt."

Maizie pushed her head back into the pillow.

"Maizie?"

Maizie shook her head.

"You know, if you didn't want me to know about those scars, you shouldn't have shown me your ass."

Maizie raised her head. Almost in tears, she said, "I forgot about 'em. God."

"Forgot about someone burning holes in your ass?"

Maizie shrugged. "Tom, please leave it be, at least for now. Maybe in some other lifetime we can talk about it, okay? But not right now."

Tom glanced toward the ceiling then nodded. "Fine. I don't like it, but if you say so, then all right."

"Thank you. God, thank you. I shouldn't have shown you my ass. I'm not thinking clearly lately."

"It's okay. Don't worry about it. Go back to resting."

Maizie buried her face into her pillow and said nothing more.

Tom angled his body so he would not be staring at Maizie's buttocks. "That woman, Ms. Morrell, is pretty tough."

Maizie mumbled into the pillow.

"You look how she's handling all this, and you have to be impressed. Most women I know would be basket cases."

Maizie raised her head above the pillow just long enough to say, "Don't be sexist."

Tom laughed then picked up a magazine.

A few minutes later, Maizie said, "You're right."

"About what?"

"Ross's girlfriend *is* tough. She's also got a temper."

"Well, I guess you would know about that."

Maizie propped her chin on her hands. "She got a little pissed at me a few times." Her words began to slur.

"What a surprise."

"You know what I think? I think Ross is like George Washington, yeah? George, I-can-not-tell-a-lie, fucking Washington."

Tom sighed. "Jeeze, you like him."

"Yeah? So what? I like everybody."

Tom laughed.

"I do. It's one of my endearing traits."

Tom shrugged and stood. "Okay, that's enough. Let's get you to bed."

"I'll tell you one thing, though. I want this case. I'm sick and tired of assholes fucking around with the George Washingtons, Tess Truehearts, and all of the Boy Scouts in the country. I'm just sick of it."

"Tess Trueheart?"

"His girlfriend."

"You keep saying that, but they haven't seen each other in ten years," Tom said. "They're not that close."

"Ah, bullshit. They're going to be like you and Mary, calling each other babe and shit."

"Suzanne, my wife's name is Suzanne." Tom lifted the ice off Maizie's buttocks.

"Yeah? Sorry. Have I met her?"

"Two or three times."

"Really? Okay, doubly sorry then. Don't tell her I forgot her name. Shit."

"Maybe you better get some sleep now."

"I bet your wife was a Girl Scout. She was, wasn't she?"

"You can ask her next time you see her."

"Christ, my butt is wet. Did it get on the sofa?"

From the kitchen, Tom answered, "It'll dry. It's just water."

As Tom helped Maizie to the bedroom, she said, "Sorry, you're right. He's probably holding back something. I shouldn't've dumped him on you."

"Get some sleep, Maizie. I'll pick you up tomorrow after I get the kids to school."

"Yeah, fine."

Tom helped her undress to her undergarments, pulled the covers back, and guided her into a prone position with a pillow under her hips. Carefully, he pulled the covers back over her frame. "Okay now? You need anything?"

"Suzanne's ass really better than mine?"

"Yup. Suzanne's got the best ass God ever made."

"Such a fucking Boy Scout."
"Get some sleep, Maizie. Get some sleep."
"God, these pills are great, you know?"

WEDNESDAY

21

There's nothing like joining the Marines to escape life.

Restless, Kay rose before sunrise from the bed in Mildred's spare room and pulled out the envelope with Harry's old letters. "Okay, Harry," she whispered, "you're holding something back from Maizie. Is it in these letters?"

She dumped them out over the top of a small table and plucked out the seven she had never read until this catastrophic week. She reread each one. Finishing the last letter, she flicked it to the top of the strewn pile. "Well, Maizie, I'm sorry. I can't see anything here that would interest you." She stuffed the letters back into the envelope. "These are mine, and you don't get to read them." She shook her head. "And if you want to find out about Harry's crappy senior year in high school, then ask *him*."

Kay remembered the homecoming dance their senior year as the last time she saw Harry happy. On what turned out to be his first-ever date, Harry had attended the dance on the arms of two girls. The next day, as had been their Sunday pattern since grade school, Kay and Harry met at her house to study. But that plan fell apart because Harry, exuberant from the affair, would not stop talking. They laughed until their sides hurt. However, everything went wrong for her best friend after that weekend.

By November, life had begun to pile up. Kay, pregnant from a former boyfriend, turned to Harry. Without a blink of judgement, he helped Kay get through an abortion that she tried to keep secret from her parents. But lying to her parents had never worked, and soon both Mom and Dad found out. She needed their support because Harry had pulled away due to his mother's terminal cancer. She passed in early January, not long after Harry's eighteenth birthday. His father, who had always enjoyed a beer before dinner, began to have two… then three. In time, he slid into a semi-functioning alcoholic haze. The slide ended in February when he was struck and killed by a hit-and-run driver while walking across a street.

Harry soldiered on by focusing on his wrestling and turned into something of a fanatic. She went to most of Harry's matches, where he crushed opponent after opponent. His focus died when, in March, he dislocated his elbow at the state championships.

In the weeks that followed, she rarely saw him.

Then in April, without consulting Kay, Harry enlisted in the Marines. He boarded a train the day before graduation to report for duty. She said goodbye at the station, where they had promised each other to stay in touch. It was the last time she saw him until the past Friday.

22

Money and Godiva begin to lose their attraction.

Dorothy flexed her fingers then reached into a bowl for a handful of M&Ms. "Yes! Got it! Nobody can keep anything from Belly Brain! Ha." Crunching away, she emailed Old Man.

```
done! how can you call this shit
encrypted?
```

She laughed. The encrypted files from Sergio's computer had actually taken most of the night to crack, but Old Man didn't need to know that. She collapsed on the sofa and placed a pillow over her eyes. Pulling an all-nighter for Old Man had become exhaustingly routine. She needed a few hours of downtime.

Fidgeting endlessly, she sat up and rubbed her eyes. "Fuck," she whispered. "He's screwing around with that moron. I know it. I know it." She sighed. "But why would he think an asshole like Carlos would care about some ex-Jarhead, good-citizen moron? And why does Old Man want to feed Carlos all that crap?"

She walked back to the desk, grabbing the last piece of pizza from a box on the floor. Folding it in half, she wolfed the triangle down before draining the remains of a liter bottle of Pepsi. She belched, looked at the bottle, then shrugged. The Pepsi was both warm and flat.

"Something sucks here," she whispered, just as Old Man sent a response.

> **i knew you could do it. how long before you can get my stuff ready?**

Dorothy snorted.

> **when do you want everything?**

> **day before yesterday.**

> **no way. maybe by tomorrow. i need to rest**

> **belly, i need it now. maybe i can help. shall i come over?**

Dorothy's heart jumped. "Christ." She wrung her hands and clenched her jaw. "Don't panic. Be cool. He doesn't know where you live." She placed her hands on the keyboard then stared at the ceiling before typing.

> **no, i'm on it**

> **i knew you wouldn't let me down. hurry, i need it right away**

Sweat ran down her face. "God fucking damn it."

> **the fake emails will take an hour. Your data will take longer**

> **that's the belly i know and love. how long for everything?**

Dorothy heaved a deep breath and wiped her face. "C'mon, c'mon. Gotta let him know I'm on top."

A few hours. and godiva ain't gonna cut it this time. this is getting crazy

i know. i can wait a couple hours but no more. things are beginning to move

then do it yourself

be nice. this is important

is this gonna save the world? or fuck it up some more?

can it be any more fucked up?

yes! it can! you're fucking with some innocents

and who, pray tell, is innocent?

the fucking good citizen moron! what are you doing to him?

ah, it's good to see you have some standards. don't worry about him, i got it covered. where do you want payment sent?

"Agghh!"

i'm serious. if this guy gets fucked over, i will personally chop your balls off

belly, time is wasting. you've been a good girl and you've been compensated well. please continue to do the job and you will continue to grow healthy, wealthy, and wise. where do you want your compensation sent?

Eyes pinched closed, Dorothy typed.

same bank same account

good girl. get it done

Belly slapped the desk then stormed to the refrigerator, looking for another Red Bull.

23

Boasting about vengeance is best done when
an enemy is dying at your feet.

Sergio groaned softly, rolled to his side, and slowly opened his eyes. The scarecrow sat at the table, working on Sergio's laptop. "Jesus. Oh, Jesus," he whispered.

Scarecrow glanced at Sergio then shook his head. Standing, he faced the computer. "You best hurry your ass, Belly. I don't like bein' alone with this turd on the floor. The temptation to squarsh him is burnin' somethin' fierce." He walked across the room and squatted next to Sergio.

Sergio knew he was awash in cocaine powder. He could smell it, feel it burning his nasal passages, and see it dusting the floor. Unbound, his hands slid toward his groin. Feeling wetness, he realized he was lying in a puddle of urine. "Oh Jesus," he whispered again.

Scarecrow laughed without humor. "I don't think Jesus is going to help you today, Sergio," he said in Spanish. "But if you get the chance, tell him I certainly appreciate your help. Yes, sir, you've been wonderfully accommodating."

Bile burned in Sergio's throat. His stomach lurched, but he was too weak to vomit.

"You know?" Scarecrow said, "I hear Carlos doesn't like his people using his product. My papa was the same way. Whatever he brewed up, he'd sell. He'd whip my hide if he ever caught me dipping into his profits." He put his nose close to Sergio's face. "You used to be something special to Carlos. Yes, indeed. Carlos liked you. He trusted you." He shrugged. "Makes you wonder, doesn't it?" Scarecrow stood.

Sergio closed his eyes. More urine slipped out.

Pacing the room, Scarecrow slid into his hillbilly patois. "Come on, Belly. Time's a wastin'. Send me the fuckin' shit. I got to git and this gots to get done afore the wrath of God and the cops barge in." He switched back to Spanish. "I tell you, Sergio, it's too bad your boss is such a horse's patoot. It's a fuckin' mystery why a smart fella like you worked for such a low-life. Carlos is stuck on revenge, and revenge is a damn poor way to run a business. Damn poor. You work for a man stuck on vengeance, and sure as shit, you're gonna find your ass in a vice. Yup, business guys like him shouldn't fuck around with vengeance. They should leave vengeance to folks like me…guys who don't worry about the fuckin' bottom line."

Sergio tried to push off the floor to his knees, but his arms buckled, his face smashing nose first onto the floor. Blood now mixed with the cocaine and urine.

"You see, Sergio, all I want today is to rile up Carlos and get his fat ass movin'. Then maybe the FBI will get off its fat ass." He moved to the computer. "Ah, there she is. My dear sweet Belly. And she's early too." He scanned Belly Brain's work which included a set of emails confirming the good-citizen moron as the target Carlos sought.

He walked back to Sergio. "Whew, you stink. Anyway, since I have a couple minutes, I thought I'd tell you what's what. After that, I'll give you something to take the squeeze off your stomach. First, I've had my eye on your operation for a long, long time. And in a few minutes, all that shit—supply lines, tunnels, boats, planes, bank accounts, everything—is going to be inside your computer. Yours, Sergio. What do you think Carlos will say about that?" He took a deep breath and clenched his teeth. "Years, Sergio," he spat angrily. "Years of watching you soulless bastards." He laced his fingers together and cracked his knuckles. "And guess what? Later today, the cops are gonna bust in here and find every damn thing. Once they find it, I believe they're going to pull off one of those major busts they're so famous for." Pausing, he punched the air. "I wonder how Carlos is going to feel about that. Hmm?" He returned to the computer.

Sergio struggled to keep his eyes open.

Scarecrow pushed away from the desk. "Well, there we go." He returned to Sergio and knelt. Using a tiny syringe, he injected something into Sergio's armpit.

"Am I going to die?" Sergio asked.

"We're all gonna die, partner."

Sergio nodded. "Are you Harry?"

Scarecrow shrugged. "Sometimes."

Sergio stiffened then died.

24

Oblivious of the old rogue's game, life rolls on.

By the time the assembly began, Kay felt she had already worked a full day. Between six and seven that morning, four teachers had called in to request substitutes. With the aftermath of the shooting, finding appropriate substitutes was proving daunting and took far more time than it should have.

She also received another text message from George.

Shopping with the boss in Saratoga tomorrow. Les Miz on Friday night with boss. It's going well.

"Saratoga?" Kay whispered with a smile. "Where is Saratoga?"

A little after seven Kay fielded a call from an angry parent, who said that her daughter would not be attending school until the security was airtight. When a break occurred in the woman's tirade, Kay proffered the agreed-upon company line regarding absences during this extraordinary time. The call took almost fifteen minutes.

Mrs. Shim entered from her office immediately after the call ended. "Don't do that, Ms. Morrell. Calls like that should be referred to Mr. Wheeler."

"I do believe our Dean of Students is probably getting his fair share of these calls, Mrs. Shim. Sharing a little of the burden is the least I can do."

"You're not sharing the burden. This is Mr. Wheeler's job, and he is very good at it."

"Did I tell the parent something wrong?"

Mrs. Shim stepped close to Kay's desk. "By not referring that call, you now need to inform Mr. Wheeler of your conversation. He needs to know which children are not in attendance, why they are not in attendance, and how he is going to convince the families to return their children to school. You do not have time for this, Ms. Morrell."

"Oh, right. I see your point. Thank you."

"You're welcome."

"May I ask you something?"

"Certainly."

"I am uncomfortable with you calling me Ms. Morrell. Would you please call me Kay? You've been calling me Kay for years now."

Mrs. Shim looked into Kay's eyes. "No. That would be inappropriate for the office." She went back to work only to return a few minutes later.

Kay looked up. "Yes?"

"The assembly is starting in a few minutes. You should hurry."

"Oh my goodness, thank you." Kay bolted for the door. When she arrived at the gym, she realized she had forgotten the note cards for her presentation. The students cheered wildly and the faculty applauded politely when Mrs. Cade introduced her. Hoping she could remember the gist of her speech, she strode toward the podium. Kay signaled for silence with upraised hands while noting that a number of the older teachers watched her with stony faces.

"Good morning." She paused and smiled. "We all go through hard times…times that never seem to get better or end…times when no matter what you do, everything goes wrong. I was going through one of these periods when one of my close friends said, *Don't let anything take you from you.*" She shrugged. "At the time, all my friend's advice did was make me angry. As bad as I felt, all I wanted to do was punch my friend's lights out."

A bit of laughter rumbled through the crowd.

"But the words never left me. I refer to those words now because on Monday a madman tried to take something from me…from you…and from the school." She paused again and stared intently at the audience, slowly turning her head to make eye contact with as many students as possible. "We can't let that happen. We can't let the actions of a madman dictate who we are or how we want to live. We just can't."

She looked down to gather her thoughts. A round of spontaneous applause made her look up. When the applause died down, she spoke of her fear when bullets smashed into the building behind her and broken glass showered her body. She spoke of Officer Cornish's heroism and of the other officers who moved into harm's way. She spoke of Mrs. Cade's leadership throughout the crisis.

Then, as soon as she uttered "Mr. Ross," the students erupted with cheers and applause. The faculty followed suit. This time, she did not signal for quiet and allowed the roar to continue until it died of its own accord. Speaking softly, she described, using as much detail as she could, Harry's charge, the life-or-death wrestling match on the grass, and the odd finale of the madman draped across Harry's lap.

A long silence followed.

She continued with Harry's progress in the hospital. Using that bit of information, she segued into the more mundane details about her temporary new job of substituting for Mr. Lee. She ended with an appeal to the audience for patience, teamwork, and open communication channels. She left the podium to another round of applause.

* * *

Her speech was a brief focal point at the beginning of the weekly operations meeting. The calendar portion of the meeting took the bulk of the time because of changes in the athletic schedule to accommodate the crisis. Mrs. Cade allowed only a few minutes for the deans to discuss the shooting before she shooed everyone away except Kay. "I don't think I've ever heard anything like the speech you gave this morning. It hit the moment right on the mark."

"Thank you. Honestly, I didn't think it would have such an impact." Quickly she changed the topic. "Um…how is Mr. Lee doing?"

"Well, according to his wife, there are signs of improvement. It's very hard to understand him with the facial paralysis, but at least he's speaking."

"My goodness, I didn't realize it was as bad as that."

"We'll continue to pray for him and hope for the best."

Kay nodded.

"Okay then, let's get back on task. I know you feel a bit overwhelmed today, but I wanted to remind you of the board meeting tonight at six. Levi has offered to—"

"Tonight?" Kay blurted. "Do I need to be there? Is this something the Dean of Faculty normally does?"

Mildred smiled. "Nobody is doing what they normally do right now. Levi and several members of the board are particularly impressed with you and asked that you be in attendance. But I am beginning to wonder if you might need a little time. A great deal had been thrown at you in the past few days, and I find it amazing that you can function at all. Tell you what: I'll let them know you won't be in attendance. You stay back and get some rest, okay?"

"No," Kay said. "I'm sorry. Of course, I'll be there."

The speech buoyed Kay until she began plowing through a deluge of teacher conferences, classroom visits, and budgetary requisitions. Most of the conferences consisted of teachers congratulating her for her speech and wishing her well. A few though took ugly turns with casual remarks that subtly denigrated her qualifications for the office. One history teacher bluntly informed her that she was not welcome in his classroom, and therefore, she was not to schedule an observation of his course.

After that teacher left her office, Kay approached Mrs. Shim. "Well, I guess the honeymoon is over."

"Were you expecting roses?"

* * *

Mid-afternoon arrived and Kay had yet to take a break. She looked at her schedule, huffed angrily, then walked into the outer office. "Mrs. Shim, please hold my calls. I'm going to take a few minutes and eat lunch."

"Certainly, Ms. Morrell."

She closed her door, dropped into her chair, then pointed angrily at the phone. "One more ring from you and you are going out the window. I mean it."

Just as she unwrapped her sandwich, the phone rang. "Mrs. Shim," she whispered, "do your duty and hold that call." Then, she heard Mrs. Shim laugh. Shrugging, she bit into her sandwich. "When in heaven's name did you develop a sense of humor?"

A few moments later, there was a rap on the door. Kay winced and pinched her eyes closed. "Yes?"

Mrs. Shim opened the door, a smile flickering across her face. "I'm sorry, Ms. Morrell, but it's Mr. Ross. He insisted that he be allowed to speak with you, and I must say he seems particularly buoyant today."

"Harry's calling?"

"Yes. Shall I have him call back?"

Kay stared silently.

"Ms. Morrell?"

"Um, no. I'll take it."

"Certainly, Ms. Morrell." Mrs. Shim closed the door.

Slowly, Kay raised the receiver. "Harry?"

"Hey, just thought I'd call and see how your day is going. Melissa said it's been a 'glowering' day for you."

Melissa? Kay thought. *He called Mrs. Shim Melissa?* "Um, how are you feeling?"

"Overall, I think I'm on the mend. My belly is sore but not so bad anymore. Anyway, there's this nurse and she's kinda cute, and she's coming in a few minutes to clean me up. I told her I'm good to go for a shower, but she insists on a sponge bath. So anyhow, I thought I'd call you for moral support."

Kay laughed. She realized why Mrs. Shim had laughed. Harry had practiced his story on her. "So, she's cute, huh?"

A short pause followed before Harry said, "Kinda cute, kinda. There's another one that's really cute."

"Okay, well, what did the doctor say about your surgery?"

"I don't think I'd mind her giving me a sponge bath, but, well, you get what you get sometimes."

Kay laughed a bit more and leaned back in her chair. "Yes, I believe that's true. But what did the doctor say?"

"I haven't seen the doctor yet today. But I've got to tell you, he's blunt. He said I was lucky."

"Well, you were. God, yes. But that doesn't sound too blunt."

"Actually, he meant that I was lucky to get him and not some other doctor. He's got a huge ego."

"Are you on any pain medication?"

"Probably…maybe…I don't know. The nurses give me stuff, like with the IV and everything. I think they're in cahoots."

"Who? Miss Cutesy Pie, Miss Kinda Cutesy Pie, and the doctor?" Kay leaned back further, slipped out of her shoes, and propped her feet up on an open desk drawer.

"Yeah, them. And their ringleader, Nurse Lei."

Kay smiled as she remembered how disjointed talking with Harry could be. "I'm glad you're feeling better. How long do you think you'll be in the hospital?"

"I think they're all trying to, well, you know…"

"Trying to what?"

"Oh, you know. They're trying to keep me in for a while. Maybe ten days. I think it's working."

"So they could give you more sponge baths?"

"Well, yeah." Harry chuckled then whispered a thin squeal.

Kay, her forehead wrinkling, listened to the squeal. When it faded, she asked, "And how are you protesting this assault on your manhood?"

Harry's squeal turned intense.

She snapped her feet off the drawer. "Harry? You there? Harry?!"

"Hey," Harry said, his voice a rasp. "Cool it already." He took a few slow breaths. "Okay, we need a new rule, a temporary one. Please don't make me laugh. Let me be the comedian."

Kay smiled and sat back. "Oh, sure. Sorry about that. You're still hurting then?"

"Kinda. It's okay. I should have prepped you better on the rules."

"You've been practicing, haven't you?"

"As a comedian? Yeah. Does it show?"

Kay chuckled. "Mrs. Shim obviously liked your story about the nurses."

"Yeah. She laughed."

"It's really good to hear your voice."

For a few moments, only Harry's breathing came over the line. Finally, he said, "Can you tell me about your day? And what is 'glowering' anyway? What did Melissa mean? Sounds like a cross between glowing and scowling. So was it like that?"

Melissa. He did it again. Kay smiled and nodded. "Yes, I suppose that's about right. What do you want to know?"

"Everything."

"Where am I supposed to start?"

"Start with something weird."

"The weirdest thing? Well, okay, how's this? This teacher walks into my office, and he tells me, 'Miss Morrell, I just want you to know that if this sorta thing ever happens again, you can count on me.' So, I thank him for his support and tell him I hope none of this sort of thing will ever happen again. Well, he stands there, nodding sagely with his hands on his hips and tells me, 'Miss Morrell, hope is one thing, but preparation in the way of a Smith and Wesson is far better than a flatulent hope in the wind.' Turns out he had a gun in his desk!"

Harry grunted again in pain.

"Harry?"

Harry continued to squeal.

A female voice came on the line. "Hello?"

"Is he all right?" Kay asked.

"Who is this?"

"This is Kay Morrell."

"Oh, Ms. Morrell, this is Nurse Lei. He'll be okay in a moment. Please be careful with what you tell him. I know you're trying to cheer him up, but his stomach is still very sore, and he seems to find humor in everything today."

"Oh God, I'm really sorry."

"It's okay, no real harm done. I think he enjoys the attention."

"Thank you. I'll be careful."

"Here he is."

"Kay," Harry said, "you forgot the rule already. I thought you liked me."

"Harry, don't make jokes. Just relax. I won't talk to you if you start laughing again."

Harry took several deep breaths. "Okay. Just tell me about your day. What did you do with the guy with the gun?"

"I sent him packing."

"Good work, boss."

She listened for him to make a joke, heard none, and told him about her speech and the rest of her day.

Sometime later she noted the time. "Oh my God. We've been talking for almost an hour. I've got to get back to work."

"Okay, boss. It's been really cool talking with you."

"I can't come over to visit tonight. I have a meeting."

"Hey, no need to be sorry. Okay if I call you, though?"

"Of course. And yes…it's been great talking with you again." She hung up, wondering why she had never mentioned the previous night's assault at her apartment.

* * *

At the board meeting that night, Kay discovered that Levi's chairmanship was in name only. True, he presided over the meeting, but it was a trio of younger members who wielded the real power. An idea by one of them led to an emergency fund-raising campaign.

The suggestion arose after the school's CFO reported that the repercussions of the attack meant unbudgeted outlays of millions of dollars. To cover those costs the school would need to delay planned capital improvements, freeze salaries, or dip into the principal of the school's endowment.

Kay jerked mildly when the man spoke of freezing salaries. She knew firsthand what that meant to the faculty.

"I believe we can raise the money," a member said. "And we should get on it right now while the school's in the news."

Kay vaguely remembered he was a big wig in some investment-banking house in San Francisco. Sitting in a comfortable armchair on the perimeter of the group, her eyes grew heavy. Kay never realized when her head dropped onto the backrest.

Mildred tapped Kay on the shoulder. She bolted upright and discovered a small knitted blanket covering her legs. Blushing fiercely, she whispered, "I'm so sorry. How long was I out? Where is everyone?"

"They just left. You were out quite a while," Mildred said.

"You were out like a candle in the barn," Levi said. "If I had gone through what you've been through, I think I'd crawl into my bed and sleep for a month. But good God, the members wouldn't stop talking about you."

"Levi," Mildred said, "let me get her home. She's had enough for the day."

For the ride back, Mildred sat in the back seat with Kay while a young FBI agent drove.

"Kay," Mildred said slowly as the car pulled out of Levi's long driveway. "I've been delegated to ask if you could possibly put one more thing on your plate."

"Um…what?"

"A committee of the board is setting up meetings next week with potential donors."

"Okay."

"Well, Mr. Kent, he's the one who had the idea in the first place. You remember Mr. Kent?"

Kay nodded. "The younger-looking one. The one with the dark-gray suit and pulled back hair."

"Yes, that one. Well, Mr. Kent believes strongly that your presence at these meetings would greatly increase, not only the odds of the school receiving a gift, but also the size of the gift."

"My presence?"

"Yes, dear."

"Because I was almost shot?"

"Well, that's part of it."

Kay turned and looked with disbelief at Mildred.

"Well, you see, my dear, Mr. Kent believes that a young heroine, a young attractive heroine is, well, as he put it, 'a great card to play.'"

"A great card to play." Kay shook her head. "I wonder what Harry would say."

"Well, Mr. Kent is hoping you could persuade Mr. Ross to be a part of this campaign. Once he's released from the hospital, that is. But he thinks you're the critical one."

Kay sat silently for a while then sighed. "When are these meetings?"

"The earliest will be next week."

Kay sighed. "This is so crazy. I can't promise Harry will do it, but if you think it's important, of course I'll help."

Mildred released a sigh louder than Kay's. "I believe it's extremely important, Kay. Thank you. I...oh Lord, sometimes I wonder if God really knows what he's doing with the human race. Um, by the way, Mr. Kent is sending someone to, well, work with you on your wardrobe, so to speak."

Kay burst out laughing.

THURSDAY

25

Friends, new and old, are worth their weight in gold.

By Thursday afternoon, Kay angrily realized the ever-growing details of her job would keep her until the evening. Worst of all, most of the work demanded her focus on mind-numbing minutia, and yet she was never left alone long enough to find a rhythm. Meetings, teacher conferences, and phone calls with angst-riven parents dominated the day.

Mrs. Shim, purse on her shoulder, stood at her door at four. "The day's over, Ms. Morrell."

"Oh. Of course. I'll see you tomorrow."

"Mr. Ross is on line two."

"He is?"

"Yes, ma'am. I'll be going now."

Kay watched her leave, looked at the stack of papers on her desk, then picked up the phone. With the barest of hellos, she vented. Harry listened calmly, and after almost thirty minutes, she finally realized he had barely spoken. "Oh, God, here I am whining and complaining, and you're the one in the hospital. I am such a baby."

"No, you're not. I need to tell you, this has been the highlight of my day, at least until Vincent gets here."

"Yeah, right."

"No, it is… It's either you or futzing around on my laptop or watching daytime TV soap operas. Talking with you is real."

"Oh, don't say that. It's all so petty, the things I do now, unbelievably petty."

"No, Kay. It's not…and I think you know that."

Kay shook her head.

As if he could see her, Harry added, "Right now, right this very moment, if you were to quit, then the whole school would fall into a mess bigger than it's already in. And you know it."

"Don't be ridiculous. I mean—"

"I'm serious. Your teachers are scared. And they have a right to be scared. The school's been shot up by a madman."

"Well, I was scared too. I still am."

Harry paused for a long time. "I know. But you didn't run. Everyone else ran."

Kay said nothing.

"The people who ran are going to want fences and more security."

Kay nodded. "We're erecting a perimeter fence, and we've hired a security company."

"Do you see a lot of teachers and kids staring at the bullet holes?"

Kay nodded again. "Well, I stare at the bullet holes too."

"Really? How many are there?"

"What? I don't know."

"You should count them."

Kay pulled the phone away from her ear and stared at it. "I don't think so."

"And after you count them, you should name them."

"Are you trying to be funny again?"

"Maybe."

Kay closed her eyes. "Well, don't."

"Okay. Sorry. Are there still cops on campus?"

"What? Yeah. So?"

"And Mr. Lee is in the hospital?"

"Harry. I know everything's in flux. I know that."

"What's Mrs. Cade doing?"

"Everything she can to keep the school afloat. This is costing the school millions…millions the school doesn't have."

"So…who's left?"

"What?"

"Who's left to run the ship, Kay?"

"Well, it's not me. It's not who I am."

Harry slid into a long pause then said, "Yes, it is. Of course, it is. It's always been who you are."

This time, Kay paused. "You really think I can do this?"

"Absolutely. And you know it, too."

"But I don't like it. I really don't. Do I have to do it forever?"

"I don't know. Ask yourself that question from time to time. Just to periodically check to see if and when enough is enough."

Kay looked at the clock and shook her head. Without thinking, she blurted, "Harry, I know why you quit writing to me. I know why you quit."

Harry turned silent.

Kay waited as long as she could. "Harry?"

"I never should have quit. Never."

"Oh, Harry."

Harry said nothing.

"You still there?"

"Yeah."

"Should I bring you some books or magazines?"

"You're coming?"

"Yeah, it'll be late though. I need to arrange it with my protection detail, but I'll see you tonight."

"Whoa. That's super."

Kay smiled. "I have a couple meetings, so hopefully I'll get there between eight and eight-thirty."

"Fantastic. Make it a book then. A big book, you know, some trashy, five-hundred-page novel with lots of sex and violence."

Kay laughed. "Got it, one low-life paperback coming up."

"Great, just great. It will go well with my sponge baths. You should see these nurses. Shameless, absolutely shameless."

Kay laughed. "Bye, Harry."

"Yeah, okay. Bye."

* * *

Kay arrived at Harry's room a little after nine, but the visit ended up a disappointment because he struggled to stay awake. Nurse Lei informed Kay that Harry had been allowed a few minutes to walk around the halls in the afternoon. But before Nurse Lei realized what had happened, forty-five minutes had elapsed. His over-taxed, feeble reserves deserted him, and he had to be helped back to bed.

"He doesn't understand what his body has been through," Nurse Lei said. "He thinks he can just get up and go, go, go."

"I'm fine," Harry croaked with barely open eyes.

Kay smiled and planted a kiss on his forehead. "Bye, Harry."

"I'll call you tomorrow," Harry mumbled. "Tomorrow."

Kay nodded and patted the spot on his forehead where her lips had touched. "Good night."

But Harry was already asleep.

She found Elizabeth in the waiting room, pacing back and forth by the window.

"Hi," Kay said.

"Hello," Elizabeth responded stiffly.

Both women stared for a while.

"You didn't need to wait," Kay said. "You could have come in. You should have. Apparently, he tried to do too much today and exhausted himself. He's sleeping now."

Elizabeth crossed her arms and nodded. "Actually, I've been waiting for you."

"Me?"

"Yes. Can we talk for a few minutes? Do you have some time?"

"I really need to get back. I have a long day tomorrow."

"Please?"

Kay sighed heavily. "Sure."

They found the cafeteria empty and sat at a corner table. Kay's FBI minder stood by the door.

"Harry's told me a lot about you," Elizabeth said. "You two must have been something growing up."

"Um, Ms. White…Elizabeth, is it okay to call you Elizabeth?"

"Sure."

"You know, I've asked that question of so many people lately." She closed her eyes and almost laughed. "Teachers, Board members, parents. 'Is it okay to call you this?' 'Is it okay to call you that?' I guess it's my teaching." She shrugged.

She found Elizabeth staring at her. "God, I just pulled a 'Harry,' didn't I?"

Smiling, Elizabeth said, "If you are referring to a tangential digression, then yes, you just pulled a 'Harry.'"

Kay smiled and shook her head. "So it's Elizabeth. What did you ask?"

"I didn't ask anything. I just said that Harry talked a lot about you."

"Oh."

Elizabeth's face lost its mirth. She wiped her palms over her legs, then interlaced her fingers and propped her elbows on the table. "Harry and I never married. Did Harry ever tell you that?"

"Actually, you did. When we met, you told me."

Elizabeth nodded. "He said you two were born in the same hospital a few hours apart."

"That's right. We more or less grew up together."

"Yes, he said that, too… You know, you were part of the reason we never married."

"I don't think—"

Elizabeth raised her hands. "A small part of the reason. I'm not blaming you. I'm nowhere near blaming you." She looked away.

"You know, I'm not sure where this is going."

"You've visited him a lot. Has he spoken about me?"

Kay shook her head. "What? No. We talk about the school and the aftermath of the shooting. Something we're both deeply involved with. But that's about it. And to be honest, I do most of the talking. Sometimes he asks a question, but for the most part, he just listens."

"Yes, I too have found him to be a good listener. But then again, once he gets started, he can go on and on and on. The funny thing is, he can be quite perceptive."

Kay looked at her minder. "Look, it's been a long week. Harry and I lost contact many years ago. I really don't know the person who ran out and got shot at my school. I don't."

"I'm not so sure about that."

"Elizabeth…I'm really sorry, but it's late. What can I do for you?"

"Harry asked me to talk with you."

"What? When?"

"Today. He said I should talk with you. So I'm just doing Harry's bidding now."

Kay clenched her jaw. "Okay. Fine. What shall we talk about?"

"Kay, I'm not trying to make you angry."

"I'm not angry."

"Harry told me about your temper."

"What?" Kay stared red-faced at Elizabeth.

"In a good way. He spoke of your temper rather endearingly."

Kay rose out of her seat. "I really think I should go now."

"Do you know why Harry said I should talk with you?"

"I have no idea."

"He said we're the two best people he knows, and that people like us need to get to know each other."

Kay said nothing.

"He told me he was going to tell you the same thing."

Kay remained quiet.

Elizabeth sighed. "But I guess they had to sedate him, and he never got the chance."

Kay took a deep breath. Her face relaxed a tiny bit.

Elizabeth watched.

"Okay," Kay said then paused. "The next time you see Harry, you can tell him that I haven't lost my temper in years. You can tell him that people grow up."

Shrugging with her eyes, Elizabeth said, "Please sit down."

Kay hesitated then sat.

Elizabeth unlaced her fingers, spread her hands, and looked into her open, empty palms. "We met at a bar in Chicago. I was there with some colleagues who were…less than polite to him. There he was, all by himself eating a sandwich and drinking something or other in our favorite booth. He was lean, you know, chiseled, and, I don't know, he had this really open body language." She paused and wrinkled her forehead. "I couldn't take my eyes off him. Even with those ears. Have you seen his ears?"

"It's from wrestling without a headgear. He used to promise his mom he would always wear a headgear. I guess he broke his promise."

Elizabeth sat back and eyed Kay. "Yeah, he told me about the promise. However, he said he made the promise to you. Anyway, I went back to Robi's every day for a week looking for him. Jesus, I felt like a goddamn school girl."

Kay laughed.

With the ice broken, the two women fell into a conversation that lasted until eleven. They discovered they shared many interests, including English literature. When they realized that tomorrow was nigh, they reluctantly said their goodnights, exchanged cell numbers, and made a date to see each other again on Saturday.

As she left, Kay realized why Harry was so attracted to the woman.

FRIDAY

26

People with a temper commonly vent on someone they love.

Kay spoke with her mother Friday morning. Dad had suffered a setback but seemed to be back on track. Would Kay be coming down for the weekend? Could she get Harry to call? In her hurried walk from Mildred's to her office, she replied to her mother's queries with generic answers.

In the hallway, she stopped by the bullet-pocked wall. The stanchions and police tape had been removed, the floor swept clean of debris, and the window covered with plyboard. "Okay, Harry," she whispered. "I have to report that I will be unable to give you an exact number of bullet holes." She looked around and found herself alone. "You see, the window's gone, so there aren't any neat little round holes to count there. Below the window, there's a bunch, but they're ragged. So, many…lots…a bunch. Satisfied now? If you want them named, you do it."

As Friday afternoon arrived, Kay marveled at the ease with which the day had passed. Harry called around two p.m. Neither spoke about the shooting. Instead, they reminisced about their days on her grandparents' farm, boosting her energy for the remainder of the uneventful day.

Charlie Cornish turned up to serve as her escort for the ride to the hospital. "The people at the FBI are all busy, so here I am."

Kay smiled then hugged the gray-haired cop. "Oh, Charlie, I'm so glad it's you."

Once in the car, Charlie's tone turned serious. "It looks like the FBI is ramping up. They've got a bunch of additional agents in the San Francisco office, and every time they call for something, it's some new voice. And you can just kinda hear the excitement in the background. Plus, my chief has been in a lot of closed-door meetings. Seems like the shit is about to hit the fan. Pardon my language."

"You mean it might end soon? Are Harry and I safe?"

Charlie hemmed and hawed for a long moment. "I can't answer that, Kay. I just can't."

In the waiting room, Kay and Charlie ran into the Tomas. Vincent pulled away from Alma and ran toward Kay with upraised arms. "Auntie Kay, Auntie Kay, Nana says you're going to live in my house. Can you read to me? Please. Please read to me, Auntie Kay. I brought lots of books."

Kay picked the boy up. Like the first time, he wrapped his arms around her neck and kissed her cheek. Again, she felt an upwelling of happiness. "Hey there, big boy, how are you?" Before Vincent could answer, she looked at Alma. "What did you tell him?"

Kenji peeled the boy away from Kay. "Well, hello there, Miss Kay. It's very nice of you to keep visiting Harry."

Kay ruffled Vincent's curls as the boy rested in Kenji's arms. "Hi, Kenji."

"Hello, missy," Alma said.

"Hi." Kay looked at the wily, old woman.

"Can Auntie Kay read to me, Nana? Can she? Can she?"

"Whoa, Vincent," Kenji said. "Slow down a bit. That's up to Auntie Kay. You need to ask her."

"But I did! I did!" Vincent said, looking for support from Kay.

Kay stared at Alma. "Certainly, I'd be happy to read if you promise to tell me all about Nana's plans. Can you do that?"

"Plans?" Vincent asked.

Alma subtly slid behind Kenji, while Kenji just smiled.

Charlie moved away then sat in a chair next to the policeman at Harry's door, where he could watch both Kay and the hallway to Harry's room.

Kay and Vincent settled on the couch and began *Where the Wild Things Are* while Alma and Kenji went to visit Harry.

A couple minutes later, Alma reappeared. "Vinnie, come. It's time to see your pops. Come."

Vincent slid off the couch and ran to Alma. Together they walked to Harry's room. Soon, Alma came out, walked purposefully to the chair adjacent to Kay, and sat. "Sorry," Alma said. "But Vinnie needs to see his pops before he falls asleep."

"What? Harry's falling asleep now? It's only six-thirty-something."

"Yeah. His doc's in there, too. The nurse says he stayed out of bed too long again and, I don't know. She said something and then more things. Yap, yap, yap. I really don't understand. Something about his whites?"

Kay rushed to Harry's room. Alma followed.

Inside, Nurse Lei administered something into Harry's IV line while a middle-aged doctor read from a tablet. Kenji held a worried-looking Vincent in his arms at the foot of the bed.

Ashen, Harry lay with eyes half-open, forcing a smile. "Hey," he whispered, "look who's here, Vincent. Dad's best friend in the whole wide world."

"What happened?" Kay asked.

No one said anything until Nurse Lei looked at the doctor.

The doctor shrugged. "I warned him infection was a possibility and that he needed to take it easy. So, guess what? He thinks he knows more than I do and tries to walk all day. Now his white count is way up."

Kay huffed angrily, turned away, and took a step toward the door. Stopping abruptly, she returned to the side of the bed, folding her arms across her chest.

Kenji quietly carried Vincent out of the room. Alma remained near the door, her hands on her hips.

The doctor eyed Harry. "Mr. Ross, you are going to remain in bed continuously for the next forty-eight hours. Are we clear?"

Harry grinned weakly. "I thought I was okay. I mean—"

"Shut up, Harry," Kay said.

"We're hopeful that the antibiotics will bring the infection under control," the doctor said.

Kay looked at the doctor, seeking the rest of his unsaid message.

Sighing, the doctor shrugged again. "If not, additional surgery may be required."

Kay stepped past Nurse Lei to the head of the bed. "Harry, what are you doing?"

Harry stared into space. "Sorry," he croaked.

"I don't care about 'sorry.' If you do this one more time, I won't come back to visit you. If your white count goes to the moon and the doctor has to rip out your insides, I will not come. Are you forgetting about your son? How can you do this to him?"

"Okay," Harry said. He struggled to keep his eyes open but still managed to nod his head.

Kay stormed out of the room. "Damn it," she huffed as she walked to the window in the waiting area. "Damn it, damn it, damn it."

Kenji carried Vincent back into the room.

"You need anything, Kay?" Charlie asked.

Kay shook her head, turned toward the window, and stared through her reflection at the parking lot. She never heard Alma come up beside her.

"You did good," Alma said. "Harry's got a hard head. He doesn't listen too much. But he listens to you. That's for sure. He needs to think about Vinnie. Good for you."

"God! Alma, will you please—" Kay spat until she noticed tears in Alma's eyes. "Alma, I have to go. Say goodbye to Vincent and Kenji for me, will you?"

Alma wiped her cheeks. "That boy's not the only one who has a hard head."

Breathing heavily, Kay turned and hustled toward the elevator. Charlie had to run to catch up.

The long ride back to Mildred's did little to quell her anger. Gratefully, Charlie remained quiet.

Mildred and her husband were out for the evening, so Kay plucked a small container of yogurt out of the refrigerator and took it to her room. She was in bed before she realized she had forgotten a spoon and almost threw the container across the room. Instead, she dropped it into her wastebasket and, seething, turned off her table lamp to hunker down and wage war with the expected onslaught of insomnia.

SATURDAY

27

Life may seem to be rolling along but perhaps it's just unspooling.

Sometime after midnight, Kay slid deliciously to the edge of sleep. Her body settled onto the mattress, and the weight of the quilt eased her fidgety leg muscles. But just as she neared the precipice, she remembered she had a date with Elizabeth on Saturday. Then she realized that it was already Saturday. Next, her temper raised its ugly head, which led to her thinking about how angry she was at Harry. Her eyes popped open.

Surrendering, she rose, donned a sweatshirt, and pulled the yogurt out of the trash. She grabbed her cell and her laptop, went to the kitchen for a spoon, then settled at the breakfast table. After she peeled the foil cover off the yogurt, she saw a missed text message from George.

We need to talk. See you on Monday.

"You're still not following the deal," she said quietly. Thoughts of George distracted her until Vincent popped into her head, reminding her of the urge to have her own Vincent. She wondered if George even wanted to be a father. In all of their conversations, parenthood had never been broached.

Shaking her head, she opened her laptop to check her email and saw an invitation to attend a December conference for administrators. "Well, maybe I can get a few days off. No…not now. Forget that."

She was just about to delete the message when the screen faded to black. She clicked her mouse all over the screen but nothing changed. Then slowly, the screen brightened and lines of text began to appear.

```
ms morell be careful. someone is
fucking around with you and mr ross
and it aint the fbi or the cops
```

The message dissolved and the invitation returned. "Hey!" Kay bolted to her feet, sending her chair crashing to the floor. She stared at the computer for another moment then grabbed her phone.

Mildred appeared at the landing at the top of the stairs. "Kay? Are you all right, dear?"

"I don't know…maybe. I need to call Maizie."

* * *

Maizie's cell chimed five times before she woke. "Cabrera here."

"Maizie, this is Kay Morrell."

Maizie eased her legs out of bed and sat on her uninjured cheek. "Is everything okay?" She looked at the clock and ran her hands through her hair.

"I don't know. I just received a message on my computer that's, um, disconcerting."

Maizie rubbed her face. "Disconcerting?"

"Yes."

Maizie shook her head and rubbed her eyes. "Okay… What was the message?"

"It…it didn't last very long, but it said, 'Be careful, Ms. Morrell. Someone is fucking with you and Mr. Ross and it ain't the FBI or the cops.'"

Shit, Maizie thought. "Anything else?"

"No, that was it. And then the message just disappeared."

Holy fuck. "Disappeared?"

"Yes. Completely."

"Have your security officer move into the house."

* * *

Within an hour, Maizie, Tom, and several other agents descended upon Mildred's home. An IT agent worked on the laptop, while Maizie and Tom interviewed Kay and the Cades. More cops roamed the campus.

An hour later, nothing had been discovered. The message would not reappear, but they did discover that the invitation was bogus. The IT agent left with the laptop.

"We're going to add to your security personnel," Tom said. "Make absolutely sure you keep in close contact with whomever is assigned."

Kay nodded. "Okay. Thank you."

Before they left, Maizie gave Kay a cell phone and charger. "Here. Keep this on your person at all times. Press 2, and it will connect you directly to me. Any time, any place, okay?"

Kay nodded again.

Maizie noted Kay's drawn face and sunken eyes. "You sleeping all right?"

Kay looked up. "What? Why do you ask?"

"I received your call around one this morning. Are you usually awake then?"

Kay smiled sadly. "No. Last night was a little rough, but for the most part, I've been sleeping fairly well."

"Okay," Maizie said with doubt in her voice. "I know the school has contracted some PTSD docs for the students. Maybe you could benefit from working with one of them."

Kay looked directly into Maizie's eyes. "Thank you for your concern. But last night's insomnia had nothing to do with this situation."

Yeah, right, Maizie thought. "Okay, then. Well, you did the right thing calling me."

Kay nodded. "Am I okay to go off campus?"

"I would prefer if you remained here, but I understand your position in the school. Whatever you decide to do, stay close to your security personnel."

28

***If you're going to be a player in the old rogue's
game, it's best to be warned and armed.***

By the time Tom and Maizie drove back to San Francisco, the predawn light had turned the world gray. Tom eased the Ford onto Marina Boulevard. "Maybe we ought to move the operation up. Get things rolling by Monday."

"The whole thing? You're kidding. There's been no final word on coordination, and the D.C. guys won't be here until this afternoon. They'll make the call."

"You should call them now and see if they can move things up."

Maizie shook her head. "They're going to say the initial raids are scheduled to start on Tuesday. They're going to want to wait."

"Yeah, okay. It was just a thought."

Maizie yawned. "There's just too much shit to get coordinated."

"I said, I know." Tom shrugged.

Maizie glanced at her partner. "What else are you thinking about?"

"That funky stuff on Ms. Morrell's computer."

"Yeah, me too. This whole case is so fucking funky."

Tom nodded but said nothing.

"Come on. What's on your mind?"

"I'm thinking about that weird warning.

"Maybe the IT guys will track it down."

"Not likely. But think about it. It was sent by someone with impressive hacking skills and that someone is involved with the whole mess."

"No shit."

"Then think about Sergio dead from an overdose. He was a top lieutenant for Carlos, and intel says none of his top guys were users."

Maizie squirmed uncomfortably on her pillow. "The stuff found on Sergio's computer…it's really good."

"Yeah… Maybe too good. Maybe his computer got hacked and someone is setting Carlos up."

Maizie glanced at Tom then nervously laughed. "Yeah, right. Computer-geek fights narco-creep."

Tom shrugged.

"Sorry, I shouldn't have laughed. I guess it's as good a theory as any right now. Christ, what if we get on with the arrests next week, and it's all a big set-up on us?"

"I don't see that," Tom said with a long sigh. "Everything on that computer has checked out, including the intel from active surveillance. And we're intercepting new emails every day. It's like Carlos doesn't know his security has been breached or that Sergio is dead." He pursed his lips. "To me, it looks as if someone is setting up Carlos by hacking into his system and planting evidence for us to find."

"So…computer-geek goes after Carlos and calls in the FBI to do his dirty work. That's your theory?"

"Well," Tom said, "it definitely has a nice funky feel."

Maizie shifted her weight again. "Make sure the D.C. guys know about your thoughts…and hey, drop me off at the deli at the bottom of my hill, okay?"

"You can manage the hill?"

"Hey, my ass is getting better every day. The doc said I can use it as long as I don't abuse it."

"Hard to imagine your ass getting any better, Maizie."

Maizie laughed. "Why, Thomas Henderson, you just shattered your fucking Boy Scout image. Whatever will your wife say?"

Tom chuckled as he pulled over. "I'll pick you up about one, then."

Maizie climbed out. "Yeah, see you."

Chas, the pseudo-hippie deli owner, always opened early on Saturday so he could play his computer games in peace, away from his wife. Maizie bought a coffee and a bran muffin and limped out the door just as her cell phone rang. The call came from an unknown number. "Hello? Who's this?"

"Ya'll best stop where you are and get back in that store and have a look-see out the window."

Maizie stopped and quickly scanned in all directions.

"Hey! Get back in the fuckin' store."

Maize hobbled back into the store and looked out the window. "What do you want?"

"Ya'll see that white Dodge halfway up the street?"

"Look, this is—"

"Hush up and look."

Maizie huffed, looked, and saw the car. "Yeah, I see it. Now, what in the hell—"

"Ya'll see the two guys in it?"

Maizie's hand twitched. "No, the angle is bad and the windows are tinted."

"OK, well, ya'll should know there's two guys in the car and they're a-waitin' for you."

"Waiting for me?"

"Ya'll best get some help." The connection terminated.

"Shit, shit, shit." She put her coffee and muffins down on the counter. "Watch these for me, Chas. I'll be back in a minute."

"Cool," Chas said, his eyes on his computer.

She opened her cell phone and speed-dialed Tom.

"Yeah?" Tom said.

"I need some help. A car is parked across the street from my building, and there's a couple men inside. It's probably nothing, but I've got a bad feeling. Will you come around and have a look-see at the intersection above my place? I'll wait for your call before I move up the hill."

"Give me five and stay on the line."

She put in her earpiece then reached inside her purse for her Glock.

Chas looked up. "Whoa, I mean whoa, Maizie. I mean, are you like a cop or something? Hey, like, I'm clean, okay?"

"Stay inside and lock the door when I leave, Chas."

"You got it. You want me to call 911 or something?"

"No, not yet. But if you hear shots, then, yeah, call in the cavalry."

"I don't think they like bring horses up here, Maizie. I think they keep them at Golden Gate Park."

"Yeah, I think you're right. And stay away from the window."

"Like whoa. This is so cool. Can I call Harmony?"

"No, don't call anyone. You got that?"

"Cool. Like, I never knew you were a cop, Maizie. Far out."

Maizie nodded then turned her eyes back to the Dodge.

"I'm here," Tom said over the phone. "I can see the car and the two men, a driver and one in the back seat. Windows are up. I don't see any weapons, but the car is idling. You were right. This is weird."

"Yeah. Can they see you?"

"No, not unless they're really good. I'm at the corner, on your side of the street. I've got good cover. I have the shotgun from the trunk. Should I call for backup?"

"Not yet. Let's check it out first. Maybe I'm worrying about nothing."

"Your call."

"I'm moving." Maizie shoved the gun into her coat pocket and began limping up the hill. She kept her head down just enough to look weary, but not enough to limit her view of the Dodge. She was almost abreast of the car when she saw the rear passenger window lowering. "Window's coming down."

"I see it," Tom said.

The man in the back seat began to turn toward Maizie. She saw the gun before it poked out the open window.

"Gun!" she shouted and pulled out her Glock. She pulled the trigger an instant before the man in the car opened fire, sending a spray of bullets into the bricks of her building's façade.

Maizie kept firing as the Dodge jerked away from the curb and fishtailed up the steep incline toward Tom's position. Tom stepped out and pumped shots into the speeding car. The gunman in the back returned fire, and Tom crumpled onto the sidewalk. The car turned left then raced up a side street and out of sight.

"Fuck!" Maizie shouted as she pulled out her phone then painfully sprinted toward Tom, who writhed on the sidewalk, clutching his abdomen. Reaching the intersection, she looked up the street and saw the Dodge stop a hundred yards away and begin maneuvering to turn around. The narrow street was a dead-end.

"You fucked up, boys." She picked up Tom's shotgun.

"Sorry, Maizie," Tom grunted.

She glanced at his white face and pulled a wad of tissues from her purse. "Keep these tight on your wound and hang in there." Pumping a new load into the chamber, she called 911. The Dodge continued to struggle to turn around.

"911, fire, police, or ambulance?"

"Police," Maizie said icily. "Listen carefully." The Dodge was still bumping and grinding, but now had its nose pointing partially downhill. "This is special agent Maizie Cabrera of the FBI. I've got an agent down and two men in a white Dodge armed with automatic weapons." She gave the name of the intersection, her eyes on the Dodge.

"Ma'am? Agent Cabrera?" the dispatcher said.

Maizie put the phone down on the sidewalk.

Tom looked up, grunting, "I screwed up. Sorry."

"Shut up, Tom."

The Dodge finished maneuvering and roared downhill. Maizie stepped away from Tom, aimed, and fired into the windshield. She pumped again and fired at the grillwork. She pumped again and fired at the front tire on the passenger side. The Dodge skewed to the right and slammed into a light pole.

Holding the shotgun to her shoulder, she watched for movement. When none appeared, she slowly approached the Dodge.

"You bastards try one stupid thing, I will blow out your brains," Maizie shouted from fifteen feet. "Throw out your weapons!"

When no one responded, she hunched over and moved closer. "I swear to God, you better not shoot! Throw your weapons out!"

When no response occurred yet again, Maizie sidled up to the car, looked quickly, then bounced back a step. "Okay," she whispered. Again, she approached and peered into the wrecked car. Black pockmarks from pellets and streams of blood darkened the driver's face. Blood seeped from multiple holes in the man in the backseat. Both men were dead.

Maizie let the barrel of the shotgun drop. "Stupid asses, stupid fucking asses." She turned away from the mess and looked toward Tom. Chas was sitting behind her wounded partner, holding him against his chest.

Sirens, lots of sirens, wailed in the distance.

29

A little booze and a new friend loosen lips… Oops.

Anxious about the mysterious email and exhausted, Kay tried to cancel her date with Elizabeth in San Francisco for lunch. However, Elizabeth offered to come to her and arrived at Mildred's at noon.

Mildred and Will had left earlier for a day of hiking on Mount Tamalpais. Kay's escort, another young FBI agent, was stationed in the front room.

Dressed casually in jeans and a hoodie, a haggard Kay met Harry's old girlfriend at the door. "Hi."

Elizabeth subtly pulled back. "Jesus. You look like hell. I'm sorry. Perhaps I should've listened and not come."

"No, it's fine. Come in. Mildred left us some salad, and there's soup heating up."

Elizabeth was dressed in gray designer slacks and a thick off-white sweater over a fitted, collared long-sleeved shirt. Her black hair was pulled back in a long, thick braid.

Kay guided Elizabeth past the escort to the kitchen.

"My God," Elizabeth said. "You have people guarding you and there are cops everywhere. This is all so strange."

"I guess that's my life nowadays." Kay filled two bowls with soup. "How about some wine?"

Elizabeth hesitated. "Um… Sure. It's a bit early, but why not?"

As they ate, they shared stories about their childhoods and commiserated about the difficulties of their jobs. In time, the conversation segued into talk about Harry and the incident that had thrown them together.

"I swear, Elizabeth," Kay said, somewhat fortified by the wine, "everyone thinks I should be feeling some post-traumatic drama sort of thing, but I don't. Even Maizie wants me to see a shrink or something."

"Kay, you were shot at."

"So what? Lots of people get shot at. Lots. Harry and Maizie got shot at. In fact, Harry and Maizie got shot."

Elizabeth leaned forward and rested her chin on her hands. "Oh, Kay. I think you may be a little drunk."

Kay rubbed her eyes. "Maybe."

"You don't drink much, do you?"

Kay shook her head. "No. I can't. It's this Japanese thing in my blood. Is my face red? It feels red. Is it?"

"A bit. You get like this after only a couple glasses?"

"Yeah... Shoot. Sorry."

"Don't worry about it. It's been a rough week, hasn't it?"

Head in her hands, Kay nodded. "Yeah...but I'm okay. It's just this job. Sometimes, I feel like everybody wants a piece of me. I even have to help with the fundraising because of this thing. You can't believe how much money it's going to cost." She paused again. "Shoot... One guy with a gun. It's just, I don't know. Ridiculous sanity. That's what this madman caused us. He pushed us into this ridiculous, over-the-top, reasonable-man sanity that we now use to make all our decisions. All of them. Now we've got fences, campus cops, new security stuff, and I don't know what else. And all the consultants and lawyers we're using. God. These experts and their expert opinions. I don't know. What makes them so smart?"

"Yeah, and they've probably never been shot at."

Kay lifted her head just long enough to say, "You're right. What do they know?"

Elizabeth leaned forward. "Oh my...are you really okay?"

"I don't know. Maybe I *am* going through some of that post dramatic trauma stuff. You should have seen the email I got this morning, and before that I almost got shot right outside my apartment, and then all this stuff about Harry."

Elizabeth jerked back.

"People trying to make me into something I don't want to be and—"

"Your apartment? You almost got shot outside of your apartment? When?"

Kay clamped her mouth shut, straightened up, and set her glass down. "Oops. I wasn't supposed to talk about it. Don't tell Harry. Please don't tell Harry. Anyway, they missed me and shot Maizie."

"What are you talking about?"

Kay closed her eyes and shook her head. "Maizie said not to talk about it."

"Maizie? Agent Cabrera?"

Kay nodded.

Elizabeth allowed a long silence to play out.

"I think I talk too much. I should learn to shut up."

"I think you've held a bunch of stuff inside far too long."

"Can we not talk about it, please?"

"Sure…but I'm glad you feel you can talk to me."

"Me, too." Kay took a deep breath and looked into Elizabeth's eyes. "I really wanted to hate you."

"I know. I saw it in your face when we first met. Anyway, now that hating me won't work…how about friendship? Will that work for you?"

"Yeah…absolutely. God, my head hurts."

SUNDAY

30

Line by line, all night and all morning, Dorothy had been working. Old Man had been very particular about this part of the assignment. He wanted the work to not only look and sound right, but it also had to *smell* right. Finally, he had been satisfied and compensation was on its way. She was done. She could relax. Maybe he'd leave her alone for a while.

She stuffed a handful of chips into her mouth. Crumbs, empty chip packages, and soda bottles littered her desk, floor, and lap. She thought about ordering a pizza just as a new message appeared. "Shit." She wiped her greasy fingers on her shirt then opened the email.

you were a naughty girl

"Fuck." Catching her breath, she stood, showering the floor with debris. Teeth bared and eyes wide, she paced the room for several minutes before returning to her computer.

```
i told you to quit fucking with
nice people

so you knew i would find out

it's the only way you would listen
```

do not, i repeat, do not contact the
teacher again. i know where you live. do
what you are told and we will sail off into
the sunset as friends

we are not friends

whatever. as rich associates then. do what
you are told. am i clear? we are trying to
stop a monster and i need you to behave

this sucks

of course it does. i'm glad you can also
think about the big picture. by the way,
here is another batch i need you to work on

31

Pathways to understanding do not exist for the pawn.

Kay slept until the sun lit up her room on Sunday morning. Feeling no aftereffects from the wine, she scanned the newspaper over toast and coffee in the kitchen.

Mildred entered, dressed for another outing with Will. "Good morning. I'm glad you slept. So, you've seen the front page then?"

Kay smiled and held up the comics section. "Not yet. Doonesbury first then the rest."

"You better have a look at it."

Kay lost her smile and pulled the front page from the stack. The lead article, topped by a four-column headline, told of a shoot-out in a residential section of San Francisco. Two alleged assailants had been gunned down and killed. One FBI agent, whose name was being withheld, was wounded and in serious condition at San Francisco General. Special Agent Maizie Cabrera was involved but offered no comment to the press. The article talked about the dead gunmen, shotguns, automatic weapons, and the normally quiet neighborhood.

Mildred turned on the radio and caught a news channel interviewing a local store owner who had aided the wounded agent.

"All I heard was pop-pop-pop and like tires squealing and then like boom, boom, and then there were more shots, and then some more. I called 911 and heard more shots. Like firecrackers, you know? And then like, crunch! I heard this crunch. It must have been when the car... Anyway, when I went out, there was this totally wrecked car smashed against this pole and like the pole was bending over. And this dude, this FBI dude, was shot, and so I like helped him."

Mildred turned the radio off. "This is getting bad."

Kay stared absently into space.

"Kay?"

"Yes?"

"I said this is getting bad. Perhaps you should do as Agent Cabrera said and stay on campus."

Kay nodded then shook her head. "We can't let them change us from who we are. I've got to call Maizie." She pulled out the new phone and pressed two.

Maizie answered immediately. "Kay, are you all right?"

"I'm fine. I saw the news. It was Agent Henderson who got shot, wasn't it?"

Maizie sighed. "Kay, I can't talk about it. Look, if everything's okay, then I have to go."

"I'm sorry about Tom. I hope he'll be all right. That's all I wanted to say."

Maizie sighed. "The doctors say he'll recover, but it was touch and go all morning. Thanks for calling, but please use the phone only for emergencies."

"I promise," Kay said and hung up.

* * *

Maizie cut the connection and looked at Tom, unconscious and pale, with IV lines to both arms. "That was Kay. She figured out it was you who got shot." She closed her eyes. "I know you can't hear me, but I thought you should know you got your wish. We're moving in tomorrow. D.C. moved everything up. I'm sorry you won't be there."

Maizie gave his hand a squeeze and left. She saw Tom's wife in the hallway and decided to take the stairs rather than walk past the woman.

* * *

Kay pocketed Maizie's cell then brought out her own phone.

"You know the agent who was shot?" Mildred asked.

"Yes. Maizie said he's going to be okay."

"Thank God."

Kay nodded as she scanned her texts and voice mail. Having received nothing from Harry, she called and reached Nurse Lei, who informed her that he was back on track. The infection seemed to be responding to treatment, and all of his vital signs looked strong. The good nurse asked if she wished to be connected to Harry's room, but Kay turned her down and said she would check in later. She wanted the day to mull things over.

She called Mom and even spent some time talking with Dad, who sounded much stronger. He even cracked a few feeble jokes.

Back in her room, she booted up a borrowed laptop and opened her email. There were no suspicious missives, so she went through several from the faculty, most of which were mundane requests.

Just as she finished the last message, she received a new one from her father's email address. She caught her breath. "No way," she whispered.

She got up and walked away before returning to the desk. Still standing, she leaned over and opened the email.

```
ms morell
do not tell the fbi about me because
you can get me killed
things might get better soon but
stay careful
I will help when I can
```

Like the previous warning, the message slowly dissolved.

She stared at the screen for several minutes then pushed away from the desk. "If that's how you want to play it, okay. But I'm not going to run around scared any longer."

She changed into workout clothes, went to the garage, and pounded out five miles on Will's treadmill. Finished, she stretched and worked through a regimen of yoga.

Later, as had been her practice for years when confronted with a problem, she decided to put her thoughts in writing. Pulling out a yellow pad and a pen, she wrote in capital letters, *WHAT I KNOW*. But thoughts tumbled on top of thoughts and refused to coalesce. She ripped the page from the pad, wadded it into a ball, and threw it across the room. "I don't know anything!" Taking a deep breath, she tried again. Thirty minutes later, with the page filled with crossed-out phrases and angry doodles, she slammed the pen down and stormed back to the treadmill in the garage.

* * *

Later, with her temper tamped down, Kay tried again to make sense of the week, this time on a computer. After a few minutes of frustration, her phone rang. "Hello?"

"Hey, it's me," Harry said. "I wasn't going to call because I was afraid you'd get angry again. But then I thought, well, maybe she's going to be upset if I don't call. So…I flipped a coin and, well, that's why I called. From my bed, by the way."

"Good. But you should know I was already angry before I saw you."

"Oh, then I guess I was the last straw sort of thing."

Kay sighed. "Not quite."

After a long pause, Harry asked, "What are you up to?"

Kay put her feet on the desk. "Well, I'm sitting here at a computer, trying to get a handle on everything that's happened."

"By writing about it."

"Yes, by writing about it. I'm an English teacher. What else would you expect?"

"Oh…okay. You're still angry."

"Yeah…sorry. I just ran about a zillion miles on the treadmill, and all it did was make me sweat. The writing is not helping either." She waited the requisite thirty seconds to allow Harry to think.

"You have writer's block, don't you?"

"Exactly. I don't know where to start. I don't know what to say. I don't even know how to say what I'm thinking. And then, just when

I get an idea, it gets overwhelmed by another. So, I just sit here while my brain goes round and round."

Again, she waited for Harry.

"Writing helps you think?"

"Well, it used to. Not today, though."

"Well, it's still a great idea. I could never do that. I hate writing."

Kay smiled. "So, best friend, do you have any ideas on how I can get going?"

"Oh man…an English teacher asking me about writing. This is something to send to the New York Times or something."

Kay laughed. "Oh God, you are so different now. I don't remember you being very funny when we were kids."

"Well, I was. A little delayed and everything, but hilarious."

Kay laughed again. "So, give me an idea."

Harry didn't pause. "You should just write the *what* part. Just describe it, you know, bluntly. Like 'the morning was sunny and warm and a herd of students were grazing in the courtyard,' or something like that. Don't try to figure out the *how* and *why* until later."

Kay laughed again. "You know, that is a good idea. However, you should know that a herd is singular and, hence, the herd *was* grazing in the courtyard."

Harry chuckled. "English teacher to the bitter end. And don't edit, just keep typing. It's not like anyone else has to read it."

Their talk turned to other topics. Kay spoke of her parents, her new position, and her apartment. Harry, for the most part, listened and occasionally related a funny story about his trek through the country. Both enjoyed the disjointed but relaxed dialogue.

By the time Kay ended the call, she was surprised by how much time had passed. She turned to her computer and began typing. *It was the first meeting of the faculty for the new school year, and Mrs. Cade's speech went overtime, as usual.*

When Mildred and Will returned home after another day of hiking, Kay still sat at the computer, fingers tapping on the keyboard.

32

*Though oblivious to much of the board, old
knights still sense a battle nearing.*

Heart pounding, Dorothy gaped at an envelope sitting on her kitchen table. She found it after stumbling out of bed in the middle of the afternoon. Inside the envelope was a handwritten note from Old Man instructing her to inform him of any movement north by Carlos. "You came into my house," she hissed. "While I was sleeping, you came into my fucking house. You sonofabitch, you said I was done." Then she thought about the money he'd paid her. It had allowed her to quit her stupid job at the bank, pay off her credit card, and buy a shitload of equipment. But all she felt now was fear. For the first time in her life, she wasn't hungry.

She sat heavily at the table and opened her laptop. A message from Old Man flashed onto her screen.

> as you can tell by now, i do know where
> you live
>
> you said i was done.
>
> i was wrong, i still need you. i need to
> know where the bastard is. i know you've
> been tracking him, so where is he? i can

**come over and help if you like. shall i
bring you something to eat?**

Dorothy shook from head to toe.

`no. i just got up. i'll get on it`

that's my girl

`fuck off`

**do you know if the bastard has crossed
the border yet?**

`no. maybe. i don't know`

you've got to find out

`ok`

She whispered, "My house. You fucking bastard, you were in my house." Then she got to work.

* * *

Jorge stood by his hotel window, looking at downtown San Francisco and the Bay, when Cobb called. "Yeah?"

"What do you want to do?" Cobb asked.

"I don't know. Apparently, Harry wants us to know he's behind all this."

"I know. Christ. But why?"

Jorge hesitated then exhaled slowly. "In case he needs our help."

"Shit. He thinks we're going to help him?"

Jorge watched a massive freighter slide under the Bay Bridge. "Yeah, he does. Have you any ideas?" After Cobb did not respond,

Jorge said, "God, I'm tired. I'm getting old and need more rest than I used to."

"Well, get your damn rest. You know as much as me. And we're going to need some sort of plan. Or at least some sort of direction before Harry brings the roof down on top of everyone. He could get a lot of innocent people killed."

Jorge sat on the small sofa. "I know, but I don't know what to say. It'd be good if Astor would call me."

"Good luck with that. Astor hates you almost as much as Harry does."

"I know. Oh well... Maybe the FBI raids will shake things loose."

"Astor says they're moving up the raids to tomorrow," Cobb said.

Jorge shook his head. "No, they're not, at least not here. I'm not sure about the ones in Texas and Arizona, or maybe even San Diego, but the ones in the Bay Area are being postponed."

"What? You're kidding. How'd you find out?"

"I may be old and on the outs, but I still have a few contacts," Jorge said. "My source says that the raids are going to be delayed because of new information."

"New information? You think Harry's behind the delay?"

"Probably. Maybe whatever Harry's planning isn't quite ready."

"Shit," Cobb said, "I bet Harry's the one feeding the FBI."

"Maybe. I don't know. You need to remember Harry doesn't have the computer skills to hack into anything."

"Fuck. Maybe he's recruited somebody. He's always been good at digging up people to work for him."

"That's because he used to have a budget from Uncle Sam. He doesn't have that anymore, and someone with those skills is going to be very expensive."

Cobb paused. "Maybe he's robbing banks or something. All I know is Harry's got something going."

Jorge watched the freighter continue on its way. "I don't know what to say."

"Why would he want the raid postponed?"

"You have to consider Harry's ultimate purpose."

"What's that?"

"Harry doesn't wish to only destroy Carlos's drug empire. He wants Carlos."

"Ah, shit."

"Indeed," Jorge said.

* * *

Clammy, chilled, and nauseated, Dorothy stretched out on her sofa and carefully balanced a bowl of M&Ms on her stomach and began stuffing small handfuls into her mouth. Within a few minutes, the sugar rush calmed her to the point where she could sit up. Wiping her face, she rose and crossed the room to her computer.

"Okay, Old Man," she whispered then typed,

```
carlos  is  coming.  crossed  the
border this morning and expects to
be in the bay area mon or tues. he
really thinks a twenty-nine-year-
old, good-citizen moron is you. how
are you going to protect the moron?
```

Old Man answered almost immediately.

```
how many is he bringing?

not sure. maybe a dozen. what about
the teacher?

carlos must be very excited

his people think he's gone around
the bend

and yet they still follow him
```

what about the teacher?

not to worry. do you want your bonus sent
to the same account?

keep your fucking money

i will donate it to a drug rehab program
of your choice

fuck off

33

Knights worry when pawns open their eyes.

Although Sunday saw no more cryptic emails or violence, Kay became increasingly edgy. During the afternoon she went back to her notes yet came no closer to understanding anything. She again attempted, without success, to burn away her lousy mood on the treadmill. At wit's end, she decided to let the matter rest until after school on Monday then spent an hour on the phone with her parents.

Dad was making progress. Both the quality and quantity of his jokes had reached a new level. Kay wasn't sure how successful she was in avoiding Mom's relationship queries, but figured Mom's peace of mind needed something to chew on other than Dad's cancer.

Dad's improved situation raised her spirits until the early evening when she reneged on her promise and read her notes again. Almost immediately, her mood darkened. With her stomach twisting, she called Harry. Because he was slated for some lab work, their conversation was brief but eased Kay's mind…for a while.

Later that night, fuming, she called again. "Hey, are you awake?"

"Yeah. Are you angry? You sound like you're pissed off."

"No, I'm okay. What've you been doing?"

"Well…I finished that book you gave me. It's, um, full of sex and violence."

"As ordered, I believe."

"Yeah…I know." After a long silence, he asked, "Did you know Cabrera was involved in that shootout downtown?"

"Yes, I did. And don't call her that. It's Agent Cabrera, okay?"

"Whoa, sorry. I didn't say it to make you mad."

"I'm not mad," Kay snapped. "And you know what? It was her partner who got shot. Remember him? Agent Henderson? He's probably in the same hospital as you are."

Harry took a few moments before he said, "I said I'm sorry. She seems to take her job very seriously."

"God, yes, she does. She cares about things and she's working like a dog. This is the second time in a week someone shot at her, and she just keeps right on going. You should have seen her the night she did get shot. She was amazing. The doctor wanted to keep her in the hospital, but oh no, not her. She's wounded and hurting and her partner is in the hospital and she just keeps at it." She paused, but when Harry remained silent, she barked, "So, show a little respect."

"I will…but wait a minute."

"Wait a minute for what?"

"Did you see her the night she was wounded?"

Kay slammed her mouth shut.

"Kay?"

Kay heaved a long sigh. "Sorry, I'm…I'm not supposed to talk about it."

Harry said nothing.

"Maizie told me not to talk about it, okay?" Kay closed her eyes, said nothing, and tapped the phone a few times against her forehead.

"You were there, weren't you? Right there."

Kay dropped her head into her hand.

"Oh God, Kay," Harry whispered.

"Yeah."

"That's why you're so kerfutzed."

"Yeah, I guess so. That's one reason…among many. Oh, Harry… I'm sorry I'm taking it out on you. Anyway, I'm not supposed to talk about it."

"Then…we shouldn't."

Kay nodded, but still said, "She got shot in the butt."

"I know. She told me that, remember? But we should talk about something else."

"Okay. What about that stuff about Maizie you said you had to think about? Can you tell me now?"

After a long pause, Harry said, "Whoa. I guess we were both told to keep things quiet."

"Yeah…but it's not working."

"Tell you what. Let's sit on this stuff for a while, maybe a day. How's that sound? If you really want me to tell you about Agent Cabrera, then okay…next time you ask, I'll tell you."

Kay's eyes popped open. "Holy cow," she whispered.

"Okay… I guess it's a good idea then."

Kay said nothing.

"Uh, Kay, holy cow, what?"

"Shh," Kay whispered. "Give me a second." Her thoughts coalesced. "Harry! I don't think he was shooting at me."

"Who?"

"He was shooting at Maizie!"

"What? Who?"

"The shooter. The one by my apartment. He didn't aim at me. He aimed at Maizie. My god! They're after Maizie."

"By your apartment? Hey, slow down! Focus. Talk to me."

"I gotta call you back, okay? I promise I'll call you back. I have to call Maizie."

"Okay. But make sure you do."

"I will. I will."

* * *

Kay closed the connection then rummaged in her purse for the special phone and hit the speed dial.

Maizie answered on the third ring. "Kay, are you all right?"

"Yes. Yes, I'm fine. But Maizie—"

"Kay, unless this is important, I need to cut you off. I just haven't got time."

"Maizie, the man was shooting at *you*, wasn't he? I mean, back at my apartment when you came to get me. He wasn't aiming at me. He was aiming at you."

"Kay," Maizie whispered.

Kay heard something in her voice. Frustration? Fatigue? Exasperation?

"Look, we considered that possibility, but it doesn't make any sense. First, the shooting happened at your apartment, not mine. Second, you were named in the press as a witness, not me. Third, the shooter was almost a hundred yards away and his weapon was not sighted-in properly, which led us to believe that he was an amateur. Fourth, he fired multiple shots which indicates a guy who doesn't aim well, which again points to an amateur. And there are other things, but I really have to go now."

"Oh." *She's lying.* "Okay, I'm sorry to have bothered you."

"You all right?"

"On and off. On and off."

"Yeah, me too. Hopefully, this thing will end soon."

* * *

Maizie pocketed her phone then took a moment to calm herself. Before she entered Tom's hospital room, she decided to keep Kay's phone call to herself. At his bedside she stared at his pale face, his IV lines, and the oxygen set-up, then closed her eyes and sighed.

"Hey, take it easy," Tom said. "I'm on the mend."

"God, I feel awful, Tom."

Tom shifted his weight then winced in pain.

Maizie jerked. "Sorry. I heard you were doing better. I'll get the nurse."

"No. I'm good. Relax. It comes and goes." He grinned. "So, what else is happening?"

"Nothing really."

"You're lying to a trained investigator. Besides, I heard about the postponement. It's not cancelled, you know."

Maizie nodded. "Of course, sure, let them shoot up a couple agents and then pull back. That ought to work."

"Come on. Maybe it's for the best."

"Well…those fucking D.C. hot shots sure think so."

"Hmm, wait a minute. You got bumped, didn't you?"

Maizie huffed. "Yeah…shit. I'm surprised they didn't do it when I got my butt shot. I should've seen it coming."

"Yeah, you should've. For whatever reason, the bad guys found out where you live and put a contract on you. You're all over the news, and there's no way the Bureau's going to want the bad PR if you get shot again."

"They've assigned a fucking security crew to me."

"What'd you expect?" When Maizie said nothing, he asked, "You still inside?"

"As long as I don't do anything," she hissed. "I'm inside because I can't go home. Fuck, they even put a cot in my office." She shook her head. "Sorry."

"No problem." Tom said. "And hey, I need a favor."

"Anything."

"I need you to talk to Suzanne."

"What? Who's Suzanne?"

Tom glared at Maizie.

"Oh, your wife, right." She looked away. "Shit."

Tom continued to glare.

"Hey, give me a break. It's always been Mrs. Henderson whenever I see her. How was I supposed to know her first name?"

"Jesus. Just go see her, okay? She thinks you feel guilty about me getting shot."

"Why would I feel guilty?"

Tom shook his head and smiled. "I don't know. It's just something Suzanne got stuck under her bonnet. I told her I'd make you promise to see her."

"Fine, I'll see her."

"Suzanne's right, you know. It's not your fault, Maizie. It really isn't."

"Yeah, whatever. You need anything?"

"Just don't let that bullet hole in your cute little ass cloud your thinking. Stay safe, Maizie, stay safe."

34

Overriding a conscience is hard work.

Dorothy, heart racing and tears running down her cheeks, shoved the bowl of cereal away, splattering milk over the table. "Fuck," she hissed before burying the heels of her hands into her eyes. "I can't do this anymore. I can't." Rising, she wiped her face then strode to her computer.

> hey! i know you're there. you've got to promise me the teacher won't get hurt

Three minutes later, Old Man replied.

> and how about all the kids and wives and husbands and brothers and sisters and uncles and aunties and grandpas and grandmas the monster has already ruined? where does the teacher fit in with those people?
>
> promise me or we're done. i don't give a shit about your reasons anymore

ah, i can tell you know where carlos is,
so tell me when and where and how many
beasts will flank his murderous soul

promise me

promise you? things are already in motion.
i promise to try and limit the collateral
damage the teacher represents. but if
the bait is pulled too quickly, well then,
everything is lost. let me know the devil's
plans

Dorothy sat, staring at the screen.

belly, you should do something about the
locks on your front door. especially with
all that computer equipment you keep. it's
just not safe

Dorothy walked away from the computer. Turning around in
the middle of the room, she pointed at the monitor and shouted,
"Fuck you and your stupid money!" She went into her bathroom
then closed and locked the door. She looked into the mirror for a few
brief moments then sat on the edge of the bathtub and cried.

Ten minutes later, dry-eyed but trembling, she typed out
another email.

a bunch of his people have already
arrived. they want it to happen tues.
not sure of the time or where. they
have people watching his school and
the hospital. i hate you

me too. keep me updated. compensation?

if   anything   happens   to   that
good   citizen   then   things   will
automatically fuck you

that, my dear, dear friend, does not
matter in the least. compensation?

Blubbering, Dorothy typed.

same

i knew you would be reasonable.

MONDAY

35

In tough times, pawns will bond.

Harry's room phone rang at 2:00 a.m. "Hello," he croaked.

"I can't sleep."

Harry said nothing.

"Did you fall back to sleep?"

"No."

"I didn't know if you were thinking or falling asleep."

"I'm awake."

"So tell me."

"About what?"

"The thing about Maizie. You said you'd tell me."

A pause. "Oh, that."

"Yeah. You probably thought I was going to call back a little sooner, didn't you?"

"Yeah."

"I'm still trying to figure things out."

"Did you call Agent Cabrera?"

Kay sighed. "Yeah. It didn't help."

Again, Harry was silent.

"So tell me. You promised."

"Okay." He paused again.

Kay heard a soft ruffling sound. "What's that? Are you okay?"

"Yeah. I'm just rubbing my face. I'm trying to focus."

"I shouldn't have called. God, I'm sorry. Go back to sleep, you can tell me tomorrow."

"No, it's okay. Just let me get my head straight." Harry yawned. "Okay, here we go. It happened a few years ago. I was running the hills north of the farm, and I found a bunch of marijuana plants. Not all in one spot but spread out in plots hidden in the gullies and small canyons. At first, I didn't think much about it. I was way off the trails and really into the run. But some of the plots were pretty big and protected by barbed wire."

"Marijuana? How close to the Toma's farm?"

"What? Oh, pretty far. Maybe seven miles as the crow flies. Anyway, I called the cops and it became a big deal and the FBI got involved. Turns out there was a lot of acreage. Then there was lots of me talking and showing them where I found the plots and then doing it all over again. Anyhow, sometime during the whole thing, I was told I could be in danger and that even Vincent and Kenji and Alma could be in danger. The agent in charge said the cartel involved was extremely violent and vengeful. And then the guy said that all of my information would be held in confidence and not to talk about it with anyone."

Kay was silent this time.

"All I did was make one phone call, and boom…cops, feds, and cartels."

"You need to tell Maizie."

Harry paused. "She already knows."

"You told her?"

"No. But Agent Henderson questioned me about it for a long time."

"So?"

Harry slowly put his thoughts together. "Agent Cabrera was part of the team investigating the case back then. She wasn't in charge or anything and I never spoke with her but I saw her working with the people I was dealing with. She stands out. She knows the case. She had to know who I am and—"

"Just because you saw her doesn't mean…I mean, maybe she was on a different case back then. Maybe you just saw her and, I don't know…maybe she didn't know about you."

"Kay…she was the one to move me from the hospital in San Rafael. And she did it within just a few hours of the shooting. And she was the one who assigned a security detail for me. I checked. It was all because of her orders. She knows about me and that marijuana deal. She started giving orders as soon she heard I was the guy wrestling with the gunman in the middle of the courtyard."

"You are not making it any easier for me to sleep."

"Sorry, but that's not the end of it. After Agent Henderson questioned me about that situation, he said it didn't make sense for a south of the border cartel to go after a guy like me just because I exposed some of their pot farms."

"But what else would make you a target?"

"Ah…the zillion dollar question. That's what I've been working on. I mean, when I'm not out hiking the halls or watching daytime soaps. Anyway, I think Agent Cabrera knows something."

Kay sadly shook her head. "You know? You were right about her."

"How's that?"

"She lies. She lied to me."

Harry said nothing.

"When she got shot in front of my building, the cops thought I was the target. But you know, I think they were aiming for her, not me. Anyway, I called her and told her and she lied about it."

"Why? Are you sure? I can tell you're not completely convinced."

Kay sighed. "Yeah, okay. I *think* she's lying, but it doesn't make sense. There's no reason for her to lie to me like that." She paused. "But then, nothing makes sense anymore. I think I'll call her again tomorrow."

"You should. But right now, it *is* tomorrow and you need to sleep."

Kay smiled grimly and walked to her bed. "Yeah, but I don't know why you think I can sleep now."

"Hey, I walked for fifteen minutes today. How's that? Lei held onto my arm the whole time. Cool, yeah? It was almost like a date."

Kay climbed into bed. "Harry, Harry, Harry. So, what else filled your day?"

Without a moment's hesitation, Harry launched into a monologue. Fat nurses, skinny nurses, and pretty nurses dominated most of his talk, but food, doctors, and interns all took a turn. Kay fluffed the pillows and let Harry ramble, and soon her eyes grew heavy.

As soon as she yawned, Harry stopped short. "Okay, it's a good thing I'm so boring. I can tell you're ready to nod off, so don't mess it up by looking at the clock. Clocks throw wake-up darts at people like you, so don't look. Just close your eyes."

"They're closed, Harry. They're closed."

"Good, keep 'em closed."

Kay yawned again. "Will I—"

"Shh."

Kay released the phone when she fell asleep, but it remained near her ear.

"Goodnight, Kay," Harry said.

36

A fuse begins to burn.

Kay's alarm buzzed a little more than four hours later. As she reached for the clock, she knocked it off the bedside table. Throwing off the blankets, she snatched the damn thing and pounded it into submission. She sat on the bed for a moment, staring longingly at her pillow. With a sigh, she glanced through the window at the cold foggy dawn before heading for the shower. After she dressed, she drained a cup of coffee then walked to work with Mildred. Her security guy followed then took his position in the outer office.

Mrs. Shim barely allowed Kay to sit down before she placed two files on her desk.

Kay looked up. "What are these?"

"The first is Brandon Steiner," Mrs. Shim said. "It's for the parent conference at nine."

"Why are we having a conference with his parents?"

"It's an expulsion conference."

"What? What happened?" Kay opened the file.

"He was caught stealing from some lockers. It's too bad. Teachers like this boy, but he's made some poor choices. His father is an extremely overbearing individual."

"Am I expected to be there?"

"Mr. Lee always attended expulsion conferences. He didn't think Mrs. Cade should be deserted for this type of meeting."

"Deserted?"

Mrs. Shim shrugged. "Left alone."

Kay softly shook her head as she held up the second file. "And this?"

"It's your schedule for the three meetings today in San Francisco with the potential donors."

"Three meetings? I thought there were just two."

"No, there are three. Ten, noon, and two-thirty."

"Three meetings for me to stand around while other people ask for money."

"That's not for me to say, Ms. Morrell."

Kay hefted the file. "It feels a little thick for just a schedule."

"I thought you would like to refresh yourself on some of the history of the school. I put together a few things for you to look at."

Kay thumbed through the pages. Test scores, family demographics, and budgetary information filled more than a dozen pages. She sighed.

"Don't forget operations at eight," Mrs. Shim said.

"This is going to be a hard day, isn't it?"

"It's Monday," Mrs. Shim said then left.

Kay stared at the door. "Maizie," she whispered. "You are just going to have to wait. I'll call you when I get some time."

* * *

In the middle of the operations meeting, Mildred left to answer an urgent phone call. Before she left, she asked Kay to chair the rest of the meeting.

Kay looked at the rest of the administrators then at her calendar. "Well, we've got a conflict for the gym on Thursday night between the set-up for the assembly on Friday morning and the volleyball game. So, who wants to score some brownie points with the new girl on the block?" The meeting lasted another quarter hour, but Mildred did not return.

Back in her office, Mrs. Shim informed Kay that Mr. Cade had suffered a diabetic attack and had to be taken to the hospital.

"Oh my God. Is Will okay?"

"It's happened before. Usually he comes home in a few hours," Mrs. Shim said. "Your parent conference is in five minutes."

The expulsion conference went badly. The mother cried, the boy cried, and the father fumed. As the meeting ended, the father asked for a few more minutes to meet privately with Kay.

"I'm sorry, Mr. Steiner," Kay said, "but that would be inappropriate. I'm terribly sorry about this turn of events and truly hope Brandon uses it to move forward. Thank you for—"

Mr. Steiner jumped to his feet and slammed the desk with the flat of his hand. "This is such bullshit! I thought this school was supposed to have some compassion. My boy made a mistake. Well, who hasn't? You guys don't give a flying fuck about anything but your stupid-ass, penny-ante rules."

Kay exploded to her feet, put her hands on the desk, leaned forward, and shouted, "Are you proud of yourself, Mr. Steiner? Did you get all that off your chest?"

Mr. Steiner's face flushed bright red.

Kay leaned closer. "Shame on you!"

Mr. Steiner, blowing hard though puffed cheeks, stared at Kay. "Why, you—"

At that moment Charlie Cornish entered in full uniform. "Why, hello there, Ms. Morrell. I'm here to remind you of your meetings in the city. I will be accompanying you and we need to get going."

While Kay and Mr. Steiner glared at each other, Mrs. Steiner and Brandon stood very still.

"Well, hey there, Jimmy." Charlie offered a big smile to the dad. "You all finished in here?"

Mr. Steiner looked at Charlie then at Kay. "We're done." He picked up his coat and stormed out of the room.

Brandon and Mrs. Steiner hesitated then followed. As they left, Brandon whispered, "Holy smokes, did you hear what she said to Dad?"

Kay, eyes blazing, watched the family depart then looked at Charlie. "That wasn't necessary. You didn't need to rescue me."

"I wasn't worried about you. I was worried about Jimmy. I've known him for a while, and I didn't want him to say something he might regret."

"I think that had already occurred."

Charlie shrugged. "Yeah, probably. But I tell you what, come tomorrow or the next day, he'll be in here, apologizing."

"What?"

"Oh, he's got a good heart, Kay. It's just buried under his temper. He'll cool down and, yeah, he's gonna feel some shame."

Kay, breathing hard through her nose, nodded.

"Anyway, here I am, your escort."

"Yeah, right…the donor meetings. Mrs. Shim!"

Mrs. Shim scurried in. "Yes, Ms. Morrell."

"Any word from Mr. Abramson or Mr. Kent?" Earlier, she had emailed their offices about Mrs. Cade not being able to attend the donor meetings.

"Yes, ma'am." She handed Kay emails from the two men.

We have the utmost confidence in your ability to represent the school in Mrs. Cade's absence. We will meet you in the lobby at the Saint Francis.

Orion Kent

p.s. Please expect questions about the incident.

The irons are hot and we need to move. Mildred will meet us if she can. Orion thinks you will be asked about the incident. I disagree but will step in if it becomes too unseemly. See you at the Saint Francis.

Levi

"The *incident*? Oh, godamnit," Kay whispered.

Mrs. Shim raised her eyebrows.

Charlie nodded as he leaned against the door jam.

"Who takes over for me while I'm gone?" Kay asked.

"Technically, Mr. Jones," Mrs. Shim said.

"Technically?"

"Mr. Jones usually defers to Mr. Chen."

"We're going to be late, Kay," Charlie said.

Kay looked at the smiling cop. "Then we'll be late."

"Okay by me."

Mrs. Shim went back to her desk.

Kay phoned Mr. Chen and informed him that she and Mrs. Shim would both be out of the office until later in the afternoon and that he should find someone to mind the phones. As she gathered the files, she barked, "Mrs. Shim."

Mrs. Shim walked in, coat over her arm, and took the files from Kay. "Do you think we can have lunch in the city? I know of a wonderful Italian place."

* * *

The fundraising meetings went well but lasted far longer than the schedule dictated. However, it was not the needs of the school that prolonged each session. As she had been warned, everyone plied her with questions about the shooting. She kept her poise primarily by steering the discussion away from herself and toward Harry.

Fortunately, Kay never had to ask for money. That task was left to Levi and Mr. Kent. When the time came for the actual request, Kay would leave the room and wait in the lobby with Mrs. Shim, where they worked on the next appointment.

"I believe you are doing a splendid job, Ms. Morrell," Mrs. Shim said during the second intersession.

Kay looked up from the notes on her lap. "What? Um, thank you. That's very kind."

"And it appears to me that you've made quite an impression on Mr. Kent."

Kay said nothing and returned to her notes.

"He seems to be quite taken with you."

Kay angrily slapped the file onto her lap. "He needs to back off."

Mrs. Shim nodded. "Yes, he does. Some of his behaviors border on sexual harassment."

"No kidding."

"My earlier comment was more about how you were managing Mr. Kent and his…affection."

"Well, he's important to the school, isn't he?"

"Yes, he is. All the more evidence of your splendid work."

Kay paused. "You're telling me all this so that I don't yell at him, like I yelled at Mr. Steiner."

Mrs. Shim shrugged.

Four-thirty arrived and, much to Mrs. Shim's disgust, there had been no time for lunch. Kay checked her phone and saw that she had missed calls from her mother, George, Mildred, and Rhonda. Nothing from Harry. She called Mildred and found out that Will had recovered from his episode but was going to spend the night in the hospital.

"The damn fool did too much this weekend and didn't listen to his body," Mildred said. She went on to thank Kay profusely for her efforts during the day and promised to make it up to her. She also added that she planned to remain at Will's side during the night, so she would not be home.

Kay decided to return the rest of the calls later.

Levi treated everyone to a late afternoon meal at Tomaso's, his favorite Italian restaurant. Much to Kay's relief, Mr. Kent opted out and went back to work. Mrs. Shim quietly gloried in the meal, which pleased Levi immensely. He plowed through his pasta with gusto, talked with his mouth full, and dominated the conversation. Kay picked at her meal, nodding and offering one-word responses to Levi's monologue. Charlie sat separately at a table that viewed the entrance.

The board begins to fill with movement.

Not far from the hospital, Juan pulled the big Dodge over to the curb just long enough for Estocio to climb in then slid back into the traffic. "Carlos arrived," he said in Spanish. "He's at the cabin near the Russian River. He wants something to happen."

"Fuck," Estocio huffed. "What're we supposed to do? The asshole's in the fuckin' hospital with a cop at his door."

Juan shrugged.

"And why in hell do we gotta work with Julio just because he's related to Carlos? The kid's a fucking moron."

Juan focused on the road. "Easy, my friend. What can we report to Carlos?"

"Report? Fuck. Tell him that the nigger lawyer visited today, but no sign of the little Asian chick or those farmers who take care of his kid. And no sign of that FBI chick either. Tell Carlos we're ready to do whatever. Tell him…shit, I don't know." Estocio shook his head. "How big a crew did he bring?"

"Nine or ten guys."

"For one fucking asshole?" Estocio said.

"He wants that fucking Harry and everyone close to him buried. It's gonna be a big job."

"Everyone? Do we even know who everyone is? Is there a list?"

"Last I heard, Carlos has Sergio working on it. For sure his kid and that FBI bitch are on the list. And probably the farm family.

The asshole's been living there for years." Juan shrugged again. "But Sergio doesn't know shit about the lawyer, and the Asian chick is just a principal or something at the school. Maybe they go on the list, maybe not."

"How the fuck is Sergio getting all this stuff? And how come he never checks in with us anymore? We're supposed to be a crew."

"Carlos's orders. He doesn't want Sergio's sources blown," Juan said with yet another shrug.

"This is so stupid."

"Shall I report that to Carlos?"

38

The fuse, once lit, has but one possible result.

Levi offered to drive Mrs. Shim home, leaving Kay alone with Charlie. As he opened the door for Kay, Charlie asked, "You want to see Mr. Ross? I mean, might as well. Traffic's gonna be terrible anyway and—"

"No. Home, please," Kay snapped angrily then cringed. "Sorry. I don't mean to be so sharp. I just need to get home and rest, okay, Charlie?" Once inside, she reclined her seat and closed her eyes. Soon, however, she gave up on sleep and sat up. Glaring at the creeping lines of cars, she spat, "Look at them! One person per car. What are they thinking? It's so damned stupid."

"Maybe you ought to put your head back down and relax, Kay. You're not doing yourself any good."

Kay sat back, whispering, "Yeah, you're right…sorry." Closing her eyes tightly, she massaged her forehead and counted her breaths. She made it to Mildred's without another outburst but still on edge.

"Okay," Charlie said as they neared the house, "we have a strange vehicle parked in the Cade's driveway. Do you recognize it? Black Mercedes?"

Kay raised her backrest and saw the car. "Oh God."

"Who is it?"

"It's George's car, George Halliday."

"I remember him from your apartment. Do you want me to turn around or maybe chase him away?"

The Merc's door opened and George climbed out.

"Too late, Charlie. Too late."

"There's a guy on duty in the house, but I can stick around if you want."

"You're an absolute saint, but no. I'll handle this. Thanks."

Charlie stopped the car and Kay got out. "You sure?"

"Yeah. And thanks again, Charlie," she said as she closed the door.

George stood by his car, nervously fidgeting with his keys.

A cop came down the walk. "Good evening, Ms. Morrell. I'm Sergeant Obanda. I'll be serving as your night officer."

The chill of the foggy night air braced Kay's lungs and offered some respite. She shook hands with the tall officer. "Sergeant Obanda, this is George Halliday. He's my friend."

"We've met," Obanda said. "He's been waiting here for a while."

"Hello, Kay," George said. He took a few steps forward and awkwardly hugged her.

Kay patted his back and kissed his cheek. "George, oh, George," she said as her eyes welled. "Darn it!" she hissed then turned away and wiped her eyes.

George took her arm, but she pulled away.

"Sergeant Obanda, George and I are going inside. We'll be in the kitchen. Can you be on duty in, say, the family room, maybe with the TV on?"

Obanda nodded. "Certainly, Ms. Morrell."

"Oh my God, are you all right?" George asked as they made their way to the house. He reached for Kay's hand, but she quickened her step and he missed.

In the kitchen, Kay silently poured two glasses of wine then sat down opposite George at the small breakfast table.

George reached across the table and took Kay's hand. "Um, I got the job, the position."

"Well, yeah. That's no surprise. You seemed pretty confident before you left."

George's eyes focused on the tabletop. "Well, one never really knows. It wasn't in the bag, but then, well…the boss and I hit it off. Everything went really, really well. We just had one of those connections."

Kay nodded again, but not a single coherent thought bubbled its way to the forefront of her mind. Tears welled again. With her free hand, she took a napkin and dapped her cheeks below her eyes.

"And so…I'll be moving to New York."

"Okay…my goodness. When?"

"End of the month."

"Uh huh. That's…I mean, wow. I don't know what to say. It's just, I um… Today's been something. I mean the whole week has been more than something and…" She trailed off then said, "So, end of the month?" She wiped more tears from her cheeks.

"Kay, you were right," George said.

"I was? Right about what?"

"About taking a week off to think about everything. You were right. Like always."

"Huh." Kay narrowed her eyes. Something was amiss. "Was I?"

"Yeah, you were. But then, you've always been right about things like this."

She pulled her hand away. "Really?"

George glanced at Kay. "Come on. Please don't get angry. You said we needed a week to think things over."

A prolonged silence fell over the table. Head down, George shifted uncomfortably in his chair.

Sitting absolutely still, Kay glared at the top of George's head. "You're dumping me. In the middle of everything, you're dumping me."

George looked up. "Kay, the week was for both of us to think."

Kay said nothing. She pushed her wine glass away.

"You know, you were the one who balked." Again, George dropped his eyes to avoid Kay's fiery stare.

"Shopping in Saratoga. You went shopping with the boss in Saratoga. Your boss is a woman, isn't she?"

Another quick glance from George. "What? Well, yes. She is. So what? What's that got to do with anything?"

"You slept with her."

This time George tried to keep eye contact with Kay. "Now you're being ridiculous."

Kay bored in with her eyes and leaned forward.

George sagged backwards and lost the staredown.

"You slept with her, didn't you?"

"What's the matter with you?" George whispered. "You need to—"

"George!" Kay shouted. "I don't care if you move to New York! I don't. I just want to know if you slept with your new boss. I just want some goddamn honesty. I am so sick and tired of… Just tell me. Look me in the eyes and tell me. Just say, 'Yes, Kay, I slept with my new boss,' or tell me, 'No, Kay, I would never do that. Not while I'm still involved with someone else. I don't do those kinds of things. Those things are wrong.' Just tell me the truth."

George stared out the window for a long time. "Oh, Kay," Finally, he looked directly into her eyes. "I slept with her. I texted you, remember? I said we really hit it off."

Kay said nothing.

"Satisfied? Are you satisfied now with your desire for honesty? Does it make you feel any better?"

Kay still said nothing.

"I think you ought to see somebody. You look terrible. You—"

"I want your stuff out of my apartment tonight."

George laughed without humor. "Come on, be reasonable. It's late. I promise I'll get everything out by the weekend."

"Tonight! Are you deaf? Tonight, or you'll find it at Goodwill tomorrow."

"Come on, Kay. It's late, and you're not yourself. I can't just move everything out tonight. You know, I came all the way out here to do this face-to-face. I didn't hide behind some email or phone call. I care for you too much. Come on. I can get the stuff by the—"

George stopped when Kay plucked her cell off the table.

She punched in some numbers and put the phone to her ear. "Charlie… Yes, I'm fine… Hey, I need a favor. Do you know any locksmiths?… Good. I'd like the locks on my apartment changed.

Can you get someone to do that?… As soon as you can, tomorrow if possible… You're wonderful, Charlie. Thanks… Goodnight."

She ended the call, glaring at George.

George smiled sadly and shook his head. "I really do care for you, Kay. Maybe someday we can be friends."

"Please leave now." Tears ran freely down her cheeks.

George got up and walked slowly out the front door.

An hour later, after three glasses of wine and a shower that used all of the house's hot water, Kay lay in bed, staring at the ceiling.

TUESDAY

39

Knowing the enemy's next move is everything.

Dorothy awoke at one in the morning, fully dressed, lying on the sofa. Slowly, she levered herself into a sitting position then looked at the coffee table, where she saw the stub of a joint beckoning from the ashtray. Picking it up with tweezers, she flicked her lighter, but nothing happened. She flicked it again with the same result. She tried over and over, until finally, she flung it and the joint against the wall.

"Fuck," she whispered then padded to the kitchen, looked at the bowl of soggy cereal on the table, the stack of half empty pizza boxes on the counter, and the layers of dishes in the sink. She shook her head. Opening the refrigerator, she pulled out a box of chocolates and began popping the morsels into her mouth.

"Gotta get some coffee," she whispered as she headed for the front door.

Sitting just inside the door was a rectangular metal box. "Fuck!" Her heart jumped as she backed away. When she finally approached the box, she found a note taped to the lid. It read,

> *My dear, dear Belly Brain:*
> *This is for you for your past, present, and future work. Consider it a bonus. Please contact me as soon as you awaken. I'm glad you're resting. It's likely to get busy.*

Breathing rapidly, she knelt and looked at the container. Dark green and filthy, it appeared to be something the army might use. She opened the lid and almost fell backwards. The box was filled with stacks of hundred-dollar bills. "Holy shit." An hour later, after counting and recounting the money, Dorothy moved to her computer.

what am i supposed to do with the money?

that's up to you

Belly wrung her hands.

what do you want me to do?

find him. i need to know where he is

i tried already

so why can't you find him?

because he's not using the internet or he changed everything which would be smart considering his current situation

you are screwing up my plans. find him. if you don't find him, i will have to use the bait more than previously agreed upon

do not fuck with my good citizen. you promised

then find satan's asshole

She stared at the money for a long while before taking the box to her desk. Setting it beside her chair, she went to work. An hour later, she still had failed to find Carlos but had managed to uncover other bits of information.

```
i have something
```

well, sweet belly, that's swell. what do you have?

Sweating, Dorothy typed.

```
i don't know where he is but he
has maybe a dozen people in the
area. they must be using throw-away
phones. the stuff online mentions
the farm where the good citizen
lives. there's also talk about
safe-houses but i can't find out
where they are. whatever they're
planning they want to head home by
thurs at the latest
```

the farm! yes! belly, you are the best! if all goes well, i'll send another can

```
are we done?
```

yes

```
done? no more anything?
```

your job is finished. a grateful world is in your debt

do not contact me ever again

my belly, my sweet potato-pie, you're
breaking my heart

40

In times of trouble, who you gonna call?

Kay tossed and turned until just past one then dialed Harry's room at the hospital.

"Hello," Harry croaked.

"Hey," Kay said through a thick lump in her throat.

"Kay… Are you all right?"

"Talk to me, Harry," Kay whispered. "I'm going crazy over here. Please talk to me."

"What happened? What's going on? Did someone else get shot? Is your dad okay?"

"No, none of that. Just talk to me, okay? I just need you to talk to me."

When Harry hesitated, Kay barked, "Damn it! Don't sit there thinking! Just talk to me, okay? God!"

"Um, okay. Can I ask you questions? Is that okay?"

"What? Whatever. Just say something."

"Okay, then. It sounds like you, um, lost your temper, right?"

Kay laughed angrily. "Oh, you could say that."

"Was it a big eruption? I mean, how bad was it?"

"Pretty bad."

"Anybody get hurt? I mean, anybody get killed?"

Kay laughed again, wiping tears from her eyes. "Oh, I don't know. Does my alarm clock count?"

"I told you not to look at the clock. I warned you about that."

Kay smiled and shook her head. "Sorry, I couldn't help it. I also yelled at one of our parents. Oh…and my duty officer, who's a real nice guy by the way. I never should have yelled at him. And then last night I yelled at my ex-boyfriend."

"Ex-boyfriend?"

"Yeah, why? You jealous?"

"What?"

"You shouldn't be. He's just another one of those jerks I can't seem to stay away from. He's not like you."

"I didn't know you had a boyfriend."

"*Ex*-boyfriend, Harry. Ex, Ex, Ex!"

Harry paused for a longer moment. "Is that all? Anybody else?"

"Well, I guess you have to count the zillions of bastards on the road who refuse to carpool or take the bus or trains or whatever."

"Bad traffic?"

"Horrible, absolutely horrible. Took us two hours to get home."

"You sound like you're still angry."

"I am, and you're not talking. Enough questions, just talk to me."

"Okay, but are you going to yell at me? Are you angry at me? I got shot, you know."

Kay let out a short laugh. "No, not right away. Not unless you start going silent on me for too long."

"Good, that's good. I'll keep my slow wits down to a minimum."

Kay smiled and wiped away more tears.

Harry said nothing.

After a few moments, Kay said, "Hey, you're still not saying anything."

"Can you tell me about work? I mean, maybe not all the times you lost your temper, but just the good things, like—"

"Harry! That's more questions. I don't want to talk about me."

She could hear Harry softly grunting.

"What are you doing? Are you in pain? Harry?"

"I'm just trying to find my bed thing. The thing that raises the back up, you know? It's hard to talk when I'm flat on my back." He paused, grunted softly again. "There, got it. I'm up. Well, I guess I had another fascinating day. A day filled with nurses and doctors. You know…like more blood tests and whatever. Oh, and I spent a lot of time doing all kinds of cool stuff on my laptop." He paused. "I even tried to call Agent Cabrera, but she was too busy, I guess."

Kay huffed. "God. All that stuff too. I forgot about all of that."

"What?"

"Hey, so I forgot. So what? Some of us are pretty busy, you know."

Harry said nothing.

"God, I'm sorry. I don't want to be angry with you. I just want…I don't know. Just talk to me, okay?"

"I'm thinking about how to make you feel better. But I'm pretty feeble-minded right now, and you're not really telling me what made you angry." He paused again. "I'm sorry you had such a bad day."

"Harry…"

"What?"

"Oh, nothing."

"What? Tell me."

Kay paused for a long moment. "Harry, do you…"

Harry took in a sharp breath.

"Sorry," Kay said. "That was stupid. What am I doing? I don't even know why I called. I'm sorry I woke you up. I shouldn't have called. Everything is just hard. God, I'm—"

"I do, Kay," Harry said softly.

"What? You do what?"

"I love you. I always have and you know it. Jeeze, what the heck."

Kay's tears flowed.

"Hey, whoa, whoa, whoa. Don't cry. Come on."

Kay dropped her head into her hands and sobbed until she couldn't breathe. In time, she stopped and took in great gulps of air then eased into gentler respirations. Finally, she blew her nose and wiped her eyes, then picked up her phone. "Are you still there?"

"Yeah. Are you done crying?"

Kay sniffled. "Yeah."

"You sure?" Harry said. "Because it's really hard to take."

"Yeah, I'm all cried out. The well is dry."

"Good."

"Harry?"

"Yeah?"

"I don't know what to say."

"That's okay. You'll think of something later."

Silence descended between the pair. Kay heard nothing but Harry's breathing, his slow respirations playing like a lullaby. Her eyes began to sag. "Harry?" she whispered.

"Yes?"

"Thanks."

"It's okay."

"I missed you. I really did."

"I should've kept writing."

"Vincent is beautiful."

"Yeah, I know. Thanks."

"I don't mean just how he looks. I mean—"

"I know what you mean."

Kay nodded. "God, I've been such an ass."

After another long pause, Harry asked, "Think you can sleep now?"

"Yeah…think so."

"Okay."

When neither hung up, Harry asked, "You going to work tomorrow?"

"Of course. And it's tomorrow already."

"I know. Just checking." He paused then asked, "Do you want me to keep talking?"

"No, I'm pretty sure I can sleep now."

"Okay."

"Thanks for listening. Thanks for everything."

"You better get some sleep now."

"Will do."

"Goodnight, Kay."

"Night, Harry."

The old rogue starts moving pieces.

Jorge climbed out of bed, shuffled to the bathroom, and took another bloody piss. He pulled up his shorts just as his cell chimed. Hustling back to the bedside table, he answered the phone. "Cobb, it's two in the morning and I'm pissing blood. This better be important."

"Harry just contacted Astor. He said the shit's gonna fly today and wants some help."

"Today? The shit's been flying since yesterday. The arrests in Arizona and southern Cal have been huge. It looks like Carlos's entire operation north of the border is going belly up." Jorge sighed. "Shit. What does he want Astor to do?"

"Astor can't do it. Harry wants you and me to do guard duty for the family at the farm where the teacher-hero lives."

Jorge's jaw dropped. "You and me?"

"Yeah. And no cops. Harry was adamant about that. He also said no vehicles…we're supposed to walk onto the property."

"Fucking walk?"

"Yeah. We gotta do it, you know. The teacher has protection in the hospital, but that family has nothing."

Jorge said nothing for a few moments. "Okay, fine. That fucking Harry. What the shit is he doing?"

"I'll pick you up in an hour."

"Whatever. You better bring me something. I left my Colt at home."

* * *

Kay went in to work early, plowed through emails, and managed a few minor school conflicts. She felt good about her focus and even chuckled at a humorous email from Rhonda that reminded her of their Wednesday date. *Is this what's going to happen?* she thought. *Massive mood swings? Get shot at and go into premature menopause?* She smiled. *Well, I guess I better enjoy it while it lasts.*

Mildred entered.

Kay rose from her desk. "Good morning. How's Will?"

Mildred sat. "He's home, swearing at the doctors and planning another hike for Sunday. I tell you, Kay, the man is an idiot."

Kay returned to her chair. "Well, at least he's a happy idiot. I'm glad he's feeling better."

Mildred smiled and clasped her hands together. "I heard about Mr. Steiner."

Kay nodded slowly. "God, I'm so sorry. I shouldn't have lost my temper."

Mildred held up her hands. "No, don't be. It is what it is. I should have been there, and you did the best you could. I can't tell you how many times I wished I had responded to some unreasonable, over-the-top parent like you did."

"Well, it didn't make me feel any better venting like that. It soured the rest of the day for me." She sighed. "I'll apologize to Mr. Steiner."

"No, ma'am. You can't do that. We'll just see how it plays out. It's not like you weren't provoked. Like I said, it is what it is. Anyway, there's a bright side to your episode."

"I beg your pardon?"

"Well, it seems that more than a few students heard you. I guess they were loitering near your door as kids are wont to do."

"Oh, God…"

"And a few of the faculty also heard you. Apparently, one didn't need to be very close to be able to hear you."

Kay closed her eyes.

"It appears you are developing into quite a legend. Several teachers have emailed me about the incident, and every single one of them has been supportive. They all think I'm brilliant for hiring you to cover for Mr. Lee."

"Oh, my goodness."

"And the students, well, students are often impressed with bouts of righteous indignation. Right now, you walk on water."

Kay smiled and raised her hands, palms upwards.

Mildred laughed. "And to top it off, Mr. Kent said you carried the day with the meetings in San Francisco. I can't tell you how thankful I am."

* * *

Later that morning, a new policeman came to Kay's office. The man was so thin, she wondered if he could offer any assistance if she were attacked. Plus, he looked older than Charlie. "I thought Officer Cornish was on my detail this morning."

"Um, yes, ma'am." The officer pulled the brim of his service cap down closer to his eyes, which were shielded with dark glasses. "Officer Cornish is taking some time off. I was called in to brief you."

"Brief me?"

"Yes, ma'am. We've just been notified by the FBI that they're pulling off your protection detail. You're now safe to return to your regular life patterns."

Kay stood. "What, really? What happened? Have they caught someone?"

Mrs. Shim entered the office.

The officer looked everywhere but at Kay. "Ms. Morrell, haven't you been watching TV or reading the newspaper? There have been raids by the FBI and local police departments all over the southwest and Southern California for the past two days."

Kay stared in disbelief. "Then…then it's over."

"Yes, ma'am."

"What about Harry? Mr. Ross?"

"I don't know about that, ma'am. I'm just doing what they tell me."

"I'm safe then?"

"Yes, ma'am. You're free to go now."

"Can I get my car?" Kay said stupidly.

"Yes, ma'am," the officer said then tapped the brim of his cap and left.

Hand to her chest, Kay heaved a deep breath. "Mrs. Shim?"

"Yes, Ms. Morrell," Mrs. Shim said with a small smile.

"Will you take me to my apartment? I'd like to go pick up my car."

Mrs. Shim's smile broadened. "Let me gather my things, Ms. Morrell. I'll be ready in a moment."

Kay nodded. "Thank you. You know, I'd like to have a look at my apartment while I'm there, maybe change clothes. I may be gone for a bit."

"That will be fine, Ms. Morrell. I'm very happy for you. I will let Mrs. Cade know. I'll call you on your cell if we need you."

Kay phoned Harry's hospital room, but no one answered. She gathered her purse and headed out the door.

In the outer office, Mrs. Shim, still on the phone, held up her hand. Kay hesitated.

Mrs. Shim hung up. "Mrs. Cade says you should take the rest of the day off."

* * *

Dorothy waddled up the stairs to her third-floor apartment, carrying a large coffee and a bag full of donuts. Grabbing the bag with her teeth, she unlocked the door and entered. It took some effort to maneuver her girth and breakfast to secure the deadbolt. Wheezing, she walked to her small living room where her array of computer equipment waited.

"Hey!" she shouted and backed up against the wall, the bag of donuts falling from her mouth.

A man in a police uniform leaned against the window frame, smiling. "Well, hey there, Belly."

"Oh shit," Dorothy whispered.

Thin as a wraith, with salt-and-pepper hair cut so close that she could see the pulse in his temples, the man shrugged. "Yup…here I am, in the flesh. I hopes I didn't scare ya'll. I got this thing 'bout me. Some folks see me and they git scared. I hopes you ain't one of them folks."

Trembling, Belly fought to breathe. Slowly, she placed her coffee on top of a pile of books. "Please go. Just please go away."

"Well, darlin', 'fraid I cain't do that. A problem's come up."

His uniform was complete, right down to the cap, the thick nylon jacket, and the radio mic attached to his shoulder. Carefully, he donned a pair of horned-rim glasses that were hanging from a strap around his neck then put his large, boney hands into his pockets. "I'm here on account of your worries 'bout your good citizen. Well, things are movin' now. I gotta get the bait out in the water but ran into a little hitch."

Belly's lips quivered.

"I'm gonna need your help just one mo' time."

Belly shook her head. "You said I was done."

Old Man shrugged again. "I brung you a nurse's outfit. Mostly, it's just these green things. Simple things, they is. Hospital folk wear 'em everywheres. I needs you to change into it. I weren't shore 'bout your size, so I brung several."

"You do anything to me now, it's gonna cause you no end of shit."

"Go get changed, Belly."

42

A weak-minded individual will assume he's powerful if armed.

Shivering in the fog, Julio leaned against a planter box outside the hospital's main entrance and tightened the drawstrings of his hood. Yawning, he angrily punched in Estocio's number on his burner. "Hey," he said in Spanish, "I need a break. It's shit-ass cold here."

"Shut your fucking whining," Estocio said. "And you better not be going stupid out there."

"Nobody's made me, man. I know what I'm doing. But I need a break."

"Later," Estocio said. "Give me a fucking report so I can call Carlos."

"Nada, nada, nada. Nobody's showed up. Not the fucking black bitch, not the little Jap, and not one FBI asshole."

"What about cops?"

"Sure. Some, but they just go in and out. And one security dude. He sits on his fat ass in the lobby."

"Just don't be stupid in front of them," Estocio said then abruptly terminated the call.

"The fuck!" Julio hissed. Seething, he hated how Estocio treated him like a little boy. Julio had been the only one with the cajones to take care of Hoffman's family. If it was up to Julio, that fucking Harry would be dead already. He had even roamed the hospital to case the job…rode the elevator right up to the fifth floor. Only one fucking cop guarded the bastard's door. Shit, he could plant a bullet in the cop's face, drop a couple into the asshole in the bed, then hustle down the stairs. Julio was fast…no one would catch him. So simple, but oh no, Estocio had other plans. As far as Julio could tell, Estocio had zero cajones.

43

A knight should ride a horse to avoid stepping in bullshit.

Cobb stopped the Jeep in the middle of the narrow dirt road then checked a map. "This ought to work. You're maybe two miles west of the farm. I need about fifteen minutes to get to the east side."

"It's gonna be a fucking long hike for me," Jorge said.

"Hey, man, according to Astor, Harry said no cops and no one on the road leading to the farm. Besides, it was your idea that we approach the place from separate directions."

"Yeah," Jorge said then checked his phone. "I've got one bar showing. We should've brought radios."

"Yeah...I know. Aim for the hilltops. We should get better reception up there."

Jorge hissed in frustration, climbed out, then reached into the back seat for his rucksack and the rifle Cobb had supplied. "I can't see any hills in this fog."

"Well, if you're going downwards, you've screwed up."

"Good safety tip." Jorge slammed the door and Cobb drove away.

With his joints crackling, Jorge ducked through the plank railings of a pasture gate and headed upslope. "Well shit, Harry, you fucking bastard, once again I'm trying to clean up one of your messes. Only now, here I am, stomping through wet grass and cow poop in the fog. Oh, well."

Forty-five meandering minutes later, Jorge's cell vibrated. "Hold on a minute," he answered breathlessly. "Let me sit down."

"Yeah, okay," Cobb said. "But don't go too far. I've been calling for a while now and finally got through."

Jorge trod heavily to a nearby line of Eucalyptus trees and sat on a flat stone then drained one of his two bottles of water. "Okay. Talk."

"You getting close?" Cobb asked, his voice barely understandable.

"Depends on your definition of close. I'm not cut out for this anymore."

"You see anything on—" The rest was fractured.

"You're breaking up."

"Can you hear me now?"

"Yeah…better. You know, this whole thing is pointless. When it's over, I'll have to walk all the way back in wet grass and cow shit."

"You have a better plan?"

"Carlos would have to be a fucking moron to come up here."

"I suppose. How close to the farm are you?"

Jorge shrugged tiredly and leaned his rifle against his leg. "About a mile. Is the family there?"

"Yeah. They're on site. The boy and the old lady are in the house. The old man is fiddling with a tractor in the yard. I gotta tell you though, something smells weird about all this."

"Yeah, the fucking cow shit."

"I mean, I feel like someone's got eyes on me," Cobb said.

Jorge paused. Cobb had been a good agent who served in dangerous places. It was not wise to doubt his senses. "What're you gonna do?"

"I'm going to reconnoiter the buildings."

"Okay."

"Anyway, I found a place where Harry might set up. It's to the east of the farm by maybe a half mile. Once you get to the farm, follow the road and you'll see it. The road goes through a deep cut in one of the ridges."

"I thought we were supposed to stay away from the road."

"I didn't say use the road. I said, follow it."

"Fine. I take it you want to meet me there."

"Yeah. It's as good as anything else I've found."

44

The old rogue can't afford to care about the lives of pawns.

At her apartment, Kay changed into a comfortable, long-sleeved, gray pullover and a pair of jeans then headed to the kitchen just as her cell rang. "Hello?"

"Hello, yourself. It's Elizabeth."

"Elizabeth! Where are you? I need to talk to you. Do you have some time?"

"Whoa, slow down, girl. My flight's at eight-something tonight, so I have to be at SFO by six-something, so yeah, I have time. Shall I meet you at the school?"

"No. My protection's been stopped, and I have my car and everything."

"Wow. Wonderful. So, it's over."

"Yes, God, yes. I'm free."

"Well then, how about Sausalito? I'll text you the address of a good place. I just said goodbye to Vincent at the Tomas so I can be there in thirty minutes."

"Cool. See you there," Kay said. Elizabeth's text came through before Kay could start her white Mini Cooper. Before she backed out of her stall, her cell rang again. "Hello."

"You've received two calls, Ms. Morrell," Mrs. Shim said. "Mr. Steiner called to apologize, and—"

"He did?"

"Yes. He will be emailing you."

"That's…whoa. How nice."

"Yes, ma'am. Mr. Ross also called and asked for your number. Shall I—"

"Harry called? Why doesn't he call me on my cell?"

"Apparently he doesn't have your number."

"He doesn't have my number? Why doesn't he have my number?"

"I don't know, Ms. Morrell. Shall I give it to him?"

"Please. Yes, give it to him."

"Yes, ma'am. Will that be all?"

"Yes, thank you, Mrs. Shim."

"You're welcome, Ms. Morrell."

Harry called just as Kay drove out of her building's garage. She connected her phone to the car's Bluetooth. "Kay, you'll never guess what happened."

"Your police escort said you're no longer under their protective custody. I was released about an hour ago."

"You too? How great is that?"

"I know. It is great. I even have my car. And I'm really glad you called because—"

"Wait, wait, you've got your car? Cool…I need a favor. I mean, if that's okay. I could really use a ride home because I can't get ahold of Kenji or Alma."

"Okay. When?"

"Right now. Well, soon. The nurse is getting the papers ready for my signature and my prescriptions, but maybe thirty or forty minutes and I'm out."

"Sure! I can be there in less than an hour."

"Great. I'll see you when you get here."

Kay immediately called Elizabeth to cancel their date. However, unable to stifle her excitement, Kay rambled to the point where Elizabeth barely got a word in edgewise. For a while, she spoke about her car, her apartment, the weather, her father's improved condition, and her mother's intuition, skirting the major issues roiling her mind.

Finally, during one of Kay's endless, disconnected monologues, Elizabeth broke in. "Kay! Stop. Take a breath."

Kay laughed. "Yes…I know. God, I'm so pumped. That's what the kids say, you know? Pumped and—"

"Breathe, Kay, breathe. I can tell you want to tell me something, so quit beating around the bush and fire away."

Kay glanced at her surroundings. "Um."

"Are you focused?"

"Focused? I, um…you know, Harry used to say that all the time when we were kids." Kay heaved a deep sigh. "You know, it's totally strange. Yesterday was so dark and mean."

"Yesterday? What happened?"

"Yeah…yesterday," Kay said. "Well, first thing in the morning, I had to expel a kid and the father yelled at me. Right after that, I had to go make nice to a bunch of rich potential donors because of what everybody's calling our *new security concerns.*"

"I heard about that. I also heard one of the gentlemen made a pass at you."

"You know about that?"

"Oh, Kay…you're in the news. Everyone talks about you, including a couple of those rich dudes you met with who just happen to be clients of my firm."

"Huh."

"What else ruined your day?"

"Well, I guess you should know that, when I got back to the school last night, my boyfriend dumped me."

"Okay…well, I know about that too. His boss is another client. I've met George a few times. He seems like an okay guy."

"He's a turd…just like all the other turds I've slept with."

"Whoa, girl. Take another breath."

Kay pulled off the freeway at the Marina exit. "Well…he's no Harry, I can tell you that."

"Aha…this is what you really want to talk about. You've finally recognized you really need Harry."

Kay was silent for a few moments. "Oh, Elizabeth…what am I going to do?"

"Hmm. You have two choices. The all-out assault or the slow and painful dating game."

"But Harry and Vincent love you."

Elizabeth took a long moment then sighed. "I know. Neither of those two have ever been able to hide their feelings. I love them too. Tell you what…as long as you and I can be cool with each other, I want you to choose the all-out assault."

Kay laughed. "I'm so glad I never hated you."

"Me too."

"God, everything's so much brighter today."

"I don't know about that," Elizabeth said with a chuckle. "It's still pretty foggy outside."

45

The enemy takes the bait and the game is afoot.

Still on watch outside the main entrance of the hospital, Julio battled with his anger. Why he had to be waiting in the cold fog while Estocio and Juan sat in the warm car was beyond him. From time to time, to ease the ache in his feet, he leaned against the lamppost, only to jerk away when the condensation on the steel column soaked through the shoulder of his hoodie.

He wanted more coffee, but he knew that it would mean another trip to the restroom inside the hospital lobby. And that was a problem. A security cop sat at a desk in the lobby right by the restroom. Earlier, when his bladder threatened to explode, he had hid his Glock in a planter box around the corner from the entrance and dashed to the restroom. Upon returning, he almost panicked when he found a fat nurse and a skinny-ass cop arguing right by the planter box. Eventually, the nurse flipped the bird then waddled toward the bus stop. The cop chuckled and turned on his heel, almost bumping into Julio. "Sorry," the cop said then headed toward the parking structure.

Frantically, Julio hustled to the planter box and found his weapon untouched.

A little before noon, he spotted someone who resembled the target. He pulled a picture of the asshole out of his pocket. It *was* him. Much smaller than Julio had imagined, the man looked harmless. Maybe under the jeans and flannel shirt, there might be some muscle, but Julio could not imagine this man causing the kind of grief Don Carlos had described. Furthermore, the man seemed like an idiot. Accompanied by a woman, he jubilantly pumped his fists and danced along the walkway outside the main entrance.

Julio pulled out his phone and speed-dialed Estocio. Casually pulling his hood lower, he walked right by the couple as they opened the doors of a white Cooper. The woman was attractive and smiling broadly. No wonder the asshole was happy.

"He's out," he said in Spanish when Estocio answered. "He and a woman just got in a white Mini Cooper. You better get your ass up here before they're gone… No, he didn't make me… No, I promise. I was cool, man. He and the woman are talking like nothing… Yeah, I can see them in the car and they're still talking. So no way he made me… Yeah, by the corner… Hurry the fuck up, they're pulling out."

The Cooper sat at a stoplight when Juan pulled up in a green Dodge sedan. Julio climbed into the back seat just as the skinny cop raced out of the structure on a motorcycle then roared past them.

"There, up ahead at the light. See them? White Cooper. I coulda done him right there, you know? The security cop was way inside the building. I coulda done him right there and you coulda picked me up and we woulda been gone, gone, gone."

Estocio shrugged. "Carlos wants to do it himself. So shut the fuck up."

"I'm just saying, man."

"Shut up," Estocio said. "Check out your piece on the floor. Carlos said the only way we take him is if it looks like he's going to run."

Julio picked up the automatic rifle and massaged the dark barrel. "You know, this is kind of crazy. Carlos said the guy's supposed to be old, like real old, fifty or something. This guy looks like maybe thirty."

"Carlos wants him. That's all I know, and that's all you need to know," Estocio said. "Probably had plastic surgery or something."

"Yeah," Julio said. "Plastic surgery. Never thought about that. I think when I get old, I want to do it, too."

Juan laughed.

Julio leaned forward. "You should think about it, Juan. You look old already. Fix your face up and maybe you won't need no whores no more."

Juan laughed again.

* * *

"Holy jeeze, take it easy," Kay said as Harry stomped his feet and clapped his hands to Creedence Clearwater's "Proud Mary" playing on the radio.

Harry rolled down his window. "Whoa, can you feel that air? God, it's great."

"It's also freezing. Roll it up."

"Hah. Better than living in a cave at room temperature for a month." Harry pushed his face into the damp fog that whipped by the car.

"Hey, you're messing around with the driver now, and that's against the rules. So roll it up. And you were only in for a week not a month."

"Well, felt like it, but you're the boss." He took one more gulp of cold, foggy air then closed the window.

"What am I going to do with you?" She stole another glance at his bandaged ear. Most of the lobe was covered by white gauze held in place by unsightly, yellowish tape. "How's your ear?"

Harry fingered the bandage then chuckled. "It'll probably be uglier than ever now. I don't think the women are going to flock to me like they used to."

Kay shook her head and repeated. "What am I going to do with you?"

When Harry said nothing, Kay realized he was thinking about an answer. "I'm glad I picked you up."

"Me too. You're way better than a taxi."

"I would hope so. Anyway, I'm glad I picked you up because I need to say something."

Harry raised his eyebrows. "Okay. What?"

Kay turned off the radio. "This is important."

Harry's face lost some of its glee. "Whoa, okay. Important, huh?"

"Yeah…it is." She paused for a long time, squeezing the steering wheel.

"Is this about last night?"

"No. I mean, yes, in a way."

"Really? I guess I'll keep quiet for a while."

Traffic crawled forward with many abrupt stops, making it difficult for Kay to focus on her thoughts.

"You want me to drive?" Harry asked.

"What? No," Kay barked as she slammed on the brakes yet again.

"I just think I should drive so you can focus and everything. I still don't know what's so important."

"It's about why you stopped writing to me."

"Oh…that."

"Anyway, I'm okay." She waited for the traffic to move then turned onto Lombard. Her throat thickened and her eyes welled. "Do you know what yin and yang is?" Traffic stopped again. "Damn it!" she hissed.

"Of course. Everyone knows what yin and yang is."

"Well, that's me this week," Kay said then mumbled incoherently.

"What?"

"Nothing. I didn't say anything. It's just this traffic."

Harry looked at her. "You don't have to tell me anything, you know."

"I know why you quit writing," Kay blurted. Traffic inched forward.

Saying nothing, Harry rubbed his thighs then clasped his hands and laid them on his lap.

Kay braked again as more tears welled in her eyes. "You must have thought I was an absolute bitch with some of the letters I sent back to you." She wiped her eyes. "Damn it!"

"You know? I think you're putting too much into this letter thing."

The traffic suddenly sped up and several vehicles changed lanes without signaling.

Kay tightened her grip on the steering wheel.

"Actually," Harry said, his tone somewhat sharp, "if I remember correctly, I thought you were basically telling me to grow up and find my own way. I thought you found my letters difficult and you knew you couldn't help me so you just tried to make it easier for me. I thought you were telling me to move on and be a stronger person, just like you used to. But you just couldn't find a way to be mean about it."

"What? Harry, stop it. You don't have to do that." She braked again to avoid another car shifting into her lane.

"Do what? You know, we should talk about something else. We can talk about, I don't know, school? How's that? Or maybe—"

"Just listen, okay?" They were still a few miles from the tollgate of the Golden Gate Bridge. But other than Kay's occasional barking at the inconsistent traffic, the pair sat silently.

* * *

Juan loosely held the steering wheel with one hand, watching the white Cooper two cars ahead, while Estocio spoke to Carlos over a burner.

"Yeah, Boss. He's headed north… Yeah, it looks like he's going to the farm… Okay." Estocio ended the call. "Juan, don't get too close. We don't want him to make us now."

Juan shrugged.

"What'd Carlos say?" Julio asked. "Can we pop him?"

"No," Estocio barked. "Carlos is gonna set up his crew at the farm. He wants to do it."

"Fuck," Julio said.

"That woman's a shitty driver," Estocio said.

"Yeah, but she cute," Julio said.

"Too bad," Estocio said. "She shoulda stayed home."

* * *

Nurse Lei arrived at the fifth-floor station and immediately noticed that no police stood guard by Harry's room. "Where are the cops?" she asked the nurse at the desk.

The nurse looked up. "They pulled off his protective detail. At least that's what the morning shift people said. I wasn't here."

"Really? Well, I guess I'm happy for Mr. Ross."

"Doesn't matter anyhow," Desk Nurse said. "He was discharged an hour or so ago."

"What? You're kidding. Who authorized that?"

46

***The pawns focus on the future, even as
death secretly knocks at their door.***

Kay tried to speak several times only to clamp her mouth shut lest she start crying. A long minute passed before she gained a semblance of control.

Harry rubbed his thighs. "You sure you don't want me to drive?"

"No. Please, I'm fine."

"But you're crying…sort of."

"Well," Kay said through her snuffling, "that wasn't my plan. I really don't know why I'm like this anyway. After last night, I think I'm about cried out. I'm not going to cry." She took a deep breath.

"We really don't have to talk about the other stuff."

"Well, I do. I need to tell you because you need to know what kind of person I really am. All these years you've been thinking I'm something else."

Harry sat silently and continued to rub his thighs.

"Okay…your letters, the last ones you ever sent. Do you remember them?"

"Um…yeah, kind of."

"Two of your friends died in Iraq, and then another one was discharged for being gay."

Harry clenched his fists.

"And then you were beaten up by some other marines who thought you were gay like your friend. You were hospitalized."

"Only for a day or two. And those guys were disciplined."

"What? Yeah. Whatever. The thing is you wrote and asked for my help and…do you remember my return letters?"

Harry said nothing.

"Well, do you?"

"Yeah," Harry said sharply. "Of course, I remember."

Kay jammed on the brakes. They had made the final move off Lombard and were now within a mile of the tollgate. The Presidio's Eucalyptus trees stood as ghostly sentries in the fog to their left.

"Damn it!" Kay shouted. "Damn it, damn it, damn it!"

They crept forward a few yards and stopped again. Kay pounded the steering wheel. "I never read your letters, okay? Those last letters. I never read them until last Saturday, the Saturday before the shooting, the Saturday after you showed up at school."

After a long pause, Harry said, "You kept my letters?"

"What? Yes."

"Really? All of them?"

"Harry. Please."

"That's…that's amazing. There must have been dozens. Maybe forty or so."

"Fifty-seven," Kay whispered.

"Fifty-seven? You're kidding."

"I know what you're trying to do, so stop it, okay? Don't change the subject. Just listen." She waited.

Harry rubbed his thighs. "Stop what?"

"It's not okay what I did to you. I should have read your letters and helped you. Instead, I never read them and just responded with crap. God, such total crap."

Traffic moved forward another hundred yards before sliding to another stop.

"You're not finished yet, are you?"

"No. I mean, yes. That's most of it." Her eyes began to fill again. "I'm not who you think I am. I'm just as mean and self-centered and crappy as everybody else. I was like all the other kids in school. Do you know what we did at sleepovers? We'd play *Trash Harry*, trying to come up with the meanest things to say about you." She paused.

"I said such horrible things about you." Tears rolled down her cheeks. "And we'd laugh. We thought it was all so funny."

Harry, staring forward, said nothing.

"I'm really sorry."

"I knew about it."

Kay trembled. "You knew?"

"Yeah. I also knew when you quit doing it in high school. It's okay. We were kids."

"No, it's not okay. After all you did for me. If it wasn't for you, I'd be…"

"You'd still be Kay," Harry whispered angrily. "Do you want me to drive now?"

Kay shook her head.

Harry quit rubbing his thighs. "May I ask you a question?"

She finally heard the angry tone in his voice. "Like what?"

"Why did you keep answering all my letters if you didn't read them? I mean, you must have kept writing for what, I don't know, a long time. Months, at least. I don't remember when you stopped. So…why did you keep writing me?"

"I don't know. God, you must have thought I was such a bitch. All that banal crap I wrote. All that absolute garbage." She raised her voice to a sing-song. "The weather's nice today, the weather's cold today, I went shopping today, Mom says hi, went to a party last night, had a lot of fun yesterday. Hope things are going well for you in the Marines." She paused. "Harry, I didn't even know you went to Iraq. I didn't even think about it. For the first time in your life you were asking me for help, and I never even bothered to read your letters."

"Uh huh. But why did you keep writing after I stopped?"

"I don't know."

"Right."

"I don't."

"Were you angry when you figured out that I wasn't writing anymore?"

"What? Of course."

"But I know when you're angry. There was no anger in your letters."

Kay paused. There it was again, that edge in Harry's voice. "Oh my goodness… You were angry with *me*, weren't you?"

Harry averted his eyes, and his hands trembled. He opened his mouth to speak several times before sharply saying, "Yes! Very angry. Not once during my tour in Iraq, did I read anything from the Kay I knew. It's like you gave up on being yourself, and that really hurt. Shoot. The old Kay would've vented at me, told me to buck up or whatever. Instead, all I got was pablum."

"God, I'm so sorry."

"Don't be. I got too wrapped up in myself. I should've realized you had your own problems. I should've kept writing." He paused. "Why didn't you read my letters?"

"Don't you get it? I didn't read them because I was too busy or too infatuated with some stupid guy. Just like always." She paused. "Are you still angry?"

Harry shook his head. "I was. But not anymore…not really. Well, talking about it pisses me off. But I can't stay angry sitting next to you." He sighed. "But back then, I went off pretty bad. Your letters are composting somewhere out there in Iraq."

Kay gripped the steering wheel with a vengeance. "I'm really sorry."

Harry nodded then shrugged.

The traffic moved. As they reached the tollgate, Kay rolled her window down.

"God, I love the air here," Harry said.

Fifty yards away from the tollgate, traffic stopped again.

"I was with someone then," Kay said. "I thought we were going to get married. He seemed to be everything. You know, all the good stuff. He was smart, funny, good-looking, lots of friends, nice house in the Berkeley Hills. And we did lots of fun things."

Kay was calmer now. She had never minded talking with Harry about her history with the opposite gender. She relaxed and looked over at him. "Anyway, the guy found your letters."

A tiny smile played across Harry's face.

"What's so funny?"

"I'm guessing your boyfriend was jealous."

"God. Yes. Very. He made me promise to stop writing you and to make you stop writing me. Yes, he was very jealous."

"But you didn't throw my letters away."

"No, I hid them."

"And you kept writing. As crappy as your letters were, I should have answered you."

"They were bad, weren't they?"

"Yeah. Especially for an English teacher."

Kay smiled. "Anyway, the guy dumped me. It was a pretty crappy time."

"You didn't write about that. You wrote about other stuff."

Kay shook her head. "Yeah, the stupid stuff. By then, you weren't writing. I didn't know what to say. I didn't know if you even read my letters. Or even if they ever got to you."

"I should have answered you."

"What? No, you did the right thing. You asked me for help, and I didn't do anything. I have no excuse."

"No. That's untrue."

"Harry, I want you to know that I'm not the person you think I am. I'm as bad—"

"Stop it!" Harry snapped. "We're done with all that, okay?"

Stunned, Kay stopped talking.

After a moment, Harry asked, "So tell me, why did you keep writing me?"

"I don't know. I really don't."

Harry said nothing.

Kay sighed heavily. "I guess I never thought you'd go away like that. Ever. I thought you'd always be around. I couldn't even conceive of you gone." Kay teared up again. "Oh God," she whispered. "Oh crap, crap, crap."

"I really think I should drive."

Kay barked a short laugh as tears trickled down her cheeks. The car crept forward.

"I'm serious. You're not focused. You're going to get us into an accident."

Kay laughed a bit harder then stomped on the brakes. The Cooper's tires chirped as they narrowly avoided rear-ending the next car.

"See what I mean? Let me drive."

Kay wiped her eyes. "I'm okay. I'll focus. Don't worry."

* * *

Estocio pocketed his cell. "Fucking area has shit for reception. I could barely hear him."

Juan shrugged. "The farm's in the boonies."

"The boss's getting pissed about the delay. He wants us to confirm that the target is heading toward the farm."

Julio, loading bullets into a magazine, said, "Fuck. Where else would he go? He's on the bridge already."

"Shut up," Estocio barked. "You better hope the guy never made you and makes a run for it."

Julio laughed. "You worry too much."

"You told him about the traffic?" Juan asked.

"Yeah. He heard on the car radio that there's an accident on the bridge."

"He can't blame us for that."

"We'll see."

47

Knights who have been put out to pasture can still smell a trap.

Jorge began to worry. Earlier he had slid by the farm and seen no one. True it was foggy, and he had kept his distance, but the place seemed deserted. And now, after hours of tramping and frequent bloody urinations, he stood on the top of a small grassy ridge, looking down into the cut Cobb had talked about. However, Cobb was nowhere to be seen. Jorge pulled out his cell, saw he had two bars, and punched in the number. Cobb did not answer.

Sighing, he scanned the vicinity. The access lane that ran from the county road to the farm occupied the bottom of the cut. To the east, a stout wooden bridge spanned a dry creek bed. An open gate at the far end of the bridge pretended to stand guard.

Jorge's worries grew. He knew that if prepared properly, the cut could be a killing zone. Almost a hundred yards long and fifteen feet deep, the gash offered no protection for anyone trapped in its bowels. If Harry was planning something, it would happen there. Carefully, he slid down the embankment to the road then walked toward the bridge. Within five yards he stopped. Spread out over the gravel was an array of tiny, three-sided spikes. "Oh shit,' he whispered then scrambled back to the top of the cut.

He was tired and had used up all his water. Sitting on the lip of the cut, he pulled his rifle from its sheath and waited.

48

Even at a standstill, the board is in flux.

When the traffic stopped again, Harry broke the silence. "You know, I remember a girl who'd walk to school with me and sit by me in class when no one else would. I also remember a girl who cowed a bunch of bullies. This girl never, ever let me crawl into a hole, and God knows I spent a lot of my youth looking for shelter. She would never let me do that."

Tears streamed down Kay's cheeks.

"Nothing you've done for the school surprises me. I bet your teacher profile is filled with accolades. I bet you love your students and they love you. Most of all, I bet you don't even think about the effect you have on people." He shrugged. "Anyhow, I think you should know that I do know who you are."

The traffic remained still. Slowly, Kay shook her head. "Harry, do you know what happens in a couple months?"

Harry looked at the ceiling then shrugged. "In regards to our present conversation, I'd have to say no… I guess you're not done yet."

"No…not yet."

"Okay. But let's not pound each other anymore. I mean, I've thought about you forever and… Let's not do that."

Kay nodded.

"Good. I got shot, and you got shot at. Twice. That should be enough pounding for a while."

"Is that supposed to be a joke?"

"Kind of. But I mean it, no more pounding."

"Okay…deal. But, going back to my question, do you know what happens in a couple months?"

"Um…in November?"

The traffic slid forward. "No, sorry. Three months, three and a half months."

"Oh. We both turn twenty-nine."

Kay huffed out an exasperated sigh. "Yeah, I know that. But—"

"Wait." Harry leaned forward. "Look, there's an accident up ahead."

"I see it."

"I think you're going to have to change lanes."

"I know how to drive, okay?" She slowed then gradually merged into a single lane. Neither spoke as they crawled toward the accident. Past the damaged cars, a tow truck backed up, and a cop stepped into the lane, stopping all traffic.

Harry looked at the people standing by the damaged cars. "Imagine those folks up there. They're like us. They're tooling along, doing the things they do, and then, *wham*! Out of the blue their entire day changes. Shoot, maybe their entire lives." He spoke easily, reminding Kay of the tone he had used whenever he helped her with her homework.

"I hope no one is hurt."

Harry rolled down the window and leaned out. "No ambulances. Maybe it's just some fender-benders—whoa, looks like five or six cars."

Kay moved a few more yards and stopped adjacent to the last car in the line of wrecks. An elderly man leaned against the car, smoking.

"What happened?" Harry asked.

"Fucking motorcycles," the man said. "Some bastard thought he was God's gift and kept racing. He roared right by me then got too close to some car up there. That car stopped too quick and, well, you know…chain reaction shit. And the fucking bastard on the motorcycle didn't even stop, just kept right on going."

"Anything we can do?"

The man shook his head.

"Take it easy. It's going to get better after a while."

"Yeah, shit." The old man tossed his cigarette, climbed back into his car, then closed the door.

"Will you roll up the window?" Kay said. "It's freezing."

Harry complied. "I think I like the cold, you know. Lets me know I'm alive."

They sat silently while the tow truck lined up with the first of the damaged cars.

"Harry?" Kay said quietly then returned to her silence.

"I'm here. I think you better just say what you want to say."

Kay took a deep breath but remained silent.

"And I think you better say it quickly. Get it out before that tow truck starts moving and you step on the gas. Your driving worries me."

Kay turned toward Harry and offered a small smile.

He leaned away from Kay. "What? What's going on? You're making me really nervous."

"Marry me," Kay whispered. She put her forehead on her hands that rested on the steering wheel. He was going to need a long time to process his response.

* * *

A few cars back, Julio said, "You know, I could do them right now. I could get out, walk up there, do them, and then drive away in their car."

"Shut up," Estocio said.

Juan laughed.

49

The trap is set.

Jorge called Cobb again, received no answer, and put his phone away. "Should have brought radios. Christ." He could hear a distant vehicle and realized he was near the county road. The noise, never much above a whisper, faded quickly. He sighed and pulled out a sandwich, believing he was headed for a very uncomfortable few hours. "Damn it, Cobb. Answer your phone."

"Pretty crappy reception in this area," a hillbilly voice said from behind.

Jorge's heart jumped. Without turning, he said, "Hello, Harry."

"Jorge," Harry said. "Pretty good of ya'll to figger out 'bout this here cut."

"Cobb found it. We were supposed to meet here."

"Huh. Ain't that sumptin'?"

Jorge did not look at the long lost, supposedly dead agent. "You called Astor. You said you wanted the farm family protected."

Harry laughed and sat next to Jorge. "Yep, I did. I certainly did. But the farm's a half mile from here. Ya'll shoulda stayed there. I never reckoned you'd come here."

Jorge faced Harry, and a shiver of fear walked up his spine. Harry's gaunt face had deep-set, unblinking eyes and a latticework of blood vessels above the paper-thin skin on his forehead. Tiny scars crisscrossed much of his face. A bolt-action hunting rifle lay cradled in his long, boney hands, the business end pointing in Jorge's general direction. Even in the chill of the breezy, foggy day, he wore nothing but a dirty brown t-shirt and jeans.

50

The pawns make an unexpected move.

Kay peeked over her hands, saw that the traffic had yet to move, then returned her forehead to her knuckles. "Harry, I'm tired, and my clock is running. I want to have children, or at least one child, before it gets too late. I don't want to be sixty when my kid is in high school. I want a Vincent like your Vincent. God, when he hugs my neck, it's like…it's just the best thing I've ever felt." She glanced at him.

Harry stared at her, his mouth narrowly open, his eyes continuously and slowly blinking under a deeply furled forehead.

Kay sighed. "C'mon, for once in your life, stop thinking. Just tell me what you feel."

Harry sat back in his seat without responding.

"I'm asking you to marry me. Do you understand that?"

Harry jerkily nodded. "Yes," he said with a catch in his throat.

* * *

Julio pulled the clip out of his automatic rifle then slammed it back in. A moment later he repeated the action. He pulled out his pistol, popped out the clip, then slammed it back in.

"Stop it!" Estocio shouted. "Stop fucking around. And make sure you don't show anything above the window. Christ, quit being such an asshole!"

"We should be moving pretty soon," Juan said quietly. "It looks like the tow truck is almost ready."

"I say we drive up right next to 'em and pop 'em from the car," Julio said. "Look what'll happen. The whole fucking bridge'll close down, and we can just keep driving. I say drive by and pop 'em."

"You want to say that to Carlos?" Estocio asked.

Julio did not respond.

* * *

Kay looked up. "Yes? Yes, *what?*"

"Kay, is this what you want? Is it really? You've just—"

"Harry!" Kay cried out. "Yes, this is what I want."

"Wait. Just wait…please."

Kay took a deep breath. "Fine."

Harry furiously rubbed his thighs. "Here's what I know. First, like I said last night, I love you. I always have. But because I do, I don't want you to… Ah, man oh man. You and I, but mostly you, just went through a very intense time. Everything happened all at once. The madman with the gun, the shooting outside your apartment, the stuff you're doing for the school, and just us finding each other again. It's been so intense and crazy." Harry closed his eyes. "I don't know if you, or I for that matter, are thinking very well right now."

Kay dropped her head back onto her knuckles.

"And then on top of all that, I know your boyfriend broke up with you. He did, didn't he?"

Kay nodded.

"I mean, you didn't break up with him, did you?"

Kay shook her head.

"And he did it last night, right?"

Kay sat up and faced him, the Harry who knew her, the Harry she knew, and the Harry she was just beginning to know. "Yes, he did." She now knew what she needed to say.

"You see?" Harry said. "We may not be whole right now. We may not be seeing things straight."

"Stop it."

"What? Stop what?"

"Pounding. You said no more pounding."

Harry's eyes slowly blinked, wrinkling his face.

"You need to know something. It's true, my boyfriend broke up with me and he did it last night. But all he really did was beat me to the punch."

Harry's blinking increased. "I… I don't understand."

"Of course, you do. I know you do. You're not a rebound, Harry. And all the craziness of the last week did nothing but crystallize everything. I want a partner to love who's going to love me when I'm old and gray and my butt starts sagging. Most of all, I want someone I can trust. And for God's sake, that *is* you. It always has been." She glanced at the unmoving traffic. "I kept writing you because I needed you. And then I lost you anyway." She heaved a deep sigh. "I can't let you go again." She took another deep breath. "You showing up out of the blue was the absolute best thing to ever happen to me."

"Whoa," Harry whispered.

"The truth is, I'm whole when I'm near you. Whole, okay? I love you, Harry. I finally figured out that I've always loved you. Always."

Harry looked out the window then at the space between his feet.

She waited as long as she could before she said, "Harry?"

"I'm thinking."

"Oh," she whispered. "Okay."

Harry, eyes on the tow truck, said, "You'll need to come up with a different name."

"What?"

"We can't have more than one Vincent running around," Harry said. "It would get confusing. We'll have to think of a new name." He sat still, stoically staring at the accident. Then he lifted his left arm and softly punched the air.

Kay reached over, snatched his hand, and kissed it.

Blushing, Harry slowly exhaled. "Okay… Whoa, this kind of stuff is going to take some getting used to."

Kay laughed, released his hand, and wiped her eyes.

"I, um, really didn't want to get back into all the letter stuff, you know?" Harry wiped a thin sheet of perspiration from his forehead. "I knew you were gonna bring it up and all, but I mean, it's the past, you know? Anyhow, I guess it was good to get it all out and everything, but shoot. And then last night I told you I loved you, and I thought you already knew and everything, and—"

Kay laughed. "You're rambling."

"Well, I guess I'm pretty kerfutzed. This changes everything."

"We'll still be best friends. That's just the way it is."

"This is quite a bit past that. You know, I think I'm a pretty good dad. I mean, how hard can it be with a kid like Vincent, but I think I do all right. Vincent's going to love you too. You know that, don't you?"

Kay smiled, nodded, and wiped away more tears. As traffic began to move, she stepped on the accelerator with a bit too much pressure, and the Cooper lurched forward.

Harry laughed. "You sure you don't want me to drive?"

"Oh, stop it. I'm a good driver."

"All evidence to the contrary."

They both laughed.

As traffic sped up to thirty-five miles per hour, Kay merged back into her favorite center lane. Just as she straightened out, the traffic slowed to fifteen miles per hour.

Kay's cell phone chimed.

Harry laughed. "Let it ring."

Kay pulled her cell out of her purse and shook her head. "It's Mrs. Shim."

"You could get a ticket if you're driving while on your cell, you know."

She smiled. "Mrs. Shim? It must be after four. Why are you still at work?" She thumbed the machine to hands free mode.

Traffic came to a standstill.

"It's three-fifty, Ms. Morrell," Mrs. Shim said.

Kay laughed silently. "Oh…right."

"The hospital is calling for Mr. Ross. They seem quite anxious to get in touch with him. I presume he's with you?"

"Yes, he is."

Harry shook his head and mouthed, *no, no, no.*

"Well then, a nurse named Lei Kalani called, and she seemed quite perturbed. She would very much like for Mr. Ross to call the hospital at his earliest possible convenience."

"Is she on the line now?"

"No."

"Please call the hospital and let them know that Mr. Ross will call as soon as he gets home."

"Certainly, Ms. Morrell."

"Thank you, Mrs. Shim. I'll see you tomorrow morning," Kay said then rang off.

"Whoa, no way, I'm not calling the hospital," Harry said. "Give me your phone."

"Why? Change your mind?"

"Nope." He played with the phone then dumped it into Kay's purse. Lastly he tossed the purse onto the floor by his feet. "There. It's on vibrate. No more interruptions because right now we need to talk."

"Oh, Harry, what took us so long?" Kay whispered as they crept forward.

Harry cautiously reached over and placed his hand on Kay's shoulder. "I don't know. Lots of things, I guess."

Kay nuzzled her cheek against his wrist.

"What do you want to be called?"

"What?"

"Your name…our name? I mean, do you want to be hyphenated?" His voice picked up speed. "Do you want a big wedding? Or maybe just some justice of the peace? Do they even have justices of the peace anymore? What the heck do they do, anyway? I mean, when they aren't marrying people off, what do they do? Justice of the peace. How do you adjudicate the peace? What if it's not peaceful? What *are* your thoughts on hyphenated names? A lot of the kids in my class have them. And what if a person with a hyphenated name marries another hyphenated person? What happens then? It'd be like John-Jacob-Jingleheimer-Smith. Or worse."

"You're going off the deep end," Kay said just as the traffic began to pick up speed.

"Anyway, there's lots to talk about."

"Yes, there is."

"Wait!" Harry shouted. "I've got it, I've got it! Get in the right lane, hurry!"

"What?"

"Come on, turn on your blinker." Harry rolled his window down. "We want the Sausalito exit."

"There's too much traffic."

"Come on, it's a heavy fog. It'll be great, really, really great."

Kay turned on her blinker, while Harry leaned out of the car and waved at the traffic in the next lane. They made it into the exit lane just as they rolled off the bridge.

* * *

"What's he doing? Is he getting off? The next exit doesn't go to the farm," Estocio said. "Get closer."

Juan looked for an opening to change lanes.

"If he gets off, we're in deep shit," Estocio said.

"He's not that far ahead," Juan said calmly. "We'll be okay."

Estocio watched the target car exit the freeway. "Shit! I fucking knew it. I knew he made us. He's running. Don't lose him."

"He didn't make me," Julio protested. "I swear to God, he didn't make me."

"Shut the fuck up," Estocio said as they finally merged onto the exit lane. "He's fucking running. Goddamn you, Julio."

"I think he turned left at the end of the offramp," Juan said.

"What? No. Look, everybody's going right," Estocio said. "He probably wants to lose us in that town."

"I'm telling you, he didn't make me," Julio whined.

"Do you have any fucking idea who we're dealing with, you little shit?" Estocio said. "Jesus Christ."

"He didn't look so special to me," Julio said.

51

Patience is required, even when the enemy's next move is known.

Jorge zipped up his trousers then returned to his seat at the lip of the cut. "How much longer do I have to wait?"

Harry, his eyes on the gravel road to the east, said, "Oh, I 'spect 'ol Carlos will be comin' round the bend right shortly. How bad's your innards?"

Jorge shifted uncomfortably. "None of your business. You know there are people who know I'm out here and—"

"You mean the fuckin' Bureau? Still bullshittin' me, ain't you?" Harry shrugged sadly. "Far as I can reckon, the Bureau's out bustin' Carlos's chops."

"No, not the Bureau."

"What? Oh…you mean 'ol Cobb."

"Jesus," Jorge whispered. "Where is he?"

"Oh." Harry reached into the back pocket of his filthy jeans. "Here's his cell."

Jorge took the phone. "Where is he, Harry?"

"Well, you see, I made this here promise to one of my frens. You know what a fren is, Jorge? Do you have any frens?"

Jorge did not answer.

"No, I 'spect not. My daddy, who was an asshole of epic proportions, still believed with all his heart that frens were the absolute essence of life. There weren't nothin' he wouldn't do for his frens, as few as they was, a'course."

Harry sat, planted the butt of the rifle into the ground, and leaned forward until his forehead touched the cold barrel. "You see, this fren of mine is special. She's all heart. Anyway, my fren asked me to pertect these here farm folk, and she has this way 'bout her that I find just plain difficult to refuse. Anyways, I asked ol' Cobb to take them outta harm's way. It took a little convincin', but he's on his way with them folks."

"I didn't see them drive out. And there's no other road to the farm."

Harry laughed. "They cain't come this way. Come on. Ol' Cobb figgered somethin' else out."

"The owners are pretty old. Are they supposed to walk out?"

"That's Cobb's problem. Last I saw him, looked like he was plannin' to use the fambly tractor."

"There's a kid."

"Yeah, I saw the kid. Little black boy. Well, as long as they don't come up this here road, they'll be fine an' dandy. Cobb's a good guy when it comes to pullin' folks' bacon outta the fire."

Jorge looked back to the road across the gully. "And you really think Carlos is coming?"

"Well, shore. Carlos has had a hard-on for me for years, and now that the shit's hit the fan with most of his business, I 'spect he's just about ready to burst through his pants."

"He's not that stupid."

"There, you see? You guys always think he's a genius or somethin'. The fact of the matter is, he *is* stupid. Oh, he's got animal sense and cajones, but he ain't no Einstein. He's comin'."

"And just what makes you so sure?"

"Well, 'cause I saw him and his compadres wait'n up on the hard pan for me to arrive from Frisco. The other me, that is."

"The teacher hero," Jorge said.

"That teacher's a regular good ol' boy with some remarkable healin' qualities."

"He's hospitalized. He was shot."

Harry laughed. "Now, Jorge, don't start gettin' all stupid on me."

Jorge paused. "Fuck. So…you got him out, and he is on his way here."

"Except he ain't comin' too soon on account of an accident on the bridge." Harry shrugged. "That lil pile up was the best I could do for my fren. She's right particular about doin' the right thing, so I had to slow things up a tad for the other me. Give him a chance, you follow?"

Jorge took another, very unsatisfactory, leak. His unbearable urge to pee ended up a pitiful pink drizzle.

Harry laughed. "Ya'll agin' pretty fast, ain't cha?"

Jorge zipped up his pants. "You want me to stay?"

"Well, you ain't leavin'. Once ol' Carlos arrives, you're gonna have a coupla choices."

Jorge felt another urge to piss. "Well, I guess the world's made up of choices."

"Yep, that be my view."

"Harry, you don't have to talk hillbilly with me. Why do you do it?"

Harry puffed his cheeks and held his breath for a moment. "Force of habit, I suppose. You try on a person long enough, pretty soon you forget it's just like a suit of clothes you're wearing."

"Maybe you've forgotten a lot of things."

Harry looked away. "Not hardly. Oh, sometimes I get them to simmer, but sooner or later they start boiling again. I have a hard time understanding people like you. You're supposed to be out to help people get on better with the world. And then you let a shit like Carlos operate."

Sitting down, Jorge asked, "So what are my choices?"

"I guess that should be pretty easy to figure out."

"Not anymore. Not today."

"Really? I guess it's true, then."

"What?"

"You aren't the same guy you used to be. Even the old bureaucrat you used to be would've recognized your choices."

Jorge huffed angrily.

Harry laughed again. "Well, one, you can choose to serve your country and help me blow the bastard's brains out, or two, you can resort to your bureaucratic sense of self-preservation and do nothing."

"Does that mean I can leave when Carlos arrives?"

"I said *bureaucratic* sense. You get to leave when the deed is done. Hell, it's time you got back in the field anyhow. You used to be quite the operator. You used to know what had to be done on a personal level. Now you're just like all the rest of those assholes in D.C. All that time you spent fucking up people's lives from behind your desk has damn near ruined you. You should thank me for giving you the chance to become human again."

"I never blew up a house with a bunch of children in it."

Harry's face darkened for a bare moment. "Well, of course you did. You sent me down there, didn't you? You sent me down there and then let that bastard rip the heart out of my friends."

Jorge said nothing. There was no sense arguing with Harry. Not anymore.

Harry's friends, a small group of informants he had cultivated, were tortured then murdered by Carlos. Initially, the FBI believed Harry had betrayed the group, especially when he slipped so far off the radar no one could contact him. In time, the legendary agent was presumed dead. Then Carlos's hacienda was fire-bombed. Twenty-three people died, including a number of Carlos's advisors, his brother, his two children, and thirteen nephews and nieces. Everyone in D.C. knew then that Harry was alive. Carlos also knew.

"You could have pulled them out, Jorge. You didn't need to keep them down there. I told you things were getting dicey."

Jorge sighed. "We couldn't. You know that. We couldn't."

"Bullshit," Harry whispered. "Oh well, shouldn't be long now."

52

The old rogue's pawn calls upon a dormant set of skills.

At Harry's insistence, Kay turned left at the bottom of the Sausalito off-ramp while the rest of the traffic turned right and headed toward the town. Kay eased the Cooper through the dense fog on a road that first went under the freeway then abruptly uphill. "This is crazy. I can barely see the center line."

Harry laughed. "Don't worry. Just keep going. You're doing great. Can I open the window again?"

"No."

Only Harry's motormouth kept her from pulling over as they crept upwards. Kay found herself alternating between gnashing her teeth and laughing. She rounded a particularly sharp turn when the fog thinned. A few moments later they burst into brilliant sunshine. "Oh my God."

"I was so hoping," Harry said. "The fog has to be just right, you know?"

They pulled over to a vista point overlooking San Francisco. Kay turned off the engine, and together they watched the blinding white fog surge past the towers of the Golden Gate.

"It's beautiful," Kay said.

"Yup, not all bad."

"It's the view on the postcard you sent me." She paused. "Do you come up here a lot?"

Harry slowly nodded.

"Because of the postcard?"

"Yeah. I told you. I've been thinking of you for a long time."

With the sun hanging above the western horizon, the wind whipped the top layer of the fog into bands of white flames that burned then flickered into nothingness. The pair exited the car to watch.

Harry looked at the empty parking area. "This place should be packed. People should see this. Why aren't there more people here?"

Kay, sweater buttoned to her neck, laughed. "Because it's cold, you dodo."

"Then they're missing one of the finer things in life." He raised his hands high over his head and danced in circles. "Whoa!"

Kay laughed. "What are you doing? People are going to think you're crazy."

"It's my Snoopy dance."

Kay took a step toward the whirling Harry. "Snoopy?"

Harry stopped short, breathing hard. "Charlie Brown's dog. You know, Peanuts? Charles Schultz? Anyway, this is the way Snoopy dances when he's happy." He stomped out a few more steps then took Kay into his arms and spun around.

"Harry!" Kay shouted through her laughter.

Harry stopped spinning and gently set Kay down on the front fender of the Cooper. Releasing her waist, he cradled her face in his hands. "This is so great."

Kay broadened her smile. "Are you ever going to kiss me or what?"

Harry's face turned serious. "You sure about all this? I mean, are you sure?"

Kay locked her arms around his neck. "You know, Harry, sometimes you just talk too much."

* * *

"There's a yellow one," Julio said, pointing to another Cooper. They had cruised through the main shoreline drag of Sausalito and twice spotted white Coopers, but both were heading north.

"Shit. Turn around," Estocio barked. "Turn the fucking car around."

"The left turn off the bridge goes up to the headlands," Juan said.

"We gotta check it out and hope they didn't head back to San Francisco."

"If they went back to the city, we're fucked," Juan said.

"We'll check the other road. If they're not there, we'll call Carlos. Hustle. They only got a few minutes on us."

Juan shrugged and hooked a U-turn at the next intersection. At least the traffic heading back toward the bridge was light, and they made good time.

* * *

"Oh my God," Kay whispered into Harry's bandaged ear.

Harry said nothing but squeezed her a little more tightly.

She ran her hands over Harry's neck then quickly pulled away and wiped them on her jeans. "You're cold as ice and you're sweating. Are you okay?"

Harry smiled. "There's no words to express how good I feel."

Kay took his face into her hands. "Come on, let's get back in the car. You're not a hundred percent, and I don't want you to get worse." Behind her, she could hear a car racing up the slope.

* * *

With the upper layer of fog burning away, Juan accelerated through a curve.

"Look!" Estocio shouted.

Parked at the lookout was the white Cooper. More importantly, the target stood outside the vehicle, locked in an embrace with the woman.

"Jesus! Slow down, slow down, I got 'em, I got 'em!" Julio shouted from the back seat. With his window but partway down, he forced his gun barrel through the narrow opening.

But Juan could not jam on the brakes and keep control of the fast-moving car. Julio would have to adjust his shots.

* * *

Screeching tires pulled Kay's attention around. As she turned, Harry expelled a furious, unintelligible shout then jerked her off the Cooper's fender. She landed on her back and gave a short scream as the air filled with a *pop-pop-pop*. The Cooper shuddered as bullets slammed into its side. The *pop-pop-pop* continued, and more bullets dug up the nearby gravel.

Crouching, Harry grabbed her by her arm and dragged her toward the guardrail. "Come on, come on."

Kay rolled to her knees and crawled alongside Harry. They scooted under the guardrail then ran, slid, and rolled for fifty feet down the steep slope before they could find any solid purchase. Just as they managed to stand, they heard men at the guardrail shouting in Spanish. The soft snap of bullets whisked by their heads as guns opened fire again. Hand-in-hand, they dashed into a line of trees bordering a dirt road. Bullets thunked into the trees, bushes, and grass-covered ground.

Past the road, they entered a larger copse of trees. Bruised and scraped, the pair lunged over a fallen log then dropped to the damp ground. The sound of shooting stopped.

Harry looked over the log. "They're coming." He pulled her to her feet. Using the fog and trees for cover, they angled to their left as the firing began again. Kay staggered in the wet grass, fought for her balance, then blindly smashed into low-lying branches. Harry grabbed her collar and pulled her along. She bucked and struggled and broke free of his grasp, only to run into a tree and fall backward.

Harry dropped to his knees and leaned closer until they were nose to nose. "Kay," he whispered, "come on. We can't panic. We can't."

Kay stared into his bloodshot eyes and saw the sweat rolling down his face. "They're shooting at us!"

He took her face into his hands. "Shh. Shh. We have to focus, okay?"

Her heart pounding, Kay held her breath then released it in a *whoosh*. Finally, she gave a jerky nod. "Okay," she whispered. "Okay."

Harry stared for a moment longer then released her face. His eyes scanned the immediate area.

From far up the slope, a heavily accented voice shouted, "Harry! Oh, Harry, you come out now. Come on, you. You come out an' we let de girl go. Hokay? You no want de girl hurt now, do you? We no want to hurt her either. Hokay? Come on out, an' we let de girl go."

Kay violently shook her head. "They'll kill us both."

Still scanning the surroundings, Harry said, "I know." Together, they rose to a crouch with Harry pointing to the east. "This way." With backs bent and heads low, they ran.

"Harry, we got your kid. Your lil black nigger kid, Harry. You betta come out now, or we gonna chop him up bad. Hokay? You wan' your lil nigga boy all chop up?"

Harry froze. Kay stopped and rested with her hands on her knees.

"Don' make me come down dere, Harry. Don' go piss me off. No one's neva gonna fin' your lil nigga boy. An' dat bitch down there, she be gone too. Dat what you want? You betta come out now."

Harry rose to his full height. Rivers of perspiration ran down his face and his jaw trembled but his eyes no longer blinked.

"Harry!" Kay whispered.

He slowly exhaled then dropped to a knee. "I have to make them stop."

"What?"

Harry straightened up, looked toward the sound of the voice, then pointed to the east again. "This way." They continued their scramble to the edge of the copse. Kay noted for the first time that they were back in the fog. She straightened, looking up the slope. Ghostly figures moved back and forth as they zigzagged downward above the narrow road. She could hear them talking but could not make out their words. "Harry, we're in the fog."

"I know." He looked toward their pursuers. One of the men slipped onto his backside. "They're struggling with the hill. I don't think they have the right kind of shoes."

"Shoes? The right kind of shoes?"

Harry nodded then pointed. "You see that old bunker?"

Across a shallow depression in the slope, a war-time concrete bunker stood. The back of the roofless structure lay open to view from the road. Kay nodded.

"I'm going over there to check it out. Wait for me here."

"No, I'm coming."

Harry hesitated then nodded. "Fine, but we have to get to the front of the bunker. There's no cover in the open area."

Kay nodded.

"Ready?"

Kay nodded again.

They clasped hands and darted across the open ground, plunged down the depression, then charged up the steps leading to the bunker's wall. The men above opened fire, but their aim was high. Kay and Harry clambered onto a narrow ledge on the bay side of the bunker.

"Hokay, Harry. If dat's de way you wan' it, your lil nigga boy is dead. You just killed him. An' dat bitch is gonna feel it before she die, Harry. Goddamn, ain't you got no cajones?"

Harry, eyes down, walked the entire length of the ledge, shoving rubble over the side. Kay followed and watched the debris rumble down the precipitous slope.

"Harry?"

"Shh."

"This won't work. We can't go down and there's no more trees that way and—"

"Shh, Kay, please."

Harry knelt and studied rods of rusting rebar that poked out of the broken lip of the ledge.

"Harry, I'm not scared anymore," Kay said quietly.

Harry seized one of the iron bars.

"Hokay, Harry, we're coming now. You fucking blew it for your kid. I wan' you to rememba dat. Everbody's gonna know what kinda gutless bastid you are."

Harry wrenched the bar upwards. "Kay, go watch them. Let me know when they're close. Stay as low as you can."

Kay walked back to the end of the ledge, lay on her belly, and peaked around the corner. "One man is coming. The other two are on the dirt road."

Gasping for breath, Harry pushed the bar downward then pulled it up again. "Is he coming down with his weapon up?"

"What? I don't understand."

"Is he pointing it at us?"

"No, he can't. It's too steep. He has to use his hands."

"What about the guys on the road?"

"What?"

"Are they pointing their guns at us?" Harry, his hands bleeding from the cold corrugated metal, bent the bar back and forth more easily now.

"No, they're just standing there."

"Has the guy reached that open area by the steps?"

"Almost. It looks like he doesn't want to go down into it. He's looking all around."

The rod, a little less than three feet long, broke off. Harry waved it in the air. "Okay. We need to go back to the trees. We can't make it here."

Kay closed her eyes and nodded.

53

Bad news arrives just as things are believed to be under control.

Maizie limped to a chair in the corner of the command room. If the day had been clear, she would have had a view of Market Street and the Bay Bridge. As it was, she could only see the ghostly images of downtown for a block or two. Happy about the staggering blow the Bureau was laying on the Carlos Cartel, she no longer fretted at being relieved of command. In a few days the D.C. boss and his crew would be gone and to hell with them. She settled down on her unwounded cheek.

"Cabrera," D.C. Boss said, "line three."

"Yes, sir. " Maizie pushed away from the wall and rode the rolling chair to an open area at the table. She grabbed a phone and cut to line three. "Agent Cabrera."

"Agent Cabrera, this is Lei Kalani, I'm a nurse at—"

"I remember you, Ms. Kalani. What can I do for you?"

"We have a problem. An officer arrived for the next shift as Mr. Ross's security, and—"

"Was the officer on time?"

"Yes. But we were informed earlier today that Mr. Ross's protection detail had been discontinued. And, as of right now, the police can't find the morning duty officer."

Maizie worked her jaw then slammed her hand on the table. Everyone in the room stopped and stared.

"Is Mr. Ross okay?"

"Agent Cabrera, he was discharged some time ago. His teacher friend, Ms. Morrell, picked him up."

Maizie's hand went to her forehead, hissing, "That fucking bastard!"

"Agent Cabrera?" Nurse Lei and D.C. Boss said simultaneously.

The table full of men continued to stare at Maizie until D.C. Boss said, "Get back to work."

Maizie ended the call then hobbled to her office. She dialed Kay's special phone but received no answer. She tried Kay's personal cell phone with the same result. She went back to operations and asked D.C. Boss for help at the Toma's farm, but he did not share her concern, and even if he did, there was no one to send anyway. She stormed back to her office.

54

Harry slid around the crumbling gun port and knelt by Kay. "Don't think about anything but getting to the trees. Run as fast as you can, get to the trees, and get low behind some cover. I'll be right behind you."

She could hear the man swearing as he slid down the embankment into the depression on the other side of the bunker.

"Go when you're ready," Harry said.

She took a deep breath then bolted. Not four steps into the run, guns began barking again, stopping only when the pair entered the copse. They angled toward a fallen tree that bridged a shallow swale.

"Goddamn it, Harry," a voice shouted from the depression. "You making dis too hard. You fucking ruint my shoes, you stupid ass sonofabitch. I tell you, I'm gonna fuck your bitch. I'm gonna fuck her and den fuck her some more." His voice trailed off into Spanish.

While Kay crawled into the hollow under the horizontal trunk, Harry raised his head. "Another one's coming down on the left," he whispered. "They want to flank us, but they'll be separated… Good." He slid into the hollow and took Kay's face into his hands.

Kay stared into his eyes. "What do you want me to do?"

Harry released her then studied their surroundings. "Okay, the guy on the right has cleared the bunker." He ran his hands through the grass until he found a fist-sized stone. Handing it to Kay, he pointed to a tree a few yards down the slope. "I'm going there. You need to stay under here and, one, watch the guy on the road. Clear?"

Kay nodded.

"Two, check for the guy on the left. He'll be careful and probably won't enter the trees very close to us. That gives us time to handle the guy on the right, okay?"

Kay nodded. "What do I do with the rock?"

"The guy on the right, his name is Julio."

"What?"

"I heard them shouting, and they called him Julio. The guy on the road is Estocio or something. I think the third guy, the guy coming down on the left, is Juan."

"What? Harry, I—"

"Julio's closest so I gotta take him out first." Harry paused then nodded as if talking to himself. "Juan's gotta be second. Then I gotta figure out Estocio. But Julio comes first, okay?"

"I understand. But what do I do with the rock?"

"Oh, yeah, number three. I need Julio to walk past the tree I'm by. He should. It's the easiest path. But if he doesn't, I need you to toss the rock into the bushes past the tree." He paused. "You'll have to throw it pretty hard. It's got to bounce and roll."

"I can do that."

Harry looked into Kay's eyes then dropped his head. "Don't let him see you throw."

Kay nodded.

"I know it's a stupid old trick…but it's all I can think of right now."

"It's okay. I'll do it."

Harry nodded then scampered to the tree.

Kay crawled higher and deeper into the hollow. Tall grass hid her from the downhill side of the log. The uphill side, however, offered little cover. Only the fog protected her from Estocio's eyes. She found it hard to believe he couldn't see her, but there he was, pacing back and forth on the dirt road, staring intently into the fog-shrouded trees, clueless to her position.

Looking left, she saw Juan about fifty yards away, calmly walking into the copse. She slid back, caught Harry's eyes, and pointed to where Juan had entered the woods.

Harry, standing erect, his back against the tree, nodded. In his left hand, the shaft of rebar hung loosely. In his right hand, he also held a stone.

Kay saw Julio, huffing and puffing, as he walked on a path that would bring him right next to Harry's hiding place. She held her breath.

Estocio shouted something in Spanish. Julio stopped and shouted something in return. Estocio moved to the right, casually holding his rifle with one hand, the muzzle pointing down.

Slowly and silently Kay hefted her stone as more shouts came from the two men. Julio shouted again then abruptly changed direction and headed straight up the incline. His new path would allow him to see Harry by the tree. Kay pulled the stone back and flung it.

At the same time, with the smallest of movements, Harry tossed his stone into the same undergrowth below the tree.

Julio jumped, lowered his weapon, and ran toward the soft thump and rambling of the stones. He shouted something in Spanish before opening fire.

With a backhanded swing of the rebar, Harry struck Julio square in the forehead as he passed the tree. Julio's head then his body snapped backward. Jumping from his hiding place, Harry straddled the moaning man then struck his head again and again.

Watching, Kay never counted the blows, but she knew that Julio stopped making noise long before the final one had landed. Blood flew in all directions, splattering the trees, the grass, the nearby shrubs, and Harry.

Harry dropped the rebar, jumped over Julio's body, and retrieved the rifle. He examined the weapon then scrambled up the slope to Kay's position.

Kay moved aside as Harry lay prone and aimed the rifle to the left.

"Harry," she whispered.

"Shh!" Harry hissed, keeping his eyes glued toward the trees.

"Julio!" Estocio shouted. "Julio!"

A moment later, Juan's silhouette could be seen darting from one tree to another, now fifty feet from their hollow.

"Juan!" shouted Estocio then added a stream of Spanish.

Kay inched over and looked up the slope. With his rifle at his hip, Estocio paced back and forth, peering into the copse. Kay again wondered why he could not see her.

Juan poked his head around a tree.

Harry slowly exhaled, and Kay felt him tense. Juan pulled his head back. Harry took another slow breath then subtly adjusted his aim.

The barrel of Juan's rifle appeared. It was low now. Juan must have dropped to his knees. Harry exhaled.

Snakelike, Juan's rifle moved around the bole of the tree.

"Juan!" Another stream of Spanish flowed from above.

Harry did not so much as flinch, yet Juan's rifle jerked angrily.

The corner of Juan's head momentarily appeared. He looked everywhere except at Harry and Kay's hiding place then snapped his head back behind the tree.

Harry took another breath.

Juan peeked around the tree again. Then, with eyes flitting everywhere, he slid his head out a little further.

Harry squeezed the trigger. A tiny eruption of blood, bone, and tissue blew off Juan's head before he dropped the short distance to the ground.

Kay gasped.

"Look out," Harry whispered.

Kay flattened, allowing Harry to squirm over her body.

"Julio!" Estocio screamed. He fired wildly from his hip into the trees. "Julio!"

Harry, prone and propped on his elbows, took his time, aimed, then squeezed the trigger. Five shots rang out in rapid succession. Estocio collapsed to the road as if the bones in his legs had dissolved.

"Wait here!" Harry said then scanned the road before backing out of the hollow. He ran to Juan's body and poked it with the tip of the rifle. Satisfied, he held the rifle to his shoulder and slogged up the slope. Several times he slipped, banging his elbows, knees, and shoulders on the steep incline, but not once did he lose the rifle or stop until he reached the road.

After prodding Estocio's body, he shouted, "We're clear! Come up! We have to get going. Hurry!"

55

Checkmate.

Still unable to contact Kay, Maizie pounded her desk, clamped her jaw, and pulled out a cell phone she had promised herself never to use inside the office. With one last huff, she dialed.

* * *

Prone on the lip of the cut, Jorge and Harry watched two large Dodge sedans appear at the far end of the clearing. Both cars rolled forward a few yards then stopped.

A phone buzzed. Jorge pulled Cobb's cell out of his pocket, but Harry snatched it away. Looking at the screen, he shook his head. "Well, shit, Jorge. I guess you aren't the only one looking for Cobb. Here, you talk. But keep it quiet and short, real short." He handed Cobb's phone to Jorge.

Jorge pressed the talk icon. "Yeah?"

"Cobb, it's all fucked up!" a female voice said.

"Astor," Jorge interrupted. "This isn't Cobb. It's me…Jorge."

"Jorge? Oh fuck…you son of a bitch. Where's Cobb? Harry's gone crazy—"

"Astor. Harry's here…right next to me. And, yeah, Harry's crazy."

After a long silence, Astor said, "Shit. Let me talk to him."

Jorge handed over the phone.

"Well, hey there, lil girl," Harry said. "I hear tell ya'll got plunked in that cute lil ass of your'n."

"Harry. Goddamn it. The fuck you doing? Where's Cobb?"

"Cobb's out takin' that farm fambly outta harm's way."

"The Tomas?"

"Yes, ma'am. So don't ya'll worry 'bout them no more."

"Harry!"

The two Dodges crept forward.

"Oops," Harry said. "You're breaking up. Shitty reception here, girlie. Anyway, gotta go. The show's about to start." He terminated the connection then handed the phone back to Jorge.

In the middle of the clearing, the cars stopped again.

* * *

"Fuck!" Maizie tossed the phone against the wall. Rising too quickly, she banged her wound against the edge of the desk and nearly fainted from the pain. With her hands on her knees, she froze until she could breathe. "Shit, shit, shit," she whispered as she gently lowered herself back into the chair. "Now, what the fuck do I do?"

* * *

Nudging Jorge on the shoulder, Harry said, "Ol' Carlos is probably a trifle distraught. I bet he wishes he had one of his Hummers. Loves those monsters like he loves his cock. Black ones, red ones, silver ones. Shit, he needs a ladder to get into some of them." He laughed. "Now he's stuck in some low-slung Dodge."

"His world's falling apart, and here he is, looking for you," Jorge said.

"Yes, sir. You get it now? He's not some fucking backwoods Einstein. You guys have been spending gazillions chasing a moron. If he'd stayed in Mexico, like the smart businessman he thinks he is, he might've been able to staunch the bleeding."

"Strange how the FBI didn't start their raids until after he arrived in California."

"Yeah, funny thing about all that. You know, my old man used to tell me that timing is everything. He was a rotten old cuss, but he was right in a few particulars. 'Son,' he'd say, 'timing is the difference between wine and vinegar, between a hero and a villain, between a—" Harry stopped talking when the lead car stopped a few yards short of the cut. The trail car closed the gap and also stopped.

"They smell a trap," Jorge said.

Harry pulled the bolt on his rifle then shrugged. "Maybe. Sure as shit, they're spooked. But maybe, just maybe, someone needs to take a piss. By the way, this'd be a good time to hold your water."

A man exited the rear door of the trail car.

"Well, shit, there he is," Harry said. "The goddamn CEO of Hades in the flesh."

Carlos, of average height but very fat, walked a few steps away from the gray Dodge, a cell phone to his ear. He paced back and forth, frantically turning this way and that. Another man exited from the front door, leaned against the car, crossed his legs, and folded his arms across his chest.

"Poor ol' Carlos," Harry said. "Not much reception down there, huh, you fat sonofabitch? I bet he wants to cut the balls off the fella that sold him that phone." He nudged Jorge again. "How many you see in each vehicle?"

Jorge sighed. "Two in the front of both cars, counting the guy that's outside waiting for Carlos. Can't see the backseat."

Harry looked through his rifle scope and aimed. "Must be a full boat, then. Four or five in each car." He chuckled. "Well, shit. We're good. We got 'em outnumbered. The bastard should've brought a few more." He continued to aim but did not pull the trigger.

Jorge understood why. Harry wanted Carlos and his people deep in the killing zone of the cut.

"Watch," Harry said. "In another couple seconds he's gonna toss that thing."

A moment later, Carlos hurled his phone at the man leaning against the car. The phone missed and burst into pieces against the car body. Leaning Man remained immobile. Even from seventy-five yards, Jorge could hear Carlos's stream of profanity as he stormed over to Leaning Man, shouting and pointing his forefinger. The man did not move or flinch or come out of his casual pose.

"Hmm," Harry said. "Could be 'ol Carlos has more to worry about than lousy reception. Looks to me like he needs to worry about the loyalty of his troops. Slippery thing, loyalty is. But you know all about that, don't you, Jorge?"

Jorge said nothing.

The two Dodges crept forward again. "All right, Harry," Jorge said, "how do you want to play it?"

"Well, Jorge, you have redeemed my faith in human nature."

Jorge shrugged. "What do you want me to do?"

"Well, you know, I do believe you'll be able to figure it out. There's no more time for planning. All I ask is you wait for me. Understand?"

Jorge sighed and nodded. His bladder ached with an urgent need.

Twenty yards into the cut, the lead car rumbled to a stop as both front tires flattened.

"Well, look at that," Harry said as he raised his rifle. "They must've run over a bunch of spikes... Wonder how they got there. There oughta be a law."

For a few seconds nothing happened. Then Harry squeezed off a shot. Jorge saw a hole appear in the windshield of the trailing Dodge. Through the starred glass, he saw the driver flop onto the steering wheel. Harry squeezed off another shot and killed the driver of the lead vehicle.

"You mind taking out their radiators first, then maybe a tire or two?" Harry asked.

While men spilled out of the doors on the right side of each car, Jorge pumped shots into each radiator before shooting out the left tires of both vehicles.

Harry popped out his clip and reloaded. "Time for the artillery. Special loads."

One man leapt away from the lead car and charged up the road, firing a pistol.

Harry chuckled then dropped the man with a shot to the chest. Aiming carefully, he shot another man whose head barely showed above the front fender, sending bits of skull flying. Next, he pumped round after round into the bodies of both cars. The special loads penetrated clear through the doors and side panels. Screams could be heard over the sounds of Harry's rifle. Only once did someone raise an automatic rifle to return Harry's fire.

Harry stopped shooting and reloaded. "Well, the time has come for Carlos to see the error of his ways. Jorge, I'd appreciate a little covering fire. Would you mind?"

After a long look at Harry, Jorge took aim at the two Dodges and began pulling the trigger.

Harry slid down the embankment then, raising his rifle to his shoulder, crouched and crossed the road. Once in line with the men hiding on the far sides of the bullet-riddled cars, he opened fire. There were no answering shots. A couple of men rose and tried to run. Jorge shot one while Harry shot the other. Neither made it ten feet.

Harry reloaded then walked slowly toward the cars. Stepping into the hiding place, he squeezed off a few more shots. Finished, he walked over to the men who had tried to run and prodded their bodies with the tip of his rifle.

Jorge slid into the cut and approached the carnage.

Breathing with difficulty through a clenched jaw, Harry turned and looked through Jorge as if he wasn't there.

Jorge stopped abruptly. "Harry?"

"Fuck. Makes you wonder, don't it?"

Jorge stood very still. "What?"

Finally recognizing Jorge's presence, Harry said, "Ol' Carlos bought it with one of them special loads. Fucker was dead before I got there." He sighed. "Too bad. I would've liked to have seen his face." He scuffed the ground with his boot. "Well, you can't have everything, not in this life anyway. That's what my daddy used to say."

Jorge no longer felt the urge to piss. "There's ten of them."

Harry moved closer to the bodies and stared at Carlos. "He killed my brother. Did you know that? And after that, he killed one of my nieces and almost killed the other."

"What?" Jorge asked, stunned to realize that Harry had relatives.

Harry shrugged. "Long time ago. I really thought this was going to be tougher. Last longer anyway." He moved away from the bodies. "You did well, Jorge. You popped a couple all by yourself."

Jorge said nothing.

"Family and friends are supposed to be everything. My asshole of a daddy sure thought so." Harry walked toward the clearing.

Jorge followed. "You did all this for your family?"

Harry laughed without humor. "No. You live long enough, you learn that some families aren't worth shit." He laughed again. "Growing up, me and my brother barely got along." Looking skyward, he gave another short laugh and said, "Once when we were young, he broke my nose with a baseball bat." A few steps later, he added, "Of course, me porking his girlfriend probably set him off."

They reached the clearing. "What are you going to do now?" Jorge asked.

Harry shrugged.

"What about the people who might be following your teacher bait? We know Carlos had people watching the hospital."

Harry shrugged. "I don't know. He should've made it across the bridge by now." He chuckled. "Look at these guys Carlos hires. Nothing but a bunch of morons." He paused and wiped his brow. "Shit, I wouldn't worry about that teacher."

"Well, the teacher might be worried."

"Can't help that. No matter what you do, folks tend to worry. My daddy used to say folks spend too much time worrying about other people's worries, which creates just a hell of a worrisome lifestyle, if you know what I'm sayin'. That ol' teacher-boy hero probly ain't even comin' this way. He ain't here now and since he ain't, there's just no point in worryin' 'bout it." He began walking again. "Slipped into my twang, didn't I? Sorry about that." He stopped and in clear English said, "Regardless, this is where you need to wait. Here by the bridge until I'm gone."

Jorge leaned against the guardrail. "Okay. Doubt I could keep up with you anyway."

Harry nodded, put his rifle over both shoulders, and hung his elbows over the stock. He took one last look around then sighed. "Well, I do appreciate the help, Jorge. Maybe someday we can hook up again." He turned and walked away.

"Well, fuck you, Harry, no thanks," Jorge said.

Without turning or stopping, Harry offered a small flick of his hand.

Jorge felt the sudden temptation to shoot him. He watched the scarecrow of a man saunter down the road until the old rogue disappeared into the fog. Jorge emptied his bladder then pulled out his cell and headed for the top of the cut, hoping to find it still had reception.

56

Stopping the bad guys doesn't always lead to Happily-Ever-After.

Once Cobb had called to let her know the Tomas and Vincent were safe, Maizie managed to control her fuming. She returned to the operations room and watched the D.C. people work. The air in the room was electric. The raids produced numerous arrests, as well as significant hauls of drugs, weapons, and cash. D.C. Boss even congratulated her, saying she would be up for all kinds of accolades. But Maizie knew that was bullshit. The accolades would fall on him.

It didn't matter. Maizie was pissed about more important things. George Washington and Tess Trueheart might be in trouble, and there was not one goddamn thing she could do about it. As her temper heated up again, she returned to her office.

Once inside, she eased into her chair, running her hands through her hair just as her cell chimed. She snatched it out of its holster and stared at the screen. "Kay? Christ. About time." She sighed, wondering if D.C. Boss was right. Maybe it was stupid to think that Harry and Kay could be targets.

"Maizie!" Kay shouted. "We need help! Please help!"

In the background she heard Harry say, "Kay! Slow down and tell her what's what. We don't have time."

"Kay! What's going on?"

Kay took a deep breath. "Three men attacked us. They said they're going to kill Vincent. You have to get some people to the farm. Vincent's there. You have to! My car won't start. They shot it up and it won't start so you have to get people to the Tomas!"

Maizie jumped to her feet and hobbled to the door of her office. "Shot up your car? Someone's shooting at you?"

"They're going to kill Vincent! You have to—"

"Kay!" Maizie shouted. "Are the men still attacking you? Are you safe?"

"What? Yes! We're…okay…safe. But we can't get to the farm. They're going to kill Vincent."

"Let me talk to Harry." She grabbed the doorknob, fought off indecision, then opened the door.

"What?" Kay shouted. "I…he went down the hill looking for the keys to the other car."

"What?" Maizie released the doorknob. The door eased shut. "What other car? Tell him to stop. Tell him I need to talk with him."

"Maizie! You have to get people to the farm! Harry can't make it without Vincent."

"We have Vincent. Tell Harry we have him. He's safe. We have the Tomas and we have Vincent. They're safe."

"Safe?"

Maizie opened the door again and took a step into the hallway. She looked around for help but saw no one. "Yes. We have them. All of them. We took them off the farm some time ago. Now—"

Kay shouted, "Harry! Harry! He's safe! Maizie says he's safe! Oh God!"

Nothing but the wind came over the cell as Maizie hobbled a few steps closer to the operations room. "Kay? Kay? Are you there?"

Kay shouted again. "No, he's okay… Maizie wants to talk to you… Yes! She says they have Alma and Kenji, too."

Maizie leaned against the wall.

"He's coming," Kay said.

"Where are you? You need to tell me exactly where you are."

Kay breathed deeply. "We're on the overlook, the view, the spot where you can see the Golden Gate Bridge. On the Marin side. Up on the hill. Way up on the hill."

"I know the spot. I'm going to send help, okay? But let me talk with Harry now. Put him on the phone."

"He's still climbing back up. They said they'd kill Vincent. You're sure he's okay?"

"Yes. I'm sure. Tell me what happened."

Kay took another deep breath. "Three men with guns attacked us. They came in a car and just started shooting. They called Harry by name and said they were going to kill Vincent and me if he didn't come out in the open. They called him by name, Maizie." Kay choked. "He's almost here. He's really tired. He's really scared for Vincent."

Maizie heard Harry's harsh breathing before she heard his voice.

"He's safe?" Harry asked. "Where is he?"

"He and the Tomas are in a hotel in Petaluma," Maizie said. "Um…an agent pulled them out some time ago. I'll have the agent call you on this number, and you'll be able to talk to them."

Harry did not respond.

Kay came on the line. "Thank you, Maizie. Thank you."

"Kay, I need you to tell me more about what happened. Are you sure you're safe now?"

"Harry!" Kay shouted. "Harry!"

"Kay! Talk to me." There was only the noise of the wind before she heard Kay and Harry talking. She could not understand, but she was relieved that she could hear their voices. "Kay!" she shouted. The door from the operations room opened with her shout. One of the D.C. boys leaned out and looked toward Maizie, questioning her with his hand.

Kay answered, "I'm here. Harry almost fainted but he's okay."

"Are you sure you're safe?" Maizie asked.

"I think so."

"Where are the men that attacked you?"

After a long pause, Kay said, "They're dead. Harry killed them."

With the phone against her ear, Maizie rushed to the operations room, shoving D.C. Boy out of the way.

* * *

Harry and Kay leaned on the Cooper after resting the rifle against the guardrail several yards away. Before she had hung up, Maizie told them to have no weapons in their hands when the cops arrived. "It's a touchy situation," Maizie said. "Everybody's going to be jacked up. You don't want to get shot because someone misreads the situation. So make sure you are far away from any weapon, and keep your hands in plain sight when the cops get there."

They waited. Harry, covered in a cold sweat and trembling, kept shifting his weight. He slid to the ground and dropped his head between his knees.

At least Harry had spoken to Vincent. Good old Charlie Cornish had called and told them about driving Vincent and the Tomas away from the farm on Kenji's tractor. They had traveled north across the fields because Charlie felt the access road would be unsafe. Harry spent a few minutes talking with his son then Kenji and Alma.

Finally, he spoke to Charlie again. "Officer Cornish, how did you know they might attack the farm?"

Charlie did not answer. Instead, he repeated Maizie's advice about how to behave when the cops arrived.

Sitting with his elbows on his knees, Harry looked up at Kay. "Are you all right?"

Kay lied with a nod. "You?"

Harry struggled to his feet then closed his eyes. "I feel better now that I've spoken to Vincent. But I worry this'll ruin us."

Sirens screamed through the fog that had risen to cover the parking area.

Kay took his hand, but when he winced, she let go. Her hand was now covered with blood from Harry's lacerated palm. Gently, she took his wrist, and pressed his bloody palm against her breastbone, whispering, "You from you."

The sirens grew louder.

57

A new friend comes running.

While standing in the first-class line ready to board, Elizabeth answered her phone. "Hello. If this is Mark, I've got to cut this short. We're boarding now."

"Elizabeth, it's Kay."

"Kay. I'm just boarding. Can I call you back when I get to Chicago?"

"Elizabeth, we need some help. Harry and I need your help. Can you come?"

The line began to move, but Elizabeth remained still. "What?"

Kay spoke in a clear, yet quavering, voice. "We're at a police station in San Francisco. Can you come?"

People jostled past Elizabeth. She stepped out of line, pulling her roller bag as she headed for the exit. "I'm coming. Give me a moment to plug in my Bluetooth, then tell me everything."

* * *

Once Maizie had told D.C. Boss _almost_ everything, and after he had blown three or four gaskets, he assigned one of his D.C. boys to handle the Harry Ross and Kay Morrell issue. Then he ordered her out of the room.

D.C. Boy proved to be surprisingly competent. He told Maizie that Harry, Kay, Vincent, and the Tomas would be brought to the

San Francisco Federal Building. Safe accommodations for all had been secured at a downtown hotel.

The Tomas arrived at six then were interviewed before being ensconced at the Saint Francis Hotel. Vincent had arrived with the Tomas but remained at headquarters under the care of a San Francisco policewoman because the Tomas had no *in loco parentis* rights. Then at seven, the policewoman and Vincent disappeared. No one, including D.C. Boy, would tell Maizie where they had gone.

Kay and Harry had yet to arrive. No one seemed to know what had happened, and D.C. Boss and D.C. Boy would no longer speak to Maizie. In fact, everyone avoided her. Of course, considering the day, D.C. Boss and his boys had a full plate managing the operation. Reports from field operatives, press briefings, and Harry and Kay's incident added to their workload. Then reports from the California Highway Patrol began trickling in about another incident, this one near the Toma farm. The trickle turned into an avalanche. The incident involved a shooting and numerous casualties. At one point, D.C. Boss charged into Maizie's office and questioned her about the incident. Maizie reported that she knew nothing, and he left in a huff.

She sat back in her chair, wincing whenever her buttocks stabbed her, and combed her memory of the day, searching for options. Her head came up and her eyes widened when she remembered the policewoman assigned to Vincent. She had met the woman a year ago. The woman had been in plainclothes then and had liaised with the FBI on some drug case. Maizie remembered her as an up-and-comer. Bright, aggressive, multi-lingual, and very athletic. But now she was in uniform. What had happened to her career? She pawed through her personal cell contact list until she found the woman's name and phone number. She dialed.

Four rings into the call a woman answered. "Hello?"

"Officer Darrow…Leticia, Maizie Cabrera of the FBI. How are you?"

There was a long pause. "I'd ask how you got my number, but I don't expect you'd tell me, would you?"

"You gave it to me last year."

"Huh…okay. You're calling about the shooting at the Marin headlands, correct? The one involving the hero from the school shooting last week."

"Yup. He and his teacher friend are supposed to be here, but no one seems to know where they are. I'm trying to find them."

"How did you know to call me?" Leticia asked.

"I saw you take charge of Mr. Ross's son."

"Not sure I can help you, Maizie."

"Ah… You do remember me then, don't you?"

"Yeah. I remember you very well."

"Then you also know my rep."

Leticia said nothing. In the background, amid the sounds of male voices and laughter, she heard Leticia say, "You guys be quiet. The kid's asleep."

"Sorry," a male voice said. Then there was silence.

Maizie waited. She heard a door open then close.

"The detective in charge is an asshole," Leticia said. "He's been interviewing the teachers for hours. Ms. Morrell brought in a lawyer, so she's done. She's getting her things. The man refused representation and so, well, the asshole is still on him. Oh…and the woman's lawyer is the boy's mother."

"A Ms. White?"

"Yeah.

"The asshole is Ricketts, isn't it?"

Leticia snorted a laugh. "You didn't hear it from me."

"I'll be there in twenty minutes." She knew which precinct Ricketts worked. "Can you tell me what Ricketts is hanging this crap on?"

Leticia sighed. Maizie could almost feel her scanning the room, looking for listeners. "Ross admits to killing the three men. And he admits to the men knowing his name, but he has no answer for that. Ricketts thinks he's hiding a connection to the cartel and he's dirty. Everyone else thinks he's God. I mean, have you seen his kid? That kid is not from some lowlife. That much I can tell you."

"I'm going to give you my personal cell number. Call me if you ever need anything. I owe you."

"I will."

Maizie left a note with one of the D.C. Boys, exited the building, then drove away in her unremarkable Ford sedan. Driving was not easy. Just sitting evenly in the driver's seat pained her, and she discovered how much the gluteus maximus was needed for acceleration and braking.

Leticia called a few minutes into the drive. "You close?"

"Yeah."

"Ms. Morrell is here in the coffee room, waiting for Ross. Seems like a nice lady, too nice for all the shit she's had to put up with over the past week or so. Did you know she was the main witness at the school shooting last week?"

"Yeah. And yeah, she's a nice lady."

"One of the interviewers came out and told me that Ricketts almost blew a gasket."

"Yeah?"

"The Ross guy takes like a minute to answer every question," Leticia said. "It's driving Ricketts crazy."

"Yeah, I've experienced that from Ross."

"Mostly I think Ricketts is really pissed because the guy hasn't flinched in his story, not once, not even a little bit. Normal people flinch with something this huge."

"And I bet the crime scene folks back up his story," Maizie said.

"That's what I hear. His story and Ms. Morrell's story check out. She was a little hazy on some of the details, but that's expected. I mean, holy shit, her boyfriend took out three hitmen barehanded."

"Barehanded?"

"Well, not exactly. He killed the first guy with a piece of broken rebar then used the guy's rifle on the other two."

"Jesus."

"He's an ex-Marine."

"Yeah, I know." Maizie sharply took in a breath as she braked for a red light. "Tell me what I want to know, Leticia. Tell me."

Leticia laughed. "No, he hasn't been arrested."

"No?"

"No. Ricketts is just grilling him on his own nickel. He's using Ross's refusal to accept representation as his go-ahead. The lady lawyer's here for him too, but because he refuses representation, she can't get in to see him."

"Shit, this is going to be duck soup," Maizie said.

58

Confronting survival is difficult, but it's
better than the alternative.

After her interview, Kay spent ten minutes in the washroom. Looking at her reflection in the mirror, she teared up. Her left eye, swollen and black, would recover in a week or so. But the lacerations across her left cheek and forehead, held together by tiny, white strips of tape, looked like they might scar. When she raised her shirt, she hissed in pain. Deeply bruised and scraped, her rib cage seeped pinkish fluid. Easing the shirt back in place, she whispered, "All right. It'll be all right. Just gotta get through today." Battling the sting of water on her cuts and abrasions, she washed her hands then gently patted her wounds with a damp paper towel.

Composed, she went back to the waiting room to care for Vincent while Elizabeth worked on Harry's situation. Kay tried holding onto the sleeping boy, but his dead weight against her injuries was too much. She laid him down on the small sofa without waking him.

Elizabeth entered the room and looked up from the copy of Kay's statement. "He's heavier than he looks."

"Yes, he is. And he sleeps like a bowl of overcooked linguini." She lifted the boy's hand a few inches off the sofa and released it. It fell with a plop, but the rest of Vincent's body did not budge. She looked into Elizabeth's eyes. "I don't know how to thank you."

"Oh, stop it. I would have been upset if you hadn't called me. Did you know they were going to send Vincent to the Child Protective Service people?"

Kay nodded.

"Someone's got to tell Harry that I'm out here."

Leticia came back from the hallway where she had made a phone call. She looked at Vincent. "Still out? Well, good. At least someone gets to sleep."

Kay nodded.

Elizabeth continued to read.

Five minutes later, Maizie limped into the center of the room followed by a cop Kay did not recognize.

Hands on hips, Maizie whispered something to Leticia and gave her a set of keys. Leticia left the room.

Looking from person to person, Maizie said, "Good evening, I'm Special Agent Maizie Cabrera of the FBI." She paused. "I will be taking charge of this situation."

New Cop, hands locked in front of his belly, looked at his feet.

Maizie faced Kay. "Ms. Morrell, is Ms. White serving as your legal representative?"

"Um, yes, she is."

Raising her eyebrows, Maizie looked at Elizabeth.

Elizabeth nodded. "Yes, I am."

Maizie smiled grimly. "Ms. White, I assume you are also here to represent Mr. Ross. Is that correct?"

"Yes, but I have not been allowed to see him."

New Cop shuffled his feet. "He has refused offers of legal representation."

Maizie huffed out of her nose. "Yes, I know. Thank you, sir, for your time. You can go now."

New Cop pursed his lips, nodded, then walked out.

Maizie gave a tight-lipped smile. "Okay now, let's get that representation thing fixed. Ms. White, please come with me."

Five minutes later, Harry emerged with Elizabeth. Both went to their son and sat. She stroked his curls, while Harry gently massaged his shoulder. Vincent woke up. "We need to go now, big boy," Harry said.

"Carry me," Vincent said.

"Vinnie, do you think you can find your feet for a while?"

"I'll carry him," Elizabeth said, picking up the boy. Vincent wrapped his arms around her neck, lay his cheek on her shoulder, and closed his eyes.

Maizie entered from the hall. "Okay, let's go. We've got a hotel for you people." She looked at Kay. "You look like you could use a shower and a bed."

Kay shrugged and took Harry's hand.

"They need a doctor," Elizabeth said.

Harry stood, wobbled, then sat back down. "Give me a minute, okay?"

"We'll have a doctor waiting at the hotel," Maizie said. "But we need to get going." She paused. "Mr. Ross, can you make it?"

Harry slowly stood. "Yeah. I'll be okay. It comes and goes."

"Good," Maizie said. "I take it neither of you wishes to confront the press now, correct?"

Kay and Harry looked at Elizabeth.

"They'd rather not talk to anyone for a while," Elizabeth said.

Leticia entered the room. "Maizie, you're right. There are a half dozen reporters and at least one TV crew outside. I moved your car."

Maizie closed her eyes. "There'll be more." She paused. "Leticia, lead the way."

Leticia nodded then led the group down the hall.

"By the way, Ms. White," Maizie said, "we do not have accommodations for you at the hotel."

"I understand. My firm has a condo in town. Kay, Harry…I'll get Vincent to the car then grab a cab. I'll call you tomorrow."

Kay stopped and rested a hand on Elizabeth's shoulder. "God, I can't thank you enough."

"Shh. Go get some rest."

Harry moved forward. "Thanks, Elizabeth."

Holding back tears, Elizabeth said, "Oh, shut up. Come on, let's get to the car."

"Yeah, really," Maizie said. "We need to move."

In five minutes, Kay, Harry, and Vincent were in the back seat of Maizie's Ford. Vincent fell back to sleep with his head on Harry's lap and his feet on Kay's. Harry gently stroked the boy's soft curls.

A few minutes into the drive, Harry said, "Thank you for coming to get us, Agent Cabrera."

"Don't worry about it," Maizie said. "That detective was way out of his depth. You guys were supposed to be brought to the Federal Building right away."

"May I ask you something?" Harry asked.

"We're putting you up at the Saint Francis. It's a great old hotel. I hope you guys like it."

"Thank you," Harry said, his voice tired and raspy. "But may I ask you something?"

Maizie tensed. "Okay."

"You had an agent evacuate Vincent and the Tomas. Why?"

"I don't think I can talk about that right now."

"On the phone you called him an agent. But it was Officer Cornish. Why did you call Officer Cornish an agent?"

"I…slip of the tongue. It was a busy day. Lots of interdepartmental cooperation and all that."

Harry's chin dropped to his chest. "Do you know why they attacked Kay and me?"

Maizie stopped at a red light. Not until the light turned green did she say, "We think it was a situation of mistaken identity." She paused. "We believe they thought you were another Harry."

"What? How can you say that?" Kay said. "They called Harry by his name, they knew about Vincent, they—"

Harry silenced Kay with a hand on her shoulder. "Agent Cabrera," Harry said, "I'm sorry you still feel you have to prevaricate."

Maizie gripped the wheel more tightly.

Harry again asked, "Do *you* know why they attacked Kay and me?"

Maizie held her breath then sighed. "All I'm trying to do is be your friend here, that's all." She paused. "Yes, I know why you were attacked. I am certain the cartel believed you were someone else."

Several blocks slid by.

"How long have you known?" Harry quietly asked.

"Known? Or suspected?"

Harry said nothing.

"I've known since the shooter came to your hospital room. I suspected the minute I saw your name connected to the school shooting."

Again Harry kept his silence.

"I'm sorry, but I'm not going to say anymore," Maizie said. "Not now, anyway."

"Can you tell me why not?"

"No." She heaved an exasperated sigh. "Other than it involves old friends."

Harry reached over Vincent and took Kay's hand. Kay felt only his cold fingers because of the bandages. She looked at him, but his eyes remained locked on the back of Maizie's head.

Even without seeing his eyes, Maizie seemed to shrink from Harry's stare.

"Perhaps you will tell us later," Harry finally said.

Kay noted no anger in his tone, but somehow his voice added to the chill in the car.

"Mr. Ross," Maizie said, "I'll tell you what. Someday I will personally come to you and tell you what I know. But it's not going to be today." She paused. "That fair enough for you?"

"Are we going to be attacked again?" Kay asked.

"I don't think so," Maizie said.

"I don't understand," Kay said. "They knew Harry's name, they knew about Vincent, you say it was a mistaken identity, and now you think it's over. Why? This doesn't make sense. Why should they stop? I mean, they seem to have legions of men willing to kill people. Why should they stop?"

"Their boss is dead."

Kay's head jerked, and she looked at Harry. His chin rested on his chest, and his eyes were closed. "Dead? One of those men was the boss?"

Harry did not move. Kay leaned over Vincent and touched Harry's cold, clammy forehead. He briefly opened his eyes then closed them again.

"No," Maizie said. "The men he killed were hired. The boss was killed elsewhere."

"By the Tomas' farm," Harry said.

Maizie squeezed the steering wheel until her hands ached. "Yes," she said. "How did you know?"

"I heard radio traffic in the police car," Harry said weakly. "I know the roads they mentioned. The people on the radio said there were five or six bodies."

Kay closed her eyes. "Five or six bodies. Oh God."

Maizie clamped her jaw then slowly released the pressure on the steering wheel. The blood returning to her hands caused a surge of pain. "There were ten bodies…ten. They were all cartel soldiers. There was a firefight, but I'm not going to say anything more about it. I'm not. So please don't ask."

Harry's head fell forward.

"Harry, are you all right?" Kay asked quietly.

Harry first shook his head then nodded.

"Is he all right?" Maizie asked.

"I'm fine," Harry said. "I just need to lie down for a bit. But all in all, I'm…" His voice slurred to a stop, and his chin dropped back to his chest again.

"Harry!" Kay whispered urgently.

"We'll be there in a few minutes," Maizie said. "We have a doctor waiting for you at the hotel. Can you make it, or do you need a hospital?"

Harry lifted his chin. "No hospital…please, no hospital."

Maizie accelerated up California Avenue and Harry said, "The Saint Francis." He huffed. "It's the only big hotel that remained standing after the earthquake."

"What?" Maizie asked.

Kay said nothing.

"It's true." Harry's head dropped back onto the headrest. "The Saint Francis was one…of the few remaining…buildings of any size…left after the earthquake."

Maizie plucked her cell out of her belt and dialed.

* * *

Leticia and a male police officer met them at the underground entrance to the hotel. She immediately reached in and lifted the sleeping Vincent out of the car. Once Harry stood, Maizie and the male cop each took one of his arms. Harry shook off their help for three paces before his knees buckled. They caught Harry before he hit the concrete floor.

Kay hustled to the elevator.

As they entered the elevator, Harry recovered some of his balance by leaning against the wall. He looked at Leticia. "You should wake him up. It's like carrying fifty pounds of oatmeal."

Leticia shifted the boy's weight. "He's okay."

Harry slid closer, put his hand on Vincent's cheek, and kissed his forehead. "Hey, big boy, time to wake up. Time to find your legs."

Vincent's eyes popped opened, closed for a moment, then slowly opened again. He shifted his weight then snuggled into Leticia's neck. "I'm tired."

"I know, big boy, I know," Harry said. "I was wondering if you could help us out and walk."

Vincent clung more tightly to Leticia's neck then pulled far enough back to see her face. "Hi."

"Hello, yourself," Leticia said.

"I'm tired."

Leticia smiled. Awake, Vincent was easier to hold. He clung with his legs and at least one arm. "It's been a tiring day."

"Put me down, please."

"You sure?"

"Have to find my legs."

"Okay." Leticia set him on the floor just as the elevator stopped.

A gathering awaited them in the hallway. It included another male cop, Kenji, Alma, and two young, attractive Asian adults, one female and one male. Kay realized in an instant that the two, were Alma and Kenji's children. The man stood as tall as his mother, while the daughter was shorter than Kenji.

After a round of introductions, the two male cops nodded to Maizie then walked to small desks at either end of the hallway and sat.

Vincent ran to the daughter. "Auntie Katt, Auntie Katt, we were at the police and we rode in a police car and Dad talked to the police and everything."

Katherine scooped up the boy and received the usual Vincent greeting. "Vincent," she said, "remember your manners. Say hello to John and Nana and Uncle Kenji."

Vincent turned back and forth in Katt's grip, waved to the assemblage and said, "Hellooo." He turned back to Katt. "But it's real, Auntie Katt, it's real. Police and everything."

Maizie went to every single Toma and shook their hands. Kay realized the family members were all familiar with Maizie. She was impressed at how quickly the tiny woman had resumed her air of command after the difficult ride in the car.

Kenji avoided Harry's bandages, took his wrist, and shook it like one would shake a friend's hand. "How are you, Harry. God almighty, how are you?"

"Hey, Harry," John said. "We've been very worried. I thought Mom was gonna have a stroke."

Alma, uncharacteristically quiet, kept her eyes on Kay.

Harry waved. "Kenji, John, hey Katherine, Alma. It's great to see you."

"Harry, thank God," Katt said.

Kay moved forward. "Hi, I'm Kay Morrell."

Katt offered her hand. "Katherine, or Katt if you like. We know who you are, Kay. It's wonderful to finally meet you. We've heard so much about you."

John shook hands with Kay. "Hi." He was about to say more but then just shook his head and smiled.

Kay hugged Kenji.

"Hey, thank you," Kenji said.

"Do I have to go to bed, Nana? Do I?" Vincent asked.

Alma had a hand on Vincent's back. "Soon, Vinnie, soon. Have you been a good boy? I've got some special things if you've been good."

"What? Tell me. I've been good." Vincent looked at Kay and Leticia. "Tell Nana how good I've been."

"He's been wonderful," Leticia said. She came forward and introduced herself to the gathering.

"See?" Vincent said.

Alma ignored Vincent and approached Kay. Taking both of Kay's hands, she bent over and, almost nose-to-nose, studied Kay's face. "You're all banged up."

Kay shrugged and nodded.

"Nana," Vincent said. "I've been good. I've been good."

"We need to get Harry to his room," Maizie said.

"I'm okay," Harry said. "I feel better." His face had lost its ashen appearance, and his perspiration had thinned to a dull gloss.

Kay, with a tiny, grim smile, kept her eyes unflinchingly on Alma.

"Harry," Maizie said. "We shouldn't keep the doctor waiting."

Harry offered no resistance. He looked toward Kenji. "Kenji, do you think—"

Alma straightened up. "Vinnie's going to stay with us tonight." She looked at Vincent. "We've got treats for him then bed."

"Yay!" Vincent said. "What did you get me, Nana? Tell me, tell me."

"Be good now, Vinnie. Don't start with me," Alma said.

Harry smiled. "Thanks, Alma. Vinnie, be good, big boy."

Vincent smiled, bounced a bit in Katherine's arms, and rocked his head from side to side. Katherine smiled broadly.

Harry, Leticia, and Maizie began to move down the hall. Kay turned to follow, but Alma kept her grasp on Kay's hands.

She faced Alma. "I'll be there in a bit, Harry."

"Okay," Harry said quietly without turning back.

Kenji, Katherine, John, and Vincent went through the door to the nearest room.

"Big room," Alma said. "John and Katt are going home, but there's plenty of room for me and Kenji and Vinnie. Two big beds. Plenty of food too. I think Kenji's going to spoil that boy tonight."

Kay looked directly into Alma's eyes. "It looks like Vincent has a lot of mothers to help him get through."

Alma squeezed Kay's hands a bit tighter. "That boy's gonna be trouble. Every damn girl falls for him."

Kay returned the squeeze. "I think I fell in love with him in less than a minute."

Alma released Kay's hands and shrugged. "I know…but he needs a mother…a real mother. Everybody else is just an auntie."

Kay sighed. "Oh, Alma."

"You don't need to tell me anything. I know everything already. How'd he ask you?"

"Ask me what?"

Jerking her head, Alma huffed impatiently. "What? Are you telling me that boy never asked you yet? Wait'll I see him."

Kay laughed, stepped forward, and hugged Alma. The tall woman stood quietly with her hands in the air before awkwardly wrapping one arm around Kay's shoulder and patting her head with the other.

* * *

Kay eventually escaped Alma and made her way toward Harry's room. Before she got there, the cop at the end of the hall stood. "Ms. Morrell, your room is one door down. I have a key for you."

Kay nodded and remained by Harry's door. "I'll be staying here tonight, Officer. But thank you."

The officer smiled, nodded, unlocked Harry's door, then returned to his chair.

Inside, a doctor and Nurse Lei tended to Harry. Maizie, reclining awkwardly on a small sofa next to the window, talked on her cell. The doctor was packing a shoulder bag and seemed about ready to leave. Harry, covered with a blanket and with an IV hanging from a lamp, sat in a large easy chair with his feet on an ottoman. Lei monitored the IV.

Staring straight at Kay, Harry said, "So Doc, I'm okay then, yeah?"

Doc looked incredulously at Harry. "You're a miracle, but no, you are not okay. You need rest and after that, more rest." He huffed. "And we need to start your antibiotic regimen all over again. Furthermore, Lei is going to stay over and check on you from time to time. You owe her big time, so listen to her."

"Lei likes me."

"You make sure it stays that way. And I don't like these spells you're going through. We'll get your blood tested tomorrow and see just what in God's name you did to your body." He paused. "And see if you can give me a stool sample tomorrow morning sometime."

Harry nodded.

"Now, get some rest. Lots of rest."

"Got it, Doc," Harry said slowly.

Doc finished packing and finally noticed Kay. "Hello there." He stared and scratched his wild mop of hair. "It's you again."

"Hi. Thanks for helping Harry."

Doc kept his hand in his hair while he carefully appraised Kay. He took a few steps closer. "Helluva job on your part."

"I, um…"

He reached forward and shook Kay's hand. Holding on longer than expected, he turned Kay's hand over and looked at the abrasions on her forearm. "Huh," he whispered. "No one's even looked at your injuries, have they?"

Kay shrugged. "I—"

"Let's see what's going on," Doc said.

"I don't think I'm hurt all that badly."

"Are you a doctor? No, you're not. Come on, let's have a look."

It took thirty minutes for the doctor to examine and treat Kay's various injuries. She was surprised to discover how many of her wounds needed stitches. Her abrasions received ointment and taped-on dressings. Finally, she found out that her ribs were just bruised.

"Should feel better in a week or so," Doc said. "Avoid sleeping on that side. In fact, try to sleep on your back."

Wincing, Kay nodded. "Okay, thank you."

He wrote out some prescriptions, which Maizie snatched and promised to fill.

The doctor looked back and forth between Harry and Kay. "Well...I must say, it's not very often I get to treat two heroes in a single house call."

Kay donned one of the hotel robes. "Thank you. I don't know what to say."

"You're very welcome." He looked at Harry. "Remember, get some rest." With that, he strode out the door.

In the silence that filled his wake, Kay moved to stand beside Harry.

Lei approached the pair. "He's a great doctor. He cares, he really does."

"He's a wonderful character," Kay said. "I can't believe he made a house call." She looked at Lei. "And I can't believe you're going to spend the night."

Maizie rose from the sofa. "Uncle Sam's nickel. Okay...we've got SFPD all over the place. But mostly, even though everything's probably over, we're going to house you here for a few days. Please remain indoors. You need anything, anything at all, check with Leticia, the officer in charge. She's a good one."

"I need some clean clothes," Kay said and immediately felt stupid for mentioning such a banal topic.

"We've already got some coming, nothing fancy, but clean and hopefully the right sizes." Maizie looked out the window. "You have a nice view. There's Alcatraz all the way to the Golden Gate, and you're higher than any building to the north, so don't worry about standing by the window."

"What?" Kay said.

Maizie shrugged. "You know, snipers. But don't worry, I'm confident it's over."

"Oh... Okay."

Harry reached out and took Kay's hand.

"Yeah, good." Maizie glanced at the floor. "We'll be in touch." She hobbled toward the door.

"Agent Cabrera?" Harry said.

"Yes?"

"Remember your promise."

Maizie nodded. "Yeah, I'll remember." She left.

Another long silence filled the room while Harry's IV slowly finished. Lei pulled the needle from his arm then looked directly at Kay. "You plan to stay here tonight, don't you?"

Kay nodded.

"May I use your room? You can get me in less than a minute if you need me."

Kay smiled. "The officer down the hall has the key. I'll go talk to him."

When Kay returned to Harry's room, she found him struggling to rise from the chair. The blanket that covered him fell to the floor. He wore nothing but underwear and a t-shirt spotted with dried blood. Gauze bandages covered the abrasions on his elbows and knees. A large but simple bandage covered the top half of his ear. The bandage covering his surgical scar bulged under his t-shirt.

"I'm going to lie down," he whispered. "I think Doc gave me something to help me sleep. I feel pretty woozy."

Kay nodded. "You look better."

Harry shrugged and shuffled the few steps to the bed. Pulling back the blanket, he paused. "Thanks for staying with me."

"Harry, we're together now."

Harry blinked slowly and nodded. He stared at the bed. "Okay if I'm on this side?"

"Yes, that's fine."

Harry nodded again. Wincing with every move, he climbed into bed.

Kay helped him with the blanket. "Do you need more pillows?"

Harry shook his head. "I just want to sleep."

But Kay saw his mouth tremble and his eyes well up. She bent over, placed a hand on his head, and kissed his eyes, tasting the salty tears. His hair felt gritty with debris, and his breath smelled slightly metallic.

They looked at each other for a while before Harry's lids began to droop. He blinked a few more times, and a few tears trickled down his cheeks. Kay dabbed them with a tissue. By the time she pulled it away, he was asleep.

Dropping the robe, Kay turned off the lights and climbed in next to Harry. With the drapes open, the lights of the city dimly lit the room. Against doctor's orders, she lay on her injured side, watching Harry sleep. From time to time she ran her hand over his face and chest, or painfully leaned on her elbow to kiss his forehead.

She did not remember falling asleep, but fall she did. Filled with uneasy dreams, she woke often. Each time, she managed a brief glance at Harry, who never moved. She also woke when Lei entered to check Harry's vitals. The good nurse fussed for a few minutes before leaving. Kay drifted back into her difficult sleep.

Then, during the umpteenth time her dreams forced her awake, Harry was no longer in bed. She thought she was in another nightmare, but the sound of the toilet flushing brought her to reality. She glanced out the window at the gray light of dawn then heard the shower. Grimacing, she sat up then awkwardly climbed out of bed. She waited until the pain eased then headed to the bathroom.

Inside, Harry stood naked, facing the shower, with one arm inside the curtain adjusting the temperature. When he heard the door, he turned and smiled sadly but made no attempt to cover his nakedness. He had peeled off all the bandages except the one on his ear. The number of raw abrasions, the largest of which covered much of his left shoulder, made her flinch. The incision for his surgery, perhaps four or five inches long, was smaller than she had expected.

"Hey," he said in a voice garbled with sleep.

"You're up early," Kay whispered.

Harry cleared his throat. "I need to wash up. My hair is full of crap, and I stink."

Kay nodded.

"I can't believe you kissed me when I smell like this."

"For better or worse, right?"

Harry blinked slowly. "Yeah."

Kay moved forward, took his face into her hands, and kissed him. He gently wrapped his arms around her only to pull away as both squealed in pain.

"I guess we'll hold off on hugging for a while," Harry said.

Kay sighed and nodded. "I might as well shower too."

"Well, it's a pretty big stall."

She smiled.

Harry waited until Kay stripped then moved aside so she could enter the shower first. She hissed as the hot water struck her abrasions. Harry followed with difficulty, likewise gasping.

Kay quickly pushed the nozzle to the side. "I guess it's going to be kind of hard to get clean, isn't it?"

Harry closed his eyes and nodded.

"Are you all right?"

"Stings. We just have to get used to it."

"Let's just stand here a minute."

Harry reached over her and pointed the nozzle back onto their bodies. With clenched jaws, they held each other's hands until the hot water no longer stung.

Soon however, Harry broke down and cried like he used to as a small boy.

Ever so slowly, Kay slid behind Harry, wrapped her arms around his torso, and let the water cascade over their heads.

When he finally gained control, Harry whispered, "Do you still want to marry me?"

Kay turned him around and took his face into her hands. "Don't you ever doubt me again, Harry. Never."

Harry nodded. "This thing may not be over, you know. They might come after me again. And you saw what I did."

Kay squeezed his face a little tighter. "Harry Ross, don't be this way. Whatever they do, they'll have to do it to both of us. We'll confront it when we have to. You did what you had to do."

Harry blinked slowly a few times before he heaved a deep sigh. "I won't think like that anymore."

"Promise?"

Harry nodded. "Sure. I promise."

SPRING

2016

EPILOGUE

A difficult promise is kept.

On a Saturday afternoon in late May, Kay, pregnant with twins, worked in the small sunroom Harry had built onto the side of the cottage on the Toma farm. With Mr. Lee on the mend but unable to return to work, Kay had acceded to Mildred's request to finish out the year as Dean of Faculty. Hopefully, the school year would end before the babies arrived.

Behind her, Harry and Vincent sat at the kitchen table playing with Lego blocks. Kay envied Harry's momentary freedom to play. His final exams had been turned in for printing, his year-end grades were nearly complete, and his classroom was as neat as a pin.

No one had expected her husband to move from his trauma into having such a successful first year. Kay knew much of the success derived from his "exalted hero" status. The students wanted to be near the guy the media raved about. Boys envied his death-defying feats and, truth be told, death-delivering persona. Girls thought he was a nice guy and hot. But Kay realized hero worship was only a part of his success. All in all, he was a born teacher. He loved history, he loved kids, and he was intensely organized.

Losing focus, Kay leaned back, looked out the window and watched Kenji working his tractor on the fields. A few moments later, she heard the screen door from the main house slam and saw Elizabeth walking across the farmyard. She was on a weekend visit and had just finished a gin rummy game with Alma. Kay waved, happy that her friendship with Harry's ex had deepened. Looking past Elizabeth, Kay saw a car come into view on the gravel road, topping the hill to the east of the barn. "Harry, someone's coming."

Harry was beside her in an instant, Kenji turned the tractor toward the house, and Alma stepped onto the porch toting a rifle. Harry laughed without humor. "Look at her. She can't even shoot. It's amazing she knows which end is which."

Kay realized Harry's laughter was forced. Everyone on the Toma farm looked long and hard at any stranger coming over the hill. "I don't recognize the car."

On his way out, Harry said, "Me neither. Vincent, stay with Kay."

Vincent came and took Kay's hand. Both watched Harry stride past Elizabeth, reach Alma, take the rifle from her hands, and lean it against a post. Alma put her hands on her hips and gave Harry an earful.

Elizabeth stopped in the cottage's front yard and watched the car approach. Shrugging, she stepped inside and moved into the sunroom. "Who in the world would drive a Beamer on that road?"

Kay shook her head.

"What's a Beamer?" Vincent asked.

"It's a type of car," Elizabeth said. "Like that black one coming down the hill."

"Why is it called a Beamer?"

Elizabeth ruffled her son's hair. "Is this how you guys meet all strangers, with Alma toting a rifle?"

Kay shrugged. "Harry worries she might shoot somebody someday. He wants Kenji to take her rifle away."

"I bet that little stratagem worked like a charm with Alma."

"Not very well, no."

Elizabeth picked up Vincent and settled him on her hip. "Beamer is a nickname for that make of car. Its real name is BMW, but people like to call them Beamers."

Vincent nodded and watched the car as it reached the bottom of the hill and entered the small valley. "If I had a name made of letters, I'd want a nickname too."

"Do you have any, I don't know, real plans for strangers coming down the hill?" Elizabeth asked.

Kay rose from her desk, her tent-like, yellow dress clinging to her legs. She plucked at it until it fell, almost reaching her ankles. "Nope. No plans, no lockdown drills, no steel-reinforced saferooms. We decided before we were married to live the way we want to live, and we don't want to surround our family with razor wire on top of walls." She sighed. "If something becomes real again…well, we'll just have to handle it as best we can. Except for Alma, of course."

Elizabeth looked at Kay's grim profile. "I guess that isn't always easy, is it?"

Kay shook her head. "Nope."

The Beamer entered the yard, stopping in front of the main house. Alma still had her hands on her hips but no longer scolded Harry who leaned against a railing. Kenji stopped the tractor a few yards from the porch. The car door opened, and Maizie stepped out into the cool May air.

As soon as she saw Maizie, Kay nodded softly with closed eyes. "I guess it takes a little faith in human nature and the law of averages." With that, she grabbed a sweater off the back of her chair and moved toward the door. Elizabeth set Vincent down and followed.

As Kay waddled across the yard, Maizie smiled. "Christ, you are God-awful pregnant. Congratulations."

"Twins," Kenji said. "Boy and a girl."

Alma nodded proudly.

"Hi, Maizie," Kay said. "And thank you."

Harry stood calmly, his slowly blinking eyes fixed on Maizie.

"Well, girlie, it's been a while," Alma said.

"Yes, Mrs. Toma, I know," Maizie said. She turned to Elizabeth and offered her hand. "Good to see you, Ms. White."

Elizabeth shook her hand. "And how are you, Agent Cabrera?"

Before Maizie could answer, Vincent stepped forward and offered his hand. "Hello, FBI lady."

Maizie laughed, leaned over, and shook Vincent's hand. "Hello yourself, big guy."

"Why are you here?" Alma asked.

"Alma," Kenji said. "Behave yourself."

Alma glared at her husband.

"That's okay, Mr. Toma," Maizie said. "Actually, I've come because of a promise I made."

Harry nodded, removed his hands from his pockets, and crossed them in front of his chest. "Well, that's good, Agent Cabrera. I had begun to give up on you."

Maizie smiled. "Please, it's no longer Agent Cabrera. I'm out of the FBI and have started my own consulting firm."

Harry, who kept his distance, shrugged.

Elizabeth knew of the underlying tension between Maizie and Harry. But no one had explained the antipathy. Indeed, Kay always spoke of the woman with a strong degree of respect.

Harry gestured to the benches lining the porch. "You can tell us your story up there. There's room for everyone."

Everyone took a step toward the porch until Maizie said, "Uh, wait. Excuse me." She scuffed the gravel. "I'm here to fulfill my promise to you, but I wish to do it in private."

As Harry's slow blinking became more pronounced, Kay moved next to her husband and took his hand.

"It's like this," Maizie said. "You can tell anybody anything you want after I say my piece. That's the chance I have to take, and there's nothing I can do about that. But that will be your call, not mine. So if you don't want to hear me in private, fine. I'll consider my promise met. I'll get back in my Beamer and leave and that will be that."

Harry stared at Maizie but said nothing.

"I'll tell you all this much," Maizie said after a few moments. "I'm convinced you won't be attacked again from any of the cartels. If you feel you need to know more, well then, you have my offer."

"How convinced?" Kay blurted.

Maizie shrugged. "Reasonably so. The man behind the attacks is dead, and many of his people are in jail. Furthermore, he was not well regarded by many of his, um, let's say, peer group."

"Other drug lords," Kay said.

Maizie nodded. "He had many enemies."

Harry continued to glare at Maizie, but she appeared not to notice.

Elizabeth marveled at Maizie's composure. After all Harry had done during that horrible week so many months ago, he had gained the aura of a mean, junkyard dog. In public, people tended to shy away from him. Strangers who wished to shake the hand of a real life hero would nervously back away as soon as their hands broke free.

For a while, Harry had laughed away the situation. But Kay had told Elizabeth it was beginning to wear on her husband. "His students are saving him. They absolutely adore him. They're not afraid of him at all." Maizie wasn't afraid either, that was clear.

"Do you mind walking?" Harry asked.

"Excuse me?"

"We can walk and be private."

"Am I going to end up walking in cow poop?"

"We don't have any cows."

"Okay, then, lead the way."

Harry nodded, pointing to a hill to the west. "This way." He turned and walked away.

Maizie looked at the hill then followed.

"Why's Dad taking her to the bench?" Vincent asked. "Is she in trouble?"

"No, they just need some time to talk together," Kay said.

"She looks like she's in trouble," Vincent said.

"No, she's not in trouble," Kay said. "I hope."

* * *

They crossed the farmyard then marched on a dirt road that bisected two small green fields. A trail appeared at the base of the hill where the road ended. As the trail steepened, a perspiring Maizie fell behind.

Halfway up the hill, Maizie stopped and bent over with her hands on her knees. "Hey! You said a walk. Slow down for Christ's sake."

Harry stopped and shrugged. "It's not much farther from here." Then he turned and resumed his march.

"Christ," Maizie said before continuing.

Once the trail leveled off, it wound around to the western slope and into a stand of wind-sculpted cypress trees. Harry stood by a wooden bench that overlooked green hills and valleys all the way to the Pacific Ocean.

Maizie sat down and stared at the view. "You build this bench?"

"No. Kenji's father did."

Maizie wiped her brow. "Kind of a Japanese meditation place."

Harry said nothing.

"Okay… Not much for small talk, are you?"

Harry faced west and stuffed his hands in his pockets.

"Well, Christ. I don't know why I'm doing this. Other than that brief moment of weakness when I made that stupid promise, I really don't think I owe you anything. I did everything I could to save your ass."

Harry folded his arms across his chest and pointed to the path. "Go then. Don't keep your promise and just…just go. "

"What? No. I'm here. I just want you to know it's not easy."

Harry sat, angling his body with one boot on the bench so that he could face Maizie. "Okay. I'm listening."

"Shit. Like I said, I did everything I could to keep you and Kay safe. I made a deal with the doctor so that you would remain in the hospital as long as possible. But somebody altered your blood tests, vital signs…everything. Your actual release from the doctor was a forgery. Your real doctor was out of town for the day. Hell, no one even thought to hunt him down for a few hours. And then, as I am sure you realize, the order dismissing your escort was also forged. That cop, by the way, has recovered from being tased. He was found in a janitor's closet."

"I know all that.

"How do you know?"

"Doesn't matter. I know."

"Huh." Maizie looked long into Harry's eyes, which no longer blinked. "Okay. I'm just saying that I thought you and Kay were protected."

"As my wife and I served as bait. As Vincent and the Tomas served as bait."

Maizie dropped her eyes and whispered, "Yes." She scuffed the ground. "It's like this. Carlos was after another Harry. This Harry was a colleague of mine in the Bureau. We were part of a special unit tasked to gather intelligence on the Mexican cartels. During our training, we were all assigned multiple aliases, but between us, the names we came to know each other by were our first choices, and he chose Harry…Harry Ross, in fact. He's always been just Harry to me."

"Oh…jeeze," Harry whispered.

Maizie nodded. "Teams were sent to Mexico to set up networks of informants. Each team would be installed in a district and essentially had to live off the land to manage their task. Most of the teams failed miserably, but Harry's team was spectacular. In six months he was sending solid intel to D.C. leading to a series of raids and arrests. Most of the raids were against the Carlos Cartel, but not all." She stopped again and looked out at a spot where a tiny triangle of the Pacific Ocean burned bright with reflected sunlight.

"But things started to fall apart. Carlos raided villages in big sweeps, gathering up dozens of people, looking for informants. A large number of the men and boys were tortured and some were executed. Carlos also allowed his men to take a large number of women and girls who were raped and then sold into the sex market. Anyway, the sources dried up. No one would talk anymore. The order to pull out came."

Maizie paused and shuddered. "Just as Harry's team started to pull out, his handler was kidnapped. The handler was posing as an American tourist in Cancun. As it turned out, the kidnappers were not directly associated with any of the cartels. They were just a bunch of assholes in another of the shitty businesses going on in that part of the world. They saw an American and went for it. Pretty soon they realized that all of the handler's documents, contact numbers, and…shit…everything was fake. Which meant ransom wasn't in the picture. They ended up selling the handler to the Carlos cartel.

"The handler was tortured on and off for seventeen days. Everything the handler knew about the operation came out: team member aliases, villages where the informants lived, communication protocols…shit…even physical descriptions. Luckily, the rest of Harry's team heard about the kidnapping and hustled back to the states. But Harry refused to leave. Direct orders, and he refused to leave. His whole goddamn world was falling apart and he stayed. No one in D.C. knew what was happening. Except for the kidnapping, of course."

Harry had become a statue on the bench.

"The cartel executed dozens of people from different towns and villages using the information derived from the handler. Most of those people had nothing to do with the operation. But that didn't stop Carlos… It was a matter of fucking honor for him."

Harry abruptly stood then paced back and forth in front of Maizie.

"What?"

"You were the team's handler, weren't you?"

Maizie glared for a moment then erupted from her seat and jabbed a finger toward Harry. "You ever been beat up then raped? Huh?"

"No."

"Well, good for you. Jolly fucking good for you. I bet you know some girls who've been raped, don't you?"

Harry stood still. "Yes…I do."

Maizie pulled her finger away from Harry's chest and let her arms drop to her side. "You know, I still don't know how many men and boys raped me. I don't know how many times I got beat up or burned with cigarettes. Here, look at my fingers." She held up her tiny hands, displaying her swollen knuckles and skewed forefingers. "They broke them with a hammer. They're the only things I can't cover up anymore. They work pretty well for being stomped on. I can still pull a trigger."

"I noticed your hands the first time I saw you," Harry said quietly. "I wondered about them."

"Yeah? Well, now you know. How about the rest of me, huh? Want to see what cigarette burns look like? Huh?" She wiped saliva from her mouth. "Ah, shit."

Harry returned to his seat and turned his eyes to the west. Maizie also looked to the west before dropping into a slouch on the bench. They remained silent for a long time.

"Seventeen days. Seventeen goddamn, fucking days. You know how I know that? Because, sure as shit, I couldn't count the days back then."

Harry said nothing.

"He told me. Harry told me. As if I really cared."

Harry remained silent.

"On the seventeenth day, I was hog-tied and loaded into the back of a panel truck. For hours it bounced across the desert and then up some mountain roads to some fucking village. No food, no water, no place to piss, and so fucking hot. When the doors open, I'm blinded by the sun." Maizie sighed and rubbed her eyes as if they still hurt. "When my eyes finally adjust, I see like half a dozen bodies, maybe more, lined up, face down in the road. All of them with their hands tied behind their backs. Mostly young men. Carlos leaving his little message for the locals. Next thing I know, a bunch of teen-age girls are shoved in with me. All of them are wailing, most of them are at least half-naked, no pants, no undies, bleeding, pissing. The smell. Christ."

Maizie beat her fists against the wooden bench. Harry stood and grabbed her wrists. She jerked away, rose quickly, and slugged him in the chest with the heel of her hand, knocking him to the ground. "Back off!" Ready to fight, she stood over him for a long time before taking a deep breath. Slowly her hands dropped to her side. "Don't you ever touch me, understand? Never!"

"Yes, okay. Sorry. I didn't want you to injure your hands."

Maizie walked away, kicking the ground every few steps and swearing. She stopped a few yards away, arms folded across her chest, and stared out toward the glimmering ocean.

Harry draped his arm over his drawn-up knees and watched.

After a few minutes of silence, Maizie said, "I apologize. I don't like losing control like that."

"No harm done." Harry returned to the bench.

Maizie glanced his way and nodded before returning to her vigil of the ocean. Soon the silence began to wear on her. "No questions, Harry? Aren't you curious about the details?"

Harry remained quiet for a long moment, then said, "I don't know what to say, Ms. Cabrera."

"Fuck, it's Maizie, okay? Christ, I just called you Harry, so call me Maizie. We're fucking intimate now, don't you think?" After another long pause from Harry, she said, "How does she do it? How does your wife put up with this thought process of yours? God."

"I don't know."

"What?"

"I don't know how she puts up with me. I don't think about it. I'm just glad she does."

Maizie rolled her head. "Shit."

"Is Maizie your real name?"

"What? What kind of question is that?"

"You want me to call you Maizie, but it's not your real name, is it?"

Maizie stormed over to the bench. "Do you think I lie about everything?"

"No. I think you do it when you need to be careful."

This time Maizie paused. "Well, I'm not fucking lying now."

"Okay."

"Do you want to hear the rest of it?"

"Yes...I do."

She resumed her slouch. "So...anyway, we were in this hot, stinking van and then we heard this motorcycle. Well, the assholes outside were laughing and talking all kinds of macho crap. The closer the motorcycle got, the louder they got. It was like Christ Almighty was coming to town." She took several deep breaths. "It stopped right by the van. There was a bunch of 'holas,' and 'que pasas' and quick little bursts of bullshit talk. Like they're all gonna hit a bar and celebrate. Then…Boom. Boom. Boom. The place got lit up. I mean, lots of guns went off. Pistols mostly. Lots of screaming and swearing in Spanish. It went on for a minute or so…not long."

She shook her head. "Next thing I know the door banged open, and there was Harry. Beautiful, fucking Harry in dirty jeans, filthy shirt, and skinny as all get out. Long hair flying all over the place." She stopped talking.

"He killed them all?" Harry asked.

"Probably. I saw maybe five dead guys on the ground with the executed villagers…might have been more." Maizie shrugged. "Maybe he had help. He was always good at getting people to work for him."

They sat quietly for several minutes before Maizie said, "He does look a bit like you, you know. Used to anyway."

Harry raised his eyebrows but said nothing.

"Well, he cut off all our bindings then got us out of the van. He stripped the dead cartel soldiers of their weapons, cell phones, and money. He even took their jewelry—watches, chains, earrings, whatever. After that, he stacked the bodies in the van. Some of the villagers started showing up then. Mostly old folks and small children. Anyhow, they just watched as he loaded up the bodies. Some of the women brought out blankets to wrap around me and the girls. Then they started coming up to Harry, grabbing at him, kissing his hands." Maizie stopped and picked at the corner of the bench for a while.

Harry looked at the ground between his feet.

"You ever been rescued, Harry? You ever have your life saved?"

Ever so slightly, Harry nodded.

"It's not all it's cracked up to be. Sometimes I think it's better to let a person die. That's what I felt like then, anyhow."

Harry kept silent.

Maizie exhaled angrily. "Anyway, Harry kept the jewelry and gave the cash to the villagers. Then he loaded his bike into the van and we left. He buried the bodies in a desert arroyo at the bottom of the mountain. I don't know what to say next. I got sick, and Harry got me home. I don't know how, I really don't. I remember the heat, the desert rolling by, and some mountain roads. After that, I spent a lot of time in a hospital. Then more time in therapy…lots and lots of therapy." She sighed. "You know, I'd have to say my shrink saved me as much as Harry ever did. God, I love that guy."

Harry stole a glance at Maizie.

Maizie used both hands to massage her forehead. "After all that, guess what? I was deemed fit and allowed to go back to work. First, it was in D.C. Little jobs, background checks, stuff like that. But it was work and it was all I knew. After a while, they found me a job in San Francisco, and, well, here I am."

Harry said nothing.

Maizie watched him. "You want to know about him, don't you? You want to know how your namesake fucked around with your life."

"And Kay's life and Vincent's life and Alma's and Kenji's," Harry said. "Yes, I believe that's what you promised."

"You never swear, do you? I mean, it doesn't take a PhD in psychology to understand you're pissed. But you never seem to swear. Why's that?"

"I don't know. I don't think about it. I swore a lot in the marines and before Kay and I got back together."

Maizie studied him a long time. "Anyway, Harry went back to Mexico and disappeared. No one heard a thing from him, no one. He was assumed dead. A year later, the FBI intercepted calls from the Carlos cartel and Harry was mentioned. Flags went up all over the place. A month after that, another intercepted call informed Carlos that he should worry about the wrath of God. That caller was ID'd as Harry.

"The wrath of God then descended upon me. I was called in with the rest of my former team. We were interviewed a dozen times. But nothing happened. No more calls from Harry, and only a few intercepts that even mentioned his name.

"Things died down until Carlos's mansion out in the boonies got blown to smithereens. A couple dozen people were killed. Women, children, old folks. The death toll included a bunch of his soldiers, his wife, his mistress, two of his sons, several nephews and nieces." Maizie paused.

"Harry blew them up?"

"Probably. I mean, yes. He did. I know he did."

"How do you know?"

"Don't ask."

"Okay."

"Anyway, for a while the Mexican army was blamed. But pretty soon the intercepts from the cell traffic were blaming Harry. And Carlos, who escaped without a scratch, was swearing revenge. The drug war intensified. People were gunned down. Tortured. Like I said, Carlos went crazy."

Maizie looked at Harry. "You got involved because…well, Carlos found a way to use the aliases I gave away. Initially, he had people search the internet and guess what? There are lots of guys named Harry Ross in some form or another. So Carlos ordered crews to cross the border and check out some of these real people. And guess what…none of them were Harry. Well, that wasn't gonna cut it with Carlos. So he concocted a new strategy…if any of these real people had just the slightest history with the drug world, they got hit."

Harry remained mute.

"The problem was, no one in D.C. figured it out. People started getting knocked off and no one paid attention. Except the local PDs of course. The local cops assumed they were all drug killings."

"How many?" Harry asked.

"How many what?"

"How many people were hit because they bore Harry's alias as a real name?"

"Oh," Maizie said. "Somewhere between eleven and twenty. They're still working on it."

"God."

Maizie nodded and shrugged.

"Someone figured out Carlos's plan, right?"

"Yeah," Maizie took a deep breath. "Harry had secured the services of a world class hacker. I don't know…maybe it was a team of hackers. Like I said, Harry was always good at getting people to work for him. Anyway, this hacker was deep into Carlos's computer network. So, yeah, Harry figured it out quickly."

Harry held up his hand and Maizie fell silent. He leaned far over his knees and placed both hands on the back of his head.

"Harry?" she asked.

"The computer hacker," Harry whispered.

Maizie nodded.

"Carlos didn't find me on the internet, did he?"

Maizie shook her head. "No…I have no proof, but I believe you're right. Harry's hacker probably found you and then filtered everything to Carlos." She paused. "The FBI found some photoshopped pictures of you on some confiscated computers. They make you look a lot older."

Harry sat up and sighed. "And you figured it out, too."

"Not immediately, but I had my suspicions. In a way it was funny. Carlos was trying to smoke out Harry by killing his aliases, and Harry smoked him out by using—" Maizie paused. "Not that funny, I guess. Not that funny at all."

After Harry said nothing for a long time, Maizie quietly said, "I told you it was about an old friend."

Harry nodded.

Maizie slouched on the bench and looked westward. The sun edged closer to the horizon. She shifted her weight from time to time, but Harry never moved. "My name is Eleanor. Eleanor Delasandro."

Harry looked up. "I know. Your mom called you Ell."

Stunned, she sat up straight. "What? How? How did you find out?"

"The first time I saw you, I thought you might be a gymnast, so I began looking on the internet. I finally found a Wisconsin site and there you were, state champ in 1998 on the floor-ex. It included a picture of you on the victory stand. Took me days to find the picture. But I had nothing else to do in the hospital. I was trying to find out why you were lying to me."

She flopped back onto the backrest. "Lying. Jesus. What a word. You know…when you're doing it, lying that is, it seems such a reasonable thing to do."

"You lied about not knowing me, then you lied about how you got shot, and most of all you lied about how I ended up being targeted."

"Well, first, I never lied about knowing you. I didn't know you from Adam until you got shot."

"But I saw you. Two years ago you were one of the agents working—"

"Oh, the pot-in-the-hills-thing." She shook her head. "I was only peripherally attached to that investigation. I was not in the loop deep enough to be introduced to any confidential source. If we were ever in sight of each other, then the lead agent screwed up. That should not have happened. It was Agent Henderson who informed me of your involvement with that situation. That's why he was the one who interviewed you regarding all that."

"Oh," Harry whispered.

Maizie sagged on the bench. "About the rest? Yeah…I lied."

"This…this friend of yours found out about my status as a confidential source."

Maizie shrugged. "Probably his hacker did. So yeah, of course he knew."

"When did you know he was setting me up?"

"I was suspicious the day you got shot…and was sure when that hitman tried to access your hospital room."

Harry nodded. "You knew his plan then, didn't you?"

Another interlude of silence passed. "He told me about it some time ago. He used to visit me from time to time. Mostly he just got drunk and wanted to talk. He lives like a hermit all over the country. So, he told me how he could get Carlos. I didn't believe him."

"Why not?"

Maizie sighed. "He always had a plan to get Carlos. He wanted vengeance as much as Carlos did. This was like the third or fourth idea he'd told me about, and all of them were crazier than the last. Besides, he wasn't the man he used to be."

Harry said nothing.

"He was a mess. His lungs were damaged, his back had been broken and didn't heal well. His legs go numb sometimes. He gets terrific headaches, and he's lost some of his hearing. Oh, and he drinks…a lot."

Harry leaned over, elbows on his knees. After a few moments, he whispered, "Okay."

"Okay? Okay what?"

Harry shrugged then asked, "So…who are you now?"

Surprised, Maizie mumbled, "The fuck if I know."

The sun slid lower, casting a pink glow on their faces.

"How much are you going to tell everybody?" she asked.

"I don't know yet. I have to think about it."

"Well, you can say whatever you like. I'm not going to hold you to any promises."

"I didn't make any promises."

Looking at him, she smiled sadly. "I'm sorry. I'm sorry for everything."

Harry nodded. He brought both feet up and rested them on the edge of the bench, his forearms on his knees.

A few moments later, she asked, "I have something to ask you."

"Yeah?"

"Harry wants to meet you. He said if you don't want to, then he'll go away. But he asked me, so I'm asking you."

Harry did not flinch. His face did not swell with anger. His hands remained relaxed. He softly stared into her eyes and whispered, "No."

She nodded. "He's my friend. I had to ask. It's all I know. He's my friend."

"Yeah." Harry stood and stared westward.

"His real name is Books, Jack Books. It's a bastardization of some Greek name. Harry never uses it."

"Like you don't use Ell."

"Something like that, I guess."

Harry ambled back and forth in front of the bench while he watched the sun near the horizon. He stopped in front of Maizie, faced her, and leaned forward. "You'll have dinner with us tonight."

"What? Are you nuts? No."

"Yes, I'm afraid so. We won't talk about any of this at dinner, but we'll talk."

She stood and shook her head. "Harry, no. This is wrong. I can't just have dinner with you and your family."

"Of course you can. And it's not just with my family. It's also with my friends. Once a week we have this dinner. Kenji cooks, Alma bakes, and Kay makes a salad and dessert. I don't know what Elizabeth is doing, she's just here visiting, but I expect she'll contribute something. Probably wine. She doesn't cook. John and Katt come sometimes, but I don't think they're coming tonight, not sure."

"What are you doing? I can't come to dinner. I can't."

Harry waved his hands across the air between them. "Stop it. Of course you can. You're an interesting person, and it's important to me to have interesting people to dinner. Do you understand that?"

She stared for a long time at Harry. He let her stare while standing completely at ease with her discomfort.

"Is this how you forgive me?"

Harry shrugged. "You know…I've thought about this, and you, for a long time. I'm not sure about the value of forgiveness. It implies a certain superiority." He paused. "I believed for a long time that your decisions were based on a set of bureaucratic values. I thought you were stuck in some mode trying to climb the FBI ladder. Clearly, I was wrong." He paused again. "I think I just want to move on. Is that okay with you?"

Maizie nodded. "Dinner with your friends then. Okay."

* * *

In bed that night, her back aching and the urge to pee almost overwhelming, Kay took Harry's hand. "I'm not sure I liked it when she called us George Washington and Tess Trueheart."

"Okay, then I'll be Tess and you be George."

"You haven't vicariously slept with enough men to be Tess, so don't be silly. I'm sure she meant that I was Tess."

"You're right, absolutely right. All old George had were those slave women he could fool around with."

"My goodness. Is that what you teach your students?"

"Let's just say I try to open the door for them to discover all of America."

"Well, as your boss, I have to hope that some patriotic parent doesn't go ballistic."

"Work, work, work. Is that all you ever think about?"

Kay scooted closer to Harry and kissed his hand. "No, not all the time." She kissed his forehead. "You know, someday you'll have to tell me everything she told you at the bench."

"She told you a bunch already," Harry said after his typical pause. "I told her we didn't have to talk about anything and there she went, blabbing about a whole lot of it."

Kay squeezed his hand a little more tightly. "Yes, yes she did. But she was pretty drunk."

"Nice of the Tomas to put her up."

"She didn't say everything, did she?"

"No."

"So someday you'll have to tell me the rest."

"I guess. But not for a while. I need to think about it."

"Even though you promised her that you wouldn't tell us anything until she said it was okay?"

Harry grimaced during his pause. "I did not promise her that."

"Really?"

He faced Kay.

She studied his face. "Sorry. It's just that you behaved like you promised her you would keep quiet."

"I didn't," Harry said then gently rubbed her swollen belly.

Kay smiled, running her hand through his hair. "So you'll tell me someday?"

"Probably. I have to think about it."

"So, Harry Ross, my little George Washington, who are you lying to now? Ell or me, your wife?"

Harry rolled onto his knees and kissed her belly. "So far, no one. Yet. I will say this, she believes in her friends."

The End